D0393718

The
Darkness
Rolling

The Darkness Rolling

Win Blevins and Meredith Blevins

A Tom Doherty Associates Book
New York

THE DARKNESS ROLLING

Copyright © 2015 by Win Blevins and Meredith Blevins

A Forge Book
Published by Tom Doherty Associates, LLC
175 Fifth Avenue
New York, NY 10010

www.tor-forge.com

Forge® is a registered trademark of Tom Doherty Associates, LLC.

The Library of Congress Cataloging-in-Publication Data
is available upon request.

ISBN 978-0-7653-7860-6 (hardcover)
ISBN 978-1-4668-6295-1 (e-book)

Forge books may be purchased for educational, business, or promotional use. For information on bulk purchases, please contact the Macmillan Corporate and Premium Sales Department at 1-800-221-7945, extension 5442, or write to specialmarkets@macmillan.com.

First Edition: June 2015

Printed in the United States of America

0 9 8 7 6 5 4 3 2 1

*Dedicated to the rolling light
that lives in every one of our grandchildren.*

Ruth, Aletha,

Caleb, Sienna,

Bailey, Blaire, Liam,

Chloe, Henry, and Peter.

This one's for you.

Acknowledgments

Hozho, or beauty and harmony, weaves the pattern of the lives of those we love. The people we take care of, and the people who take care of us. It is the great balancing act of living a peaceful life.

We would like to thank Barry Simpson and Steve Simpson of Twin Rocks Trading Post for firing our imaginations. Also, of course, as invaluable sources of story, joy, and friendship.

Thank you, Jen Mouton, for a place to write and dream, bonne terre cottage. We are ever grateful for your love and support.

Bob Diforio, agent extraordinaire, is our champion and more. Kristin Sevick Brown, our editor, thank you for your energy, enthusiasm, and brains. And to Bess Cozby, ever good-natured, for making certain we are on track.

Finally, we thank our bighearted community—a strange and wonderful brew of Anglos and Navajos, always on the edge, always opinionated, irascible, loving, kind, loyal, and smart. We are two of the luckiest people alive to count ourselves as among the 300 Bluffoons.

Win Blevins
Meredith Blevins
Bluff, Utah 2015

The First Holy Wind
Saad T'áálá'í Diyin Nílch'i

Holy Wind comes from the place life began,
    it is said.
    Shí, Diyin Nílch'i, nishlí aádóó iina silíí, jiní.

Wind is the same within us all,
    Nílchi át'é t'áá nihii,
But there is an evil wind-part called Darkness
    Rolling.
    Jó éí díí nichoó ei chahalheel yimasii wolyé.
It runs the large, bad thoughts within us.
    Ii'háhejeehée, baahágii nitsékeestsoh.

If it happens that a person dies, it is said,
    Éhooniilgo diné ádin,
There was one moment when their heart stopped
    listening,
    Jiní Nihijéiyée niiltli',
And they let the Darkness Rolling come inside.
    Áko kodóó Dinétah dine sodiszin, yéilti'.

We listen to this earth from where life first began.
Aádóó iina silíí,
Good and Evil, Sun and Darkness Rolling,
Aádóó iina silíí,
We remember—Holy Wind made them all.
Ya'at'eeh nchó'i ako doo yá'áshóo da.

Holy Wind comes from the place life began,
  it is said.
Shí, Diyin Nílch'i, nishlí aádóó iina silíí, jiní.

Traditional Navajo prayer
translated by Meredith Blevins

The
Darkness
Rolling

One

I was itchy. Tingling. My skin felt like foaming surf breaking on sand, and my brain was buzz-busy, just like the
soldiers who had decided to stay in San Diego after the war.
Possibilities. Worlds of them. I felt them, too.

Women who'd traded their love for gasoline and stockings
walked the singing sidewalks. High heels clicked, and the
sun raised their red lipstick to a promise. Happy to have
their young men back home. High times.

I stood on one foot, then the other. Yes, itchy. The radio
operator tried again, and this time I heard her voice. After
the official shortwave palaver, he said, "Mrs. Nizhoni Goldman?"

"Yes."

"I have Seaman Yazzie Goldman here for you."

I leapt in, probably too loud.

"Hello, Mom." I hadn't said that in six years. Hard for

me to get in touch while in the service, and no phones at home on the rez.

"Yazzie!" Her voice was a cry, the kind that's elation and tears at once.

"Mom, this has to be quick. It's against regulations, and the last thing I want to do right now is get tossed in the brig."

No words, but I could hear her, so far away, out in the red rock desert where silence has the muted voice of a monsoon. I got the feeling she couldn't speak, so I kept on.

"I'm mustering out on Tuesday, Mom. I've got my railroad ticket, and I'll be in Flagstaff at 7:14 Wednesday morning. Can someone pick me up?"

I heard a sound in the background, something between a bear growl and a coyote yowl.

"That was Grandpa, saying the biggest *yes,* in his way. Jake Charlie will be in Flag for you."

"Hi, Grandpa!" I hollered into thin air to the man who was my compass. "Then it's home Wednesday night, Mom. Gotta get off now, before I get caught."

"Wednesday night!"

"You bet."

The radioman broke the connection. He looked up at me, grinned. In an imp tone, he said, "You paid back now, Yazzie?"

"We're square," I said. I ran out the door, raised my arms, and whooped. Then I whooped some more.

Two women, wearing polka-dot dresses that blew in the breeze, walked arm in arm chattering with each other. They turned their bright faces to me, shiny as a cloudless sky.

I bounded off. No particular direction, just my feet

wanting to take my heart and body for a dance. The war was over—so many terrible stories I knew—but my home was still standing firm. Still welcoming. Waiting for me. How lucky I was.

❖❖❖❖

"How you gonna get to town?" the guard said.

Zopilote said, "Steal a car."

The fool guard grinned and put his hand to his forehead to protect his face from the sun, as if that was possible. "Don't steal a new one. The first just been made since the war started, and they're conspicuous. Lots of metal."

Zopilote, the "buzzard man," didn't bother to fake a grin. He took his packet of ragged belongings, wrapped in newspaper and tied up with string. He turned away. March 1, 1946, he saw on the front page. He would remember that. May as well have been a different century.

On the side of the highway he felt a warm wind on his neck, and it shivered along his skin. His insides prickled with hatred. His mind was blood-soaked. Finally, trudging through the dust alongside the highway, he was free. Free to act out his treasure-lust of dreams, the ones he'd been hoarding for twenty-five years.

He'd be damned if he'd look back at the Arizona State Prison. So much time lost. Years eaten. Plenty of reason to hate and to get even.

The yearning for revenge had grown until it filled every corner of his soul, assuming he still had one. He intended to kill those who had betrayed him—his own family!—and who had locked him away in prison.

An early-season dust devil whipped his feet, rising from

the ditch beside the highway. That was all right. Let the dust devil lick him—maybe it had come spinning in from his home to greet him. No paved highways on the Navajo rez, but plenty of dust devils. He felt sort of like a whirlwind himself, a being that roiled with primal chaos. Home would be good. Plenty of red-orange dust and plenty of buzzards.

It was behind bars that he'd given himself the name Zopilote, the Mexican word for the black bird with the red head. Scorched Buzzard, that's how he liked to think of himself now. That's who he was.

A Mexican, a guy he talked to a lot, this Mexican said to him, "You're like the *zopilote*."

"What?"

"The *zopilote*. The buzzard." The Mexican had pointed to the piercing sky, where several of the big birds circled.

"That huge vulture with the bald head, like it had been burned—that thing?"

"Yeah. The *zopilote*, he's like no other living creature. People kill, all creatures kill, and then they eat. The *zopilote*, no, he eats only things that he finds already dead." The Mexican looked at him and smiled. "So he eats death to create life, his own life."

Then the Mexican guy shrugged, waited for some words from the Navajo. Didn't get any. "You, you're one crazy Navajo. You keep yourself alive by feeding on the death of these people you hate, whoever they are. Not their real death, but your thoughts about it."

You never have true friends in jail.

But he took that story back to his cell with him. He liked it. The next morning he told the other prisoners to call him Zopilote. Forced them with his fists when necessary. He'd learned a few things in prison. To speak English and read it. To pick a lock and break into any building. To fight really mean. To kill with bare hands when he wanted to.

To change his name? No problem.

He also learned, later, that the *zopilote* sometimes *is* like human beings and other predators—it kills first and then eats. But that was rare, a last choice. It might, sometime, be *his* first choice. He could hear the future's drumbeat and the rhythm made his days. Most avidly, he dreamed of his wife's death.

Over and again he heard the words she spoke against him in court. He also spent hours remembering her father's testimony against him, word by daggered word, and he pictured knife-blade revenge.

Sometimes Buzzard thought of his child. At the trial his wife had been big with his offspring, but he had never known whether the child was a boy or a girl, alive or dead. He didn't dwell on this child, because it confused his feelings.

So back to images of his traitor wife and her turncoat father. He would descend upon them and bring terrible deaths to each.

In the Navajo way, to touch a dead body was taboo. The part of the dead person that was evil, the *chindi*, might enter your body and spirit, might take you away from the good path. An Enemy Way ceremony was required to heal the ill, to restore *hózhó* to the victim—harmony, beauty, balance, and health. Men returning from war especially needed this ritual.

The thought of deliberately *consuming* death—how much more horrifying that would be to his clansmen. That's why Zopilote relished the idea. Revenge was the shrine in his heart. He gave himself wholly to it, he made it the sole devotion of every moment of his life, he prayed to be transformed by it. He rejected *hózhó*. He cursed harmony, beauty, balance, and health. Zopilote, Scorched Buzzard, sought evil. In turn, evil had befriended him.

Two

Jake Charlie and I had been bumping along the dirt road headed north out of Flagstaff all day, baked by a murderous sun, racked by every rut and rock in the dirt road. A few times we got stuck in the sand and had to shovel out.

All that day I'd been worse than restless. My thoughts churned inside my chest. I wanted to sound off, to banter, to tell jokes and ask questions, but Jake Charlie, at the wheel, had a way of neither listening nor speaking.

Was going home supposed to be this kind of hard? Good question. Being here, in red rock country, after living so close to the ocean? My body had started feeling like it was salt water and driftwood instead of blood and bones. And from where I sat, next to a quiet Jake, this world seemed like it couldn't be home to anything except lizards, bluffs, and buzzards.

Except for one thing. A squirmy part of me was excited to be here. Home echoed. I felt it to the very center of my heart. All in all I was a Ping-Pong ball going over a red-dirt net, and it was no wonder.

Yes, yes, I had not walked in harmony, as my people say. I'd enlisted in the navy and been gone from Dinetah, our land between the Four Sacred Mountains, for six years. After the first two years I'd gotten caught up in a conflict that killed many human beings, so many human beings. A planet-wide combat. Mother Earth was waist-deep in the gore of her children. A terrible thing.

So, an Enemy Way ceremony would be planned for me, and then I would listen to the deep, quiet part of me that *knew,* that part I didn't have words for yet. So far, that quiet part had told me only, "Live your life the way you want." I damn well meant to.

I would answer my own questions—how did I really feel about my people's traditional ways? There were other questions that were hard to speak out loud, hard to put into words.

I'd grown up at a trading post in a place near Monument Valley called Oljato, which means Reflection of the Full Moon on Water. The water was the spring that persuaded my grandfather to build his home and business there. I was expected to take it over. But now I'd changed, I'd seen some of the big world. And I had been on shore patrol, a different kind of job that gave me ideas, ones that maybe leaned into the future. Maybe not.

Shore patrol wasn't a big deal, but I liked keeping order, and I liked seeing inside people's minds. Thinking about what they might do before they did it. Did I want to go back to hanging out in the post, jawing endlessly with other Navajos about how many sacks of Bluebird flour they could get on credit? Those memories didn't frost my cake.

But Monument Valley? The land was a glory. Straddling the Arizona–Utah state line, it is in every photo that people see when they think of the word "west." Horses, courage, isolation, cutting lose, outlaws, being wild, and layers of geologic time peeled back like a naked lady strutting her stuff. Yes, it is home. Yes, it tugs at me in a way no other place does. But, those sandstone monuments, no matter how magnificent, they are always, day after day, unendingly the same. My taste of city life, the possibility of a different kind of life than the trading post, plus a whiff of the glamour of being around movie people . . . I doubted that the glow of a full moon on water could satisfy me, but doubts come and they fly off. You cannot trust your doubts.

Altogether, my soul was in trouble. I didn't know where I belonged.

As we came around the curve that river-winds between orange and rust cliffs, and I knew I was about to see the long vista of the huge stone gods of my homeland for the first time in six years, I took a deep breath. This was the test. Was it a joyful homecoming? Or was it drinking from a pond turned to scum?

Suddenly, there it was, unexpected and magnificent. Another mile or so and I saw something new, yet familiar. Pushed upside the folds of Monument Valley, and laid out perfectly, stretched the false-front street of an Old West town. A big gang of white people crowded up together near the road, there was a camera with some guys working beside it, and lights mounted all around. Beyond them stood two circus tents, the white canvas tinted orange at the bottom from dust. My pulse soared, and it thumped two words, *movie crew, movie crew.*

Jake Charlie cracked open his jaw and squeezed out in Navajo, "Mr. Ford and them, they come here right before I pick you up. You remember 'em."

"Remember" was a weak-tea word. Mom must have given herself a secret smile by writing me nothing about the shoot and telling Jake Charlie to let me be surprised. He hand-rolled a smoke and clamped it between his lips.

The first movie that was ever shot in my homeland was *Stagecoach,* a couple of years before the big war. I had watched every day of the filming and had worked on it, and the movie turned into a big hit. Now, with the war ended, John Ford and his crew were back.

I felt like hollering for joy, right out loud. Yes, I was glad to think of the money the movie people would bring our trading post. Mostly I was beside myself because Mr. John had told me he'd have work for me when he returned. Also, I admit, I was starstruck.

"Stop!" I said.

Jake Charlie slitted his eyes and lip-pinched his smoke in disapproval, but he braked. I got out and edged my way down the shaley slope, knowing Mr. John would be right by the camera. He picked me out first off with his good right eye and waved me over. He wore a patch on the left eye, I never knew why, and sunglasses. He called over the heads of several people, "Howdy, Groucho."

I went into Groucho Marx's funny chicken-lope of a walk.

As I got close, Ford said, "Mrs. Goldman, why do you have so many children?"

It was an old routine of ours.

In a falsetto voice I said, "Because I love my husband."

"I love my cigar, too, but sometimes I take it out of my mouth."

Everybody around Mr. John burst into laughter, me the loudest.

"Welcome, Uncle Miltie," said the man next to Mr. John, who was his brother-in-law and assistant director, Wingate something. Wingate was calling me out to do one of the bits from the Milton Berle show *Stop Me If You've Heard This One.*

I responded on cue, "You monkies is the cwaziest peoples." It got a laugh. All silliness leftover from the last shoot years ago, and I almost felt light-headed.

I'd started out as an extra playing a red savage chasing heroes on horseback. We were supposed to be Cheyenne Indians, never quite sure about that, but they painted us up in ways that no one in the Southwest has ever seen. I hung around—listening, learning—until the actors noticed the curiosity that is me, Yazzie Goldman, a tall muscular Navajo with a Jewish last name, able to speak three languages fluently—Navajo, English, and Spanish—and pretty hep to white people's ways.

We'd gotten along great right from the start. They'd egg me on, and I'd launch into my mimic routines, stolen straight from radio broadcasts. First I tried my Groucho imitation on the camera crew. "The world would not be in such a snarl, had Marx been Groucho instead of Karl."

They loved it—the absurdity of the little guy's New York voice coming out of a tree-tall Navajo. Then I'd roll out some other lines. It was good times.

All this shtick came from the radio, not Grandpa. He didn't talk one bit like a Borscht Belt guy. But those Hollywood people were mostly New York Jews. I looked at them and their glamorous lifestyle, and I thought, *Maybe these are my real people. My real tribe.*

Regardless, I got a bunch of good buddies right quick. When Mr. John discovered that I could translate Navajo and Spanish into English without blinking an eye, he kept me close by for the whole shoot.

I would have worked for Ford forever, but the filming ended, and the cast and crew went back to the magical place where they lived, Hollywood. Someplace mystic near the shining sea where Changing Woman wrapped her dusky arms around her husband, the Sun-Bearer, every evening. That's what I imagined.

Now, looking at the movie people . . . we had all changed. The war snuffed out a lot of people's happy fantasies, and it near killed Mr. John at Normandy. I'd read that while I was doing nothing big or important in San Diego, he got to chase right into battle with his camera and got wounded and decorated.

"Good to see you hale and hearty, Mr. John," I said, offering my right hand the white-man way.

"Yazzie. Good to see you." He'd long since learned to shake Navajo-style, a touch like moth wings.

We had some time to talk while they set up for the next shot. I had to decipher his mumble through the linen handkerchiefs he chewed every minute of a shoot, don't ask me why.

He said, "Damn glad you're back." He took off his sunglasses. "Still want a job?"

He fixed me with that one blue eye, the way white people look right into you, probing. You had to watch out for Mr. John. According to his mood, that look made him a friend of heartfelt understanding or a Jehovah about to send you straight to hell for your sins, ones that only he knew about.

"Damn straight," I said. "Raring to go." I'd started cussing from being around swabbies who peppered and salted their talk with profanity.

"People say you got cop experience."

"Shore patrol." My unheroic war.

"I can use you for security. Ready to start now?"

"Yeah." I was screaming inside not to get excited so big that Mr. John would see the thump of my heart. He was Hollywood, and might offer me less money.

"I got an actress ready to come out here. Big star, bigger ego. Linda Darnell." I kept my face straight. Who didn't know her name? Most beautiful woman in show business, the movie mags called her. "She needs"—he shrugged— "escorting."

I looked at him, waiting for more. I wasn't about to push Mr. John, just kept standing there, studying the sky.

He did a double sigh. "She has a way of getting involved with men," he said, "who think her attentions mean more than they do."

"Got it."

"Problem is that she also has a way of getting involved

with men who have money and power, and they don't like getting dumped."

"They're used to being on the leaving end, and money gives a person plenty of ways to cause trouble," I said.

Mr. John patted me on the shoulder and looked at that same patch of blue sky. "Exactly. What I need from you is to make sure trouble and Miss Darnell are strangers, at least while she is working on this movie."

A job that was a natural fit. I could try out some of my cop instincts in a bigger way, and I was strong enough to take care of trouble. Not only did I speak the languages needed in my wild piece of country, I had read the classics and knew which fork to use. In other words, socially presentable. A lady of the silver screen crossing a desert full of Navajos, Hopis, and Mexican guys, some of them outcasts and others fresh out of the service, would be a lot safer with me than any Anglo.

"She coming in from Flagstaff?"

"No, Winslow."

"So," I said, "she's riding the Super Chief, and she wants to spend a night at La Posada."

"What else? The Train of the Stars, the hotel of the stars." Ford hated actors who paraded around like big somebodies.

But whoa! The Super Chief, the Santa Fe Railroad's ultra-luxurious passenger train from Los Angeles to Chicago. I'd read all about it, forward to backward and then all over again. Forty-one hours and forty-five minutes for the one-way trip at speeds up to a hundred miles an hour, only occasional stops, and every amenity—Pullman sleeping compartments, plus posh dining cars run by the Fred Harvey Company serving fancy foods, all the way up to oysters, champagne, and caviar.

The whole thing was one of my pictures of heaven—blasting across deserts and mountains at top speed while being served fine food on white tablecloths. When the Super Chief started running in 1936, and until I went off into the navy, I spent every possible minute during the trips Grandpa and I made to Flagstaff standing at the train station. Watching the trains roll in, and then trembling to my soles as the Chief flew by. Those diesel locomotives powered my dreams.

The Super Chief didn't make many stops, and the Santa Fe chose Winslow instead of Flagstaff. Fred Harvey built a luxurious hotel there called La Posada, designed around Southwestern Indian motifs and art. The rich people thought it was just too exotic to pass up.

"The lap of luxury," Ford said sarcastically. "She wouldn't have it any other way. And neither would the studio." Mr. John was a down-to-earth kind of guy. I knew he liked life in our wide and lonesome desert better than being around telephones, traffic, and movie moguls.

"I'll give you a car and driver." He named a figure for a week's work that was more profit than our trading post made in a month of Sundays.

"I'm good for it, Mr. John. Listen, could you fix things for me to get on the train at Seligman?" That was the last stop before Winslow, 140–150 miles west, roaring nonstop through Flagstaff on the way.

"What for? Miss Darnell will just be getting up, eating lunch, that sort of thing."

"Check her back trail, that'd be a good idea."

Not exactly honest. The truth was, I wanted to ride the Super Chief.

"All right. The studio will get you on board at Seligman. Julius will drive you there and follow with the car to Winslow."

"When?"

"How far from here to Seligman?

"About two hundred sixty to seventy miles."

"Two days?"

"One and a quarter. Second part is paved."

"Ollie!" he called.

An assistant director trotted up, got instructions to check on the Super Chief's arrival times in Seligman and in Winslow the day after the next day, no room for mistakes. Miss Darnell was valuable property. When Ollie brought back the times—one o'clock in Seligman and about four at Winslow—Ford said to me, "Make damn sure you're at the train platform on time."

"Yes, sir."

Ouch. My stomach went south for a minute or so. The prospect thrilled me, and it stung. It meant that after more than six years, I'd get only one night at home with Mom and Grandpa before running off again. But, I told myself, we needed the money bad.

"And, again, keep your eyes open," said Mr. John. "She's a hot commodity in many ways, and her marriage doesn't slow her down." Here, another sigh so long that it almost hit the ground. "Plus, that damned Zanuck is feeling fussy."

I'd heard plenty of griping about Darryl Zanuck, head of Fox. Mr. John spat out a handkerchief, which was pulped.

"The security we've got around here? Sadly lacking in experience and in guts."

He turned to face me again with his look that could melt metal. "I'm counting on you."

"Good with me." I'd carry my sidearm. Second nature, and no one had to know.

"Ollie!" More trotting. "Introduce Seaman Goldman here to Julius." He focused his good eye on me again. "You two get it set. Deliver my actress like a baby in a cradle."

Julius spared me one blip of his attention. He acted bored, probably pissed off that a Navajo was made Linda Darnell's bodyguard. I noticed that he was packing, which meant he wasn't just a driver, he was part of location security. I hoped he hadn't heard Mr. John's remark that included the words "no guts." No one wants to hear that. I'd do the best I could to get along with Julius, but it didn't seem like it was going to be easy. He wore a gray cloud around himself.

We agreed that he would pick me up tomorrow at sunrise. As he talked, an unlit cigar as thick as my thumb jutted out, probably as permanent in his mouth as his teeth.

Now I had to face up to a knotty problem, a personal obligation. Jake Charlie had made just enough words to let me know what rough shape the trading post was in and how much work Mom had planned out for me. I needed to come up with a way to get that done for her.

Not impossible. A score of Navajo men were hanging around the movie location, holding their horses, watching the shoot and hoping for work as extras. Mr. John paid eighteen dollars a day, which would buy a lot of coffee, beans, bullets, and flour.

I had some dough. During the war years, '42 through '45, I hadn't gotten the thirty days of annual leave I was due. I could have taken those last four months at the end of my second enlistment, like some guys did, to get home early. And I would have done just that, except I got a letter right then saying Grandpa was gone to the hospital in Santa Fe and would be there for weeks or months. Mom was with him, and the trading post was closed up for a while.

I wanted to see Mom and Grandpa. But I am Navajo—I don't go into hospitals unless I get dragged there. And so there were more reasons we'd need money. Medical bills. I worked right to the end, and left the navy with mustering-out money plus four months wages. I carried it in cash, naturally. The nearest bank was all the way to Flagstaff.

I scanned the faces of the waiting hopefuls for my clansmen. Spotted two standing right together, Katso and Oltai Neez, brothers. I'd known them all my life.

"*Ya'at'eeh,* Katso, Oltai."

"*Ya'at'eeh,* Yazzie." No wasted words.

"I got some work if you want it. Fixing corrals, repairing roofs, whatever else Mom needs doing."

I didn't need to say anything about Grandpa. They knew. They waited patiently.

"Five dollars a day, probably ten days of work."

I waited.

"*Haghwhoochii,*" which means in Navajo, 'Okay,' or 'It's a deal.'

No haggling. We all knew I could have gotten them to work for less. They realized I was practicing generosity, a basic Navajo virtue.

"Early tomorrow. Mom will tell you want she wants done."

"*Haghwhoochii.*"

Glory be. Done in a flash. Home duties taken care of, hired for a good job, and money pouring into my pocket.

What danced through my mind now was beyond belief as my reality. Riding the Super Chief. A movie actress on my elbow. Getting paid for living the high life. Definitely the luckiest guy in the world.

I got into the truck with Jake Charlie, who hadn't moved from the steering wheel, and I started to say "home." There was a pang, and the word got caught in my heart. I felt like a traitor. I wanted to see my family, to hold them. My attention went out especially to my grandfather because of his . . . what had happened to him.

But my mind was running off the track. For years I'd been hot to ride that train to Los Angeles and see the movie stars. Six years in San Diego, I never had the bucks for the Chief and hadn't seen a single movie star. This is the kind of time when you think, *Life is one crazy ride.*

Sure, there was plenty to like about Southern California. The balmy weather was only half as hot and half as cold as the Navajo rez. And I loved—no way to put this delicately—I loved how amorous the white women were. Lonely ladies. A guy who is six feet six inches tall, red-skinned, spruced up in a white uniform, good-looking, *and* a twenty-four-year old man instead of an eighteen-year-old boy like the other sailors. It made for some fireworks.

My body was headed home, and my heart was opening to receive Grandpa and Mom. But my mind was riding in a studio car, no doubt a doozy, and flirting with Hollywood's most beautiful woman.

So who the hell are you, Yazzie Goldman?

❖❖❖❖

Scorched Buzzard staked his stolen horse and watched from the top of a rise. A dozen Navajo men sat halfway down the hill, observing. He studied them, making sure none was old enough to remember him. Bit by bit, watching and listening, he came to understand what he was seeing. Some people from out in Hollywood were making a movie. They had put up a fake town, the fronts of their buildings running along a newly bulldozed road. That machine with men gathered close to it was the camera, and the actors were play-acting in front of those lights.

He remembered well the one movie he'd seen as a young man, a bunch of fighting between white men and fake red men. Silly, but it explained why the Navajos were waiting. They wanted work, in front of the camera or not, any work that paid.

He thought of going up to the trading post that overlooked everything, the one called Goulding's. It hadn't been here a quarter century ago. It was fancy, a big, rambling building for trading and living plus three cabins built of sandstone. Maybe the movie people built those cabins, or maybe the traders had put them up for tourists. A funny idea, tourists in this far, far end of the rez, a place with grass and water enough only for a few sheep and many fewer people. Zopilote wondered which *bilagaanas,* white people, owned this post, and how they made enough money to run such a big business in this remote piece of Dinetah. He had gotten squat from his native land.

Before he rode on—before he found *her*—he wanted only one answer. He was curious about the young Navajo standing near the camera, outfitted in the dress whites of the navy. What could a Navajo sailor have to do with this movie foolishness?

He led his horse over to a couple of the young Navajos who were waiting. *"Ya'at'eeh,"* he said.

"Ya'at'eeh," came back.

All three of them watched in silence. The young men were polite enough to wait for their elder to say what he wanted.

"That Navajo sailor," Zopilote finally said, "the one in uniform." Pause. "Who is he?"

"Yazzie Goldman," came the answer.

"Goldman," Zopilote said casually. "Some relation to the old Jew at Oljato?"

"His grandson."

Grandson. Grandson. Yazzie Goldman?

As if struggling to remember, Zopilote said, "I know that family. That sailor is the child of Nizhoni?"

The young men looked at him closely. He shouldn't say much more.

At last one of them said, "Only child."

Zopilote nodded.

Only! And from his looks he was in his mid-twenties.

Zopilote had to get away. He shrugged, like it was nothing to him.

He stood slowly and duck-footed up the slope. Her only child. *Yazzie Goldman. My son. MY son.*

He mounted and walked his horse slowly along the road. Beyond the first hill he would gallop. He had to get to Oljato Trading Post right now. It was only an hour's ride away. She was there. He would watch her. And the old man. And sooner or later he would see his son.

Buzzard soared to the thought of what he would do to that family.

Three

My mother, Nizhoni Goldman, sat on the post's wide stone gallery, watching. *Nizhoni* means beautiful in Navajo, and at forty-two Mom had not only beauty but style. She showed off her love of flamboyant colors in velveteen blouses and full skirts. Her magnificent squash-blossom jewelry was a declaration. That was Mom all the way—"if you've got it, flaunt it." Her regal bearing and family turquoise marked her eminence as the queen of her realm, Oljato and the surrounding mesas. And it wasn't all show. Mom knew that her regal bearing brought in business, red and white, and served as a cornerstone for negotiations.

She didn't need to tell me that even through recent lean times, she never gave an inch in her appearance or demeanor. At just five feet, she commanded far more respect around Oljato than me. She was generous with neighbors and hard-boiled to outsiders. She advanced local people supplies even though she knew we'd never get paid in full, but she drove a hard bargain with tourists. She had spoiled me rotten. All this without setting down her scepter.

After six long years I ran to her, picked her up, whirled her around, and gave her the world's biggest smooch. She smelled like melting honey on hot fry bread. A smell that sang, "You are home."

"Stop that!" she said, feet flying out behind. I spun her all the way around again. At that moment a dust devil fussed up and blew a handful of dry cottonwood leaves in my face.

"See," she said, "unruly boys get their faces slapped."

I set her down, and she looked at me with the depth of feeling only a mother has. I don't know if there's any words for that.

I looked over the top of her head at Jake Charlie. He wasn't used to displays of affection.

"Jake Charlie got all the trading stuff you asked for," I told her. "We better unload." Most of what we sold was delivered in a big truck by an outfit named Babbitt, but it was cheaper in Flagstaff. We always needed the supplies of everyday life, like coffee, sugar, and beans, for ourselves and for the folks that came in wanting to swap a basket or tell stories.

"Unloading can wait," Mom said. "Sun's almost down."

She called, "Jake, go to the sheep now. Get YouKnow-Who on her way back down here while there's still light."

Who on earth could YouKnowWho be? Since when did Mom hire a woman to watch the sheep?

"No questions," Mom said. She could always read my face.

Jake Charlie soft-footed it back to the truck, a loyal shadow.

I looked at my mother. Simply looked at her.

"No questions," she repeated, "and don't think I'm going to let you out of my sight for one minute. Not yet, anyway."

She took my hand and led me through the bullpen—the trading post, the first big room of our house—then through our living room and into the kitchen. She lifted the lid off a bubbling iron pot. The steam swamped our faces. The gravy aroma was thick, rich, better than any restaurant in San Diego. It was part of me. I've only had one kitchen my whole life, so maybe they're all like that. It's the center, and everything good comes out from there.

"I've been cooking two solid days for you," she went on in Navajo. "*Ha-nii-kai.*" A stew of lamb marrow and white corn, my favorite.

She led me to a window. The tone of her joy fell a few floors down an elevator. "You saw how things are outside?"

I had. Stock pens collapsing, barn doors hanging by lone rusty hinges, their sky-peaked roofs sagging, corrals barely strong enough for the horses. Plenty more of the same everywhere I looked. For sure, Mom had the next month all planned out for me, and who could blame her, but . . . *Sorry, Mom, I've got other plans.*

"Are you ready to see him?" She took me by both hands, and her face turned grave.

"Yes," I said.

"No, you're not. But it's time."

Mom led me back into the living room of our home, past

the eight-foot sofa that was Grandpa's prize, and to the door of the rug room.

"He's waiting for you," she said, and urged me forward. Clearly, Grandpa wanted me to see the circumstances of his new life in this special place, the center of the art that he loved most. Large, beautiful Navajo rugs of every design, each priced to keep it from selling, or at least to fetch enough to let him buy two that he liked even more. One step through a passageway . . . I faced the man who was my grandfather and father in one, whose life had been changed unalterably while I was a thousand miles away.

In the middle of the room, he raised himself tall in his wheelchair, and parked on an eye-dazzler rug made by a great Navajo weaver. He had known, cultivated, and loved her as an artist and like a daughter. He was smiling. I suppose you could say, smiling broadly. The left side of his mouth rose into a kind of grin, and the right drooped. That entire side of his face drooped. His enormous beard actually lifted a little on the left. The overall effect was surreal. Heartbreaking. My big strong grandfather. Right then I hated the slap of time.

Mom had written me about it. The stroke made the right side of his body nearly useless. Rehabilitation had helped, but he was still in the wheelchair and could speak only mangled words. True, he was improving daily, Mom said, and he was only sixty-four years old, so hope lurked around the corner. But my grandfather would never again be the man I had known all my life—my hero, the legendary king-size Jew of the Desert, Trader Supreme.

She was right. No way to be ready for this. None. My trembling knees betrayed me.

And yet. His presence throbbed with energy. I understood that he really was smiling, and he beckoned me to him with his left arm. I got down on my knees and leaned into his one-armed embrace. It was fierce. His laugh was a little odd, but I could tell he was trying for big and hearty. Grandpa's spirit was still inside there, rough and rollicking as ever.

He held me at one arm's length and embarked on a demonstration of how cleverly the wheelchair worked. On the left side it had two big wheels instead of one. When he pushed one wheel, he pivoted to the right, the other, to the left. With a shove on both wheels at once he could make the chair roll forward or backward, fast.

With his left hand he tapped his right bicep. I squeezed it lightly, and it felt like cooked noodles. Then he slowly made his right index finger point to his left bicep. That arm felt like the thick root of a tree.

He grinned—I was coming to know it as a grin. He wheeled off at a scary speed through the bullpen and the living room, past the kitchen, where Mom was cooking fry bread, and to the door of his bedroom.

The legs of the bed, once high, had been cut down about a foot. He turned his dead side to the mattress, pushed with his left leg and left arm, and levered himself onto the bed.

He held up a finger to say a demonstration was coming. He rolled across the bed, got the position he wanted, and flipped his bottom squarely onto the chamber pot.

What a relief that he had his pants on.

Up popped the finger again. He rolled onto the bed and across, and then took a small blackboard from a pouch tied to the black metal arm of his chair. He chalked with his left hand, though he was right-handed, WORK ARM + LEG. He slipped the blackboard into the pouch again.

Then he hoisted himself one-handed and one-legged into a new-fangled walker at the end of the bed. He started hobbling. A twig the thickness of my thumb would have supported his huge body as well as that right leg did.

He hobbled jerkily back to the rug room and to its right wall. He showed me the cover of the record he intended to play now. He flipped a switch, put the 78 on the spindle of the turntable, and placed the needle arm on the record, all one-handed. In the white noise that preceded the music, he turned back to the middle of his beloved eye-dazzler rug.

From the speakers came the piece I knew he loved best of all music, the fourth movement, Adagietto (he insisted on teaching me such terms, but I was never real clear about what they meant), of Mahler's Fifth Symphony. Not my kind of music—I go for swing—but definitely his. This piece was an elegy, and now it swept me high on emotion about the transformation from the giant of a man to this. . . . It was not what he intended, I knew, but I felt like a culvert in a gully washer of grief.

After a few moments he lifted the needle. He mouthed distinctly, "Talk Mom," and pointed toward the kitchen.

He started his recording again, lowered himself by the rungs of his walker to the center of the rug, pulled his legs halfway to a cross-legged position, and molded his face into deep absorption.

Understanding that he wanted to be alone with Mahler and his feelings, I padded away.

I wandered through the living room and slid back

through my eighteen years here. Sepia photographs of Grandpa everywhere, a lot of them with my grandmother. Others of him working, butchering a sheep for a ceremony, fleecing off wool, building a sandstone wall. The photo I loved most was Grandpa mounted on his black stallion, both man and horse of mythic proportions. Eighteen hands for the stallion, and Mose Goldman matched his mount at six feet eight inches, a rare height for anyone, but especially a Jewish man—that's what he told me, and I believed him. The picture was shot when Mr. John made *Stagecoach* here.

Duke Wayne and my grandfather had gotten to be friends during that movie. Gone hunting and shooting together with some of Grandpa's well-kept guns. Caught fish out on the San Juan River, scraggly things that looked prehistoric, but John Wayne loved this land, even bought some property around here.

When the shoot was over, Duke had gotten one of the wardrobe guys to take an army campaign hat and dye it black for Grandpa, so it looked kind of like the hat Hasidic Jews wear. A photo was taken, and there were laughs all around. It was half-heroic and half-comic, and underneath it was the label DON QUIXOTE. It was the way Grandpa came at life, a mix that tickled me and touched my heart.

Sometimes I've hoped the oddity that is me, Yazzie Goldman, could grow to be half-heroic and half-comic. I still hope so. Whatever I was, or will become, my grandpa, Mose Goldman, made me. Not one inch of me existed that did not love my grandfather. Now his body lurched and was bent—I was coming to peace with that change. He was still, and ever, my hero.

❖❖❖❖

Zopilote circled wide around the trading post, approached it from the west, hobbled his pony beyond a rise, and found a good hiding place behind some rocks above the well. In the last of the light he let his eyes feed on the familiar building—he had lived there for nearly a year—and the hot feeling boiled up in the buzzard man again. Volcanic hatred.

He knew that in the darkness—*my true home, the Darkness Rolling*—he would not be seen. From here he had an end view of the post, including the front and back entrances. He could tell by the over-bright light that Mose had wired the post for electricity. Lantern light would glow mellow. If the buzzard man slipped close, he'd be able to see into most of the windows, where the drapes were only half drawn.

Yisté'! Look there! Was that really her? Yes, the hints of silver in her hair did not fool him. She watered a potted plant in the window, inspected her work, added a little more water, and disappeared. A moment later she walked out the back of the trading post and followed a path to the outhouse. He would know her walk anywhere—he had once been entranced by it. She disappeared and reappeared. On her way back she stooped to pick something up, studied it, and put it in her apron pocket. He got a good look at her face. *In essence, unchanged after twenty-five years. Beautiful. And unchanged inside. Treacherous.*

She slipped through the back door.

The ridiculous trial—his memory held it in the brightness of a thousand suns. His own wife and her father, the trader, testified against him. Zopilote never doubted what the verdict would be. His stomach juices were runaway horses of anger.

Of course, he was not surprised that she was carrying his child. She had caught the baby from his breath in the first month they had spent together.

White people were funny. They thought you made a baby by sticking your cock into a woman. Stupid idea. Babies were conceived in the exchange of breath, and of spirit, when a man and woman came together.

He remembered that morning, all those years ago, right at sunrise. She took him by the shoulders, looked into his eyes, and told him that they had created a new human being last night. Two moons later she told him again. Yes, the child that swelled her belly was his.

And now that infant was grown into *this*, this . . .

Even at the moment she told him, he had understood that her words were intended to tether him, to keep him at home. But he was a man and would do as he wanted, and what he wanted was to ride broncs, drink, gamble, drink, gamble, and then drink and ride some more. Why not? People deserve the kind of life they want.

I picked Grandpa's ancient edition of *Don Quixote,* printed in Spanish, off a shelf and sat down on the big leather sofa intending to browse through it. But my thoughts took me wandering.

I was pretty sure I was the only person on the rez, right then, reading Cervantes. I was odd all right, and it didn't come from being the grandson of a Jew, the son of a

Navajo-Jewish woman, and being brought up in a trading post. Not really. It came from what my grandfather taught me. Make your own rules. Be fair. Be aware. Be bold. Take care of family. Learn. Learn more again. Love adventure. Sometimes, live on the edge.

Grandpa's ancestors had been driven out of Spain to Mexico, fleeing persecution, and then out of Mexico City to a remote province of New Mexico, living among Catholics, pretending to be Catholic, but in secret practicing Judaism. They learned that when you run from tyrannical authority, you can take only one thing with you—what you know. So he hammered education into me.

I grew up in a sea of Navajo language, but he taught me English, Spanish, and enough Hebrew that I could have been bar mitzvahed. He had less patience with formal religion than I did, and he was not an observant Jew. But he saw the Torah as a book of wisdom, and I would have bet he still read it, one-handed.

Cervantes rustled his pages at me.

I didn't hear her come in, so quiet as a deer she moved. She sat on the arm of the sofa, patted my arm.

"It's right to have you home. The third person here has been named Empty."

She looked at the book I was reading. "It's not just me who's missed you. Grandpa, you're his twin, his son, his grandson—all those things."

"He turned me into a big reader."

"He did that for both of us," my mother said. "You know the rhythm of life. It swings from blasts of hard work to bundles of blank time, time filled best by reading and stories."

I looked at my mother, my mother the woman. When I

left she was simply my mom. Now I could see her as a beautiful woman, the aging and wise person with infinite patience but who sometimes tore up the world like lightning. Big brains. Had she been lonely? It had never occurred to me that she was a real person with desires and hopes that had nothing to do with me. Selfish, childish, but true.

"Have you been okay? You wear yourself so fiercely, sometimes I forget, everyone around here forgets, that you're not Superwoman."

"Life is good, Yazzie. I have my relatives, my ancestors, their spirits. All of that keeps me warm."

Sure . . . I thought. And then she crept right inside my mind.

"Okay, a good man would have been nice, but that's not in the cards for everyone," she said. "Are you happy to be home, Yazzie? Some part of you feels half gone."

I smiled at her. "Mothers are terrible things," I said, and could not believe I'd said it. I expected her to cave. Her with no mother, and me with a big mouth.

"Don't look at me like that," she said. "Believe me, I have had enough aunts to understand about mothers, and I have been mother enough for ten kids to you. Let's forgive each other."

"For what?"

"Needing each other too much. Not always being honest."

And pretty soon I was going to tell her that I'd be gone in the morning. This was not going well for my insides, and it was going to get worse when I laid it all out on the table.

"And think of your grandfather," she said. "You idolize him, but he hasn't always been easy—no one knows that better than me. During winters by the woodstove or in blazing-hot summers, we had four strict hours of reading, writing, and arithmetic. Sometimes," she said, "it seemed like running this place was an interruption. Like our customers were a nuisance. It's a miracle we've had one dime to rub against the other."

I had enjoyed learning time, and it's true, sometimes I thought the customers were a bother, too. Reading by kerosene lamps, we rampaged through Homer to Shakespeare, from Dickens to Mark Twain. A herd of poets galloped with us, his favorite, Walt Whitman.

She put her head back and laughed.

"What?" I said.

"You think that you're an oddball? Think about how my side of the family sees us."

I didn't want to think about it. I knew how the whole thing worked, and it still made my head hurt. So many relations, everyone connected.

"They think we're pathetic," she said. "Some of them envy us the trading post, although I can tell you that not one of them would want to run it."

"I think you're proud of yourself."

"About running the trading post? Maybe. But that is a business, and money comes and goes. What I do have is blood relations galore, and relations matter. Gatherings matter. Counting aunts and uncles as parents, and counting nieces and nephews as kids, I have enough family to make a herd. I wrap them around me like a blanket. You and your grandfather, you never warmed to doing that."

She was right, but I felt defensive. "Grandpa loves his family in Santa Fe."

"Of course he does. He's always glad to welcome them and just as happy to see them head home."

She was right.

"That wasn't fair," she said. "He does love them very much. They sit with him in the center of culture, of the music and books that he loves. And you," she said, "fall in the middle of our two tribes."

"Not accepted by either," I said, "and accepted by both. Sometimes—"

"Stand up."

"What?"

"Right now," she said, "stand up."

I did.

"Ask me what will bring your two hearts together. Let me help you."

"Who is my father? What I carry of him is that question. . . . He died before I was born, I know that. You and Grandpa never utter one word about him. I don't even know his name."

She stood up in front of me and put both hands on my chest.

"You are several tribes, and there is no split. If you were being introduced to a Navajo family you didn't know—believe it or not, that might happen one day—then you will say who you are. Tell me. Say it."

I felt ridiculous, but I said it. Long time since I did that, in the Navajo way of introductions. "My Grandfather is born to Jew and born for Jew, no Navajo. My mother is born to the Bitter Water people and born for Jew. I am the same, my mother's clan and my grandfather's." Here I got stuck, but just a little. "I do not use my father, because I don't know his name or his clan. And, in our way, the father is the man who stays to raise the child. So my clan is my grandfather's."

She looked up at me. "And that is everything you need to know."

My father stayed where he had always been with my mother. *Don't know, don't care.* "Your son, Yazzie Goldman," I said to her, "born to the Bitter Water people, born for Jew."

Her eyes smiled and her back was straight. "You've got to get used to being who you are, Yazzie. It's time."

And then there was something. A noise, a feeling? Something.

"What is that?" I said.

"What?"

"That sound outside the window. A rustling."

She sat still and straight, shook her head. "Nothing. You've been living around so much noise that country silence sounds like a roar."

She stood and walked into the kitchen, the heart of our home, to finish cooking dinner for the family. I moved the curtain to the side, looking and listening. Probably just a passing wind tossing the squawberry branches. I closed the curtains, sat back down, and buried myself in Cervantes.

❖❖❖❖

Twenty-five years ago, when Zopilote came back from that last long ride on the whiskey—for three moons he had been gone—he found his boots and a worn-out saddle on the front porch. That was the time-polished way for a Navajo woman to say, "You're no longer my husband. Take your belongings, get going, and don't come back."

In that moment on the porch he stood transfixed, rigid

with a desire to have words with her. Mose Goldman opened the door and stood behind the latched screen, glaring at him. Then, without making a sound, he slowly closed the heavy door in the face of the discarded husband.

Zopilote had left his belongings, rode over a low rise, tied the pony, and walked back. Though he was sober, he wove and stumbled like a drunk, feeling for the first time the stirring of the Darkness Rolling that Holy Wind had breathed into him.

He hid in some rocks and watched the post. Not that he damn well couldn't guess what had already happened. What was going to happen.

It didn't take long. A Mexican was hovering around his wife, a friend of the big Jew from Santa Fe. This man had come out the previous autumn with some rich white men who brought big cameras and wanted to be packed into Rainbow Bridge for an exploration. Mose had accommodated them as packer and guide.

And now his wife, Nizhoni, had surely accommodated the Mexican in bed. Their bed.

When the three went to the dinner table that night, Zopilote crept to a window and listened. Everything he needed to hear was in one word. The Mexican called Zopilote's wife by the fond name Novia. Betrothed. Zopilote knew the odd Mexican custom of a couple's declaration of plans to wed—becoming *novia* and *novio* to each other—and then a ceremony in one of their fancy churches. *Very holy, getting permission from the gods to bed another man's woman. My woman.*

That evening the Mexican did not even come out and pretend to go to his sleeping place in the barn loft. The lanterns went dark in the main part of the house, but not in the bedrooms. Zopilote flew like a raptor outside the bedroom he'd shared with his wife, screwed his eyes into a corner of the window, and saw what he trembled to see. The *novia* and *novio* stripped off every stitch and got into bed together. Then, madly, she straddled him.

Rage exploded inside Zopilote. He crept to one side of the outhouse and waited. By chance, they walked out of the house together, carrying a single lantern. The Mexican waited while his wife—*wife!*—went inside. As the door closed, Zopilote struck.

His blade dug deep and hard into the chest. The Mexican roared with pain. So did Zopilote. That rage and agony, bullhorned, was the most satisfying moment of his life.

His wife burst out of the outhouse screaming. While she watched—he *wanted* her to see him, he wanted her to know who had burned her new life to ashes—he grabbed the Mexican's head from behind and pulled it back. Fixing his eyes on his wife's face, he slit the Mexican's throat.

Her screams brought her father running with a shotgun. Zopilote threw the knife at him. As the Jew dodged, Zopilote dashed behind the outhouse and sprinted into the darkness. He heard the bang of the weapon but felt not a single pellet touch him. He ran laughing into the darkness, his personal darkness.

On that terrible and magnificent night, Zopilote gloried in the thought of the Mexican's death. If the Mexican's spirit was still nearby, if the Mexican wanted him . . . *Come to me!* He shouted in his mind. *This is the beginning.*

Now, at the climax of those years, stoking his fire of hatred in the heat of prison, he yearned to see them. He decided to sneak close. He wanted to taste a thin slice of the life stolen from him. He found a crack in the curtains and peered through.

His son sat on the familiar leather sofa, holding a book. His wife, the boy's mother, Nizhoni, chattered at him like a bird. Women.

Zopilote's eyes recorded the details of the room. Scores of photos, probably displays of all the happiness these three had enjoyed and taken from him, this family that should have been his, all of their doings. The old man's shotgun, there where it had always been, a relic. Family smiles inside picture frames. Jokes. Remembrances. The sight of gold sunsets, turning to red and purple. The smell of dawn air. The feel of monsoon rains on parched skin. The rhythm of a good horse sprinting. The touch of a woman. The deep tang of whiskey. Hints of what could have been. Perhaps more children.

During those years his own spirit thirsted, and the Holy Wind parched his soul.

One day, after they had been punished, when her body lay violated nearby, Zopilote would walk around that room, study those photos at his leisure, and rejoice.

His soul reveled. He was home.

❖❖❖

Mom interrupted my reading, sat down on the sofa close to me. "The stew needs just a few more minutes."

She looked at me for a long while. Her mind turned to fretting, the other side of my mother's coin. She rattled on about the problems of the trading post. We sold very little. We did trade, Navajo to Navajo, even when we knew we

couldn't resell the items for a decent price. The post was
barely afloat. Then the worst: In the last few months, when
Grandpa was sick and then in rehab, she had to close down
and lose their customers to Goulding's. Mike Goulding,
Harry Goulding's wife, had done everything possible to help
them out, and sometimes she'd paid them more than their
stock was worth.

"We were okay in Santa Fe," Mom said. Though Grandpa's relatives had mostly scattered, his sister Frieda still
lived in the old family house, which was said to be grand at
one time, and no one went hungry there. Mom had spent a
fortune on Grandpa's medical bills, sold off treasures at half
of their value, and still she would have a hard time paying
off the rest without my help.

"When we got back from Santa Fe, your Grandpa and I
would have wasted away except that my family and our
neighbors brought us quarters of deer meat." Mom looked
down at her hands, folded in her lap. "Very tough time."

Her family's tribute to their legendary benefactor, Mose
Goldman.

From time to time she glanced out the window, probably
watching for truck lights.

"But a new year came, and what a difference," she said.
"That call from you saying you were headed home? What a
blessing."

"Then," I teased her, "the news about John Ford that you
kept from me."

"A giant boost for us. For the whole valley."

My mother wrote to storekeepers and traders we knew in
Flagstaff, promised them good discounts on our wool, our

rugs, our everything. Our necks stuck out on the chopping block farther yet.

"We've never lived high on the hog, but we weren't in debt. Now . . . ?"

Lights flicked across the living room windows. You-KnowWho was turning the pickup toward the hitching post. The mystery woman.

Mom jumped up. "Good that Mr. Ford is back," she said, her eyes dancing. "And you've come home just in time. Just in time."

The back door scraped open a few inches and got stuck.

"Yazzie, help her with that." Mom ran into the kitchen, and I followed after. Grandpa sat at the pine table, using his weak arm to lift a can of beans over his head. Back down on the table. Up over his head again. His barbell, a can of beans.

Looked like I would have to rehang that door. A lift up from inside and there stood . . .

Who's this?

A young woman slipped by, olive-skinned, with crinkly black hair down to her waist. She could have been a Navajo, except that she was wearing pants and had a kitten on one shoulder.

"Hi, Grandpa," she called. "Hi, Nizhoni, hi . . ." She noticed me standing behind the door. "You must be Yazzie."

A good face. Never mind the almond shape, pert mouth, and bowed nose. She had eyes big as dinner plates and the blue-violet color of forget-me-nots.

She stuck out her hand. "I'm Iris." I shook, and she gripped like a white man.

Then she smiled big and her face turned a funny corner. One of her two upper front teeth twisted half-sideways like a door ajar. I smiled, and I stared right at the open door in her mouth. Rude, but it caught me off guard. "I came out with your Grandma Frieda. Oh. I know. Very original teeth!" She touched the tooth with the tip of a finger. And then she laughed.

Perky beauty with a kitten friend.

I wondered how Grandma Frieda got into this picture. Then I remembered—she'd mentioned a daughter, her daughter, in some of her letters to us from New York. Those letters that came, regular as clockwork, even before she'd moved back to Santa Fe. Frieda was Grandpa's baby sister.

Iris sat down next to Grandpa and kissed him on the cheek. He didn't miss a beat with that can of beans.

"Wait," I said, "you're my aunt?" My head started to pound. This Navajo family relations business could give a person a headache.

She cocked her head.

I said, "I call you Aunt Iris?"

"You want a black eye? It's Iris," she said. "But I get it. Navajos call their mother's sister 'mother,' and you call our grandmother's sisters 'grandmother.'"

She was kind of an exotic wise-ass. Good-looking, probably a couple of years older than me. Strange to think of her as my aunt.

I couldn't take my eyes off the kitten.

"You want to hold him?" She reached the cat out to me, and I took it. Not bad—cuddly.

"His name is Cockeyed."

I looked a question at her.

"Take a gander at his right eye."

I held the kitten up in front of my face. Sure enough, while the left eye looked straight at me, the right one pointed out and up, seeing who knows what?

"I'm cockeyed in one tooth, and he's the same in one eye."

"Where'd you get him?" Definitely not from around here—he would have been coyote chow by now.

"When Mom and I drove Uncle Mose and Nizhoni out here, I brought him along for company. He was barely weaned, and he's still just a kitty."

"Don't let him run around outside—you won't have him long."

My mother had ladled food into beautiful hand-beaten silver bowls and onto Pueblo pottery serving dishes. She took one last look around the kitchen and announced, "Dinner is ready!"

I walked into the dining room and flipped on the lights above the table, bulbs affixed to a wagon wheel, the local version of a chandelier.

Iris put Cockeyed on her shoulder and quick-footed it in the direction of food, carrying serving bowls to the dining table. She went back into the kitchen, her hands ever-moving. It seemed that was her way, hands never still, body in perpetual motion. It was like she was dancing to a tune only she could hear.

Grandpa wheeled himself to the head of the table. Mom slid a tray of hot fry bread next to him and plunked down a jar of honey. She sat at Grandpa's left, Iris next to her, and I sat across from the women, still mystified.

Mom's face was animated now. "How do you like our surprise?"

Grandpa grinned in his distorted way.

Mom jumped in. "Frieda knows what family is. Which is why she drove out, got Grandpa and me, and carted us right back with her to Santa Fe when we needed help. What a woman, sixty years old, more like twenty, and driving that dirt road from Flagstaff? Then your grandfather decided he'd had enough rehab"—she gave Grandpa a look of disapproval—"and Frieda drove us back here. Iris came along. . . ."

"And I fell in love with the place."

"Now we can't get rid of you." Mom tried to grin.

"You've been herding sheep?" I said. Unbelievable.

"Am I enamored of that part of life here? I think not. Who would love camping out and watching sheep curl their wool and squirt shit five days a week? And what has Nizhoni sent me out to eat but canned Spam and biscuits? I mean, awright, I'm no observant Jew, but *Spam*? And the biscuits, cold and stale? Thank God I had Cockeyed to talk to."

Iris's accent was strong, and I'd heard women say cuss words before, although not many.

"Mom's not really tough," I said. "She's just trying to promote you to Jake Charlie status."

Iris stuck out her tongue at me.

My aunt had pizzazz.

"Why did you come from New York, which to me might as well be Paris, to this far end of the planet? And stay?" The whole family had visited us, but not since Great-Grandpa died, maybe eight years ago. Centuries ago, it felt like.

She smiled. "Not now. But, if you're a good boy, I'll show you in the morning."

There it came, another corkscrew of guilt. I'd arrived just before dark, would be gone as soon as the sun came up, and I still hadn't said a word about it. My mother was right. We weren't always great about being honest with each other.

"Are you excited to be home?" said Iris. "You are, right?"

More and more guilty.

Mom got up and went to the kitchen. I knew she didn't, could not, see the big rejection coming. Or what would feel like to her as rejection.

I faked a grin. I said, lowering my voice as if I was some newscaster on the radio, reading the latest from the front:

"Headline: WAR SURVIVOR KILLED BY BOREDOM

"Subhead: OVER ONE HUNDRED SHEEP ARE SUSPECTS IN DEATH OF SEAMAN GOLDMAN"

Iris threw her arms high, and Cockeyed slid into the crook of her neck. "Why not follow my lead?" she said. "Get delirious to be here. This place is pure magic. Maybe you need to see it with fresh eyes, not with your memories."

I didn't know what to think about that. Iris fit on the rez like an Arab at Yom Kippur. Navajos are soft-spoken people, always patient and courteous, and we go to any length to avoid dispute. A New Yorker? That's probably as far from Navajo as you can get.

Passing the food, we started filling up our bowls and plates. The scent, the steam. It was pretty close to heaven.

"You want to tell me about the world war?" Iris said. "You know, the one our country didn't get into until Hitler had killed half the Jews in Europe?"

"For me, what war?" It was good to have an audience.

"When I enlisted, which was 'thirty-nine, no one really expected a war, at least not in Asia. They sent me to San Diego, and I got a blue-water assignment as a seaman. Water to the east of us, waves to the west of us . . ."

"Oh, poor baby."

"Hey, I signed on to see the world—'Go Navy!' What I saw, total, was Pearl Harbor for a refueling stop. We got eight hours of liberty and hopped right back onboard. I didn't get to see one grass skirt."

"Bet you wanted to do more than see," said Iris.

Grandpa made a coughing sound that seemed to either be his try at laughter or putting a lid on it for Mom.

"When we got back to San Diego, I asked for shore patrol duty. A lot of sailors hate it, but I thought it was good work and good times. At first it's just patrolling, you know, the bars and—"

"Whorehouses," Iris chipped in.

Jeez, what a tongue on a woman. I fumbled my way forward. " . . . And finding sailors who are drunk and getting them back on board before they get into trouble. Sometimes you have to rap a head with a baton, but usually nothing much. Made me think that maybe, when my tour was over, I might want to be a cop. Something like that."

"Such talk," Mom said. "Let's think of a nicer topic for the dinner table." Meaning no talk about anything but me spending the rest of my natural life at the trading post.

Cockeyed curled up in Iris's lap, fifth diner at the table. Even before her first bite, Iris asked me, "You ever fire your piece?"

Mom glared at her. Evidently, Iris didn't put much stock in "nice."

"I shot into the ground one time. That put a quick stop to a scrap that was brewing up. That was about it.

"Something good came along, though. Two things, actually. One, I asked for long-term duty on shore patrol. For most guys, it's just the duty of that particular day, but having one sailor in every patrol who has a lot of experience works well. So I got what I wanted.

"Then came my real break. I showed some of the NCIS guys—that's Naval Criminal Investigative Service—I showed them that I wanted to learn how to investigate crimes and do it right. You know, like suppose a real crime was committed, let's say assault or assault with a deadly weapon, and the perpetrator, or the victim, was a sailor. In comes NCIS."

"A cop? No kidding?" Iris tore off a small bit of lamb and fed it to Cockeyed on her lap. My aspirations didn't seem to impress her.

"Almost all the NCIS guys are officers, you know, above everybody else. But one man, a warrant officer, took to me and offered help. He said if I passed the exam and went up one more grade, he'd ask that I be on his team. I passed and got the duty. So guess what? I got to be a real cop."

Iris leaned her forehead into her hand. "Oy vey."

"I loved it. Actually, my thought was . . ." Normally, I wouldn't have said this—why did Iris make me talkative? "Actually, I'm thinking with that experience, maybe I'll look for work as a railroad dick."

Iris grinned at the word.

"I've always loved the sound of that train coming in and out of Flagstaff, and add that to my cop experience? It seems like a natural."

Mom interrupted, and she dismissed my talk with one wave of her hand. "Enough of all this. Time for dessert. You three adjourn to the sofa."

Grandpa settled his wheelchair at the end of the big leather couch. Iris and I found seats at each end. Mom cleared the empty plates. I took Cockeyed, held him, and studied his crazy eye. Weird and sort of hypnotic, both . . . kind of like a New York aunt being here in Navajo-land.

"Where do you think that off-eye looks?" said Iris.

"Into the great unknown," I said.

She was pleased by that.

Just then Mom came out from the kitchen with a cobbler made of dwarf peaches. I'm sure the Anasazi didn't have anything like that peach cobbler. I'm also sure they enjoyed the dwarf peaches, the sticky juice running down arms, as much as we do. She was really putting on the dog for me, and I loved it. Grandpa had gotten our trees from a Hopi trader as saplings decades ago. We stored the dried peaches in the root cellar over the winter and reconstituted the slices in water for treats. Mom handed us full bowls and sat facing us across the coffee table.

"Ummm, this is pure bliss," said Iris. Then she eyed me. Eyebrows arching, she said, " 'Dick' is exactly the right word, isn't it?"

It's like I'd erased my mind when we left the dining table, and my face went hot. Then I remembered. The railroad. "You're having way too much fun razzing me."

She tilted her head and pursed her mouth, trying not to smile. She took a big bite of cobbler. I decided that waiting for her to have a mouthful of food was the perfect time to talk.

"And, yep, that's really what they're called, the railroad detectives—'dicks.' And, yes, I really want to work on the Santa Fe Super Chief."

"The Super Chief!" Mom practically yelled. "You've gone *degeez!*" She looked sideways at Iris. "Sorry, it means 'crazy.' "

Ride the Super Chief! Travel like a rich man. Explore L.A. Chicago!

I could see it. I could taste it. I wanted it.

I went on before Mom went completely wild. "Mom, if I got that kind of job, I could pay off Grandpa's medical costs. Which otherwise would take forever."

Mom waited, then drew herself as tall as a five-footer could and acted out her high-style queen of the roost. "You will stay here and run this place. Iris is sweet to help out, especially with Grandpa being like this, but it's temporary."

Iris said, "Why shouldn't I stay? I love it here."

"Yes, but you want to paint, paint, paint, and not the kind that needs doing—house painting."

I was trying to avoid conflict, acting calm inside, but it was getting hard to carry off. What was Mom going to say when I told her I was leaving tomorrow morning? So I said to Iris, "You paint?"

She shrugged in a way that meant 'Later.' Cockeyed rode up and down Iris's shoulders, one eye fixed on me, the other seeking the mysteries.

Mom came at me again. "You want to lose the horses?

You want rain to ruin Grandpa's rugs? And rain in our beds?
What on earth are you thinking?"

Mom wasn't acting a bit Navajo. But she was raised by a
man who could get in your face as well as anyone. Second,
she never knew her own mother. And third, she was a trader.
She could talk tough to white people as easy as act nice with
Navajos. This was that lightning part of her, and it was
damned hard to stay clear.

"I'm waiting," said Mom.

I gave in. "Okay, sorry, but I can't talk about this. Not
right now."

Everybody sat in the silence that is rightly called dead.

><><><

Zopilote watched the talk, the fun, the intimacy, with acid
in his throat. He mouthed one word over and again—
"family." Family was what they had cheated him out of.
All those years he had never realized. When his wife and
the old trader sold him out, this circle of relationship,
this warmth, this hearth of affection—*this is what they stole
from me.*

He had never understood. Not clearly.

In county jail, during the trial, and during the years in
prison, every day Zopilote replayed that awful picture of her,
legs spread wide, hips rising and falling, until she shrilled
out her pleasure. Then his enemy flipped her over, quick
and hard, and climaxed inside her.

Zopilote raged at the theft of flesh, the flesh of *his*
woman.

The Mexican's life was no payment for her treachery. Nor

had she paid for the twenty-five years of Zopilote's life slain, sunrise by sunrise.

In all his years behind bars, Zopilote got only one communication from the outside world. It arrived shortly after he was locked up in the state pen, a letter from the old trader. It was written in English and had to be translated for him. After he learned to read, he looked at it and mumbled the words over and over, until the paper crumbled.

Yes, your ex-wife is with child. She knows it is your child. So do you.

But you abandoned her, and she threw you away as a husband.

This child's father will be me.

It is my great pleasure to slap your face with this knowledge. You will never see your own offspring. You have no wife. You have no child. You will spend your life in a cage and have no solace.

—Mose Goldman

Zopilote dismissed the letter as a vain attempt to squash his spirit, and he resolved to make it do the opposite.

Now he grasped the meaning of the letter in a more tortured way. *I have been robbed of family.* This truth burned hot.

❖❖❖

I stroked Cockeyed. He purred on my lap, the only sound in the room. But the cozy comfort started to feel like a cold ocean. I was swamped, awash and drowning in guilt.

And so I came right out with it. "Listen up. This is a hard thing to say. Mr. John hired me today, while I was on my way home with Jake Charlie. Tomorrow I'm going all the way to Seligman and then on to Winslow. Then I drive back."

"What are you talking about?" That was Mom.

"Mr. John hired me as a bodyguard, from the train all the way to Monument Valley, for an actor who's coming in for his new movie. I'll be gone about four days, maybe less." Although, I was hoping maybe more.

Mom marched around the coffee table and plopped on the couch next to me. She almost sat right on my hot cobbler, but I fast slid it away.

"You'll be back as soon as possible, you say, and all of this"—she motioned with her chin to take in our entire property, inside and out—"has to wait for a few more days. I hope," she said, "he's paying you enough to make up for the time you'll lose here."

"Mom, we need the money."

Her face went white. "You've been gone so long that you think money answers every problem."

I was ashamed for being a bad son. What had I been thinking of? Myself. Gone six years, and I turn around and leave. She wrapped her arms around my neck, and I felt her tears, wet against my skin.

She pulled herself together quick and made a little distance between us. She spoke low and flat. How long would I be gone this time? Exactly? Who else was going? Why did I need to do this thing? Exactly? Why now?

Grandpa's look was impossible to read. He was waiting for the whole story before he got out the scales and weighed the worth of my actions. The cat got up, stretched, and padded onto Iris's lap. She stroked it, but its tail curled and uncurled, over and over.

I put an arm around Mom, and she brushed it off. She let me rest my hand on her shoulder, and I answered her questions. I told her the truth, most of it.

"Mom, I'm trying to do what's best. I'll make a lot of money working for Mr. John. This place needs fixing, the money will pay for that. The medical bills, money will take care of that, too."

Mom's voice sizzled. "I need you here. I'm counting on you. What if you decide not to come back? What if you head straight from Mr. John to a train job?"

"Mom, you need to listen."

"No, you need to listen. I have shared you with the government of the United States. You wanted to go, and it was also a duty. Mr. John is not a duty. The war is over."

"I have a present for you," I said.

"And here is something else you may not have thought about, while—"

Grandpa uttered something garbled. He raised his good left arm and flailed it. His garbled talk was hyped-up. I didn't understand it. Mom either. More flailing. He pulled out his chalkboard.

He pointed to his daughter, and then to me. GIFT + LISTEN.

She pulled back a little. Nizhoni Goldman studied her father's face. He urged her with his eyes.

"You have a gift for us," she said. "I will listen to you."

I plunged in with enthusiasm. "I hired Katso and Oltai

Neez to do the fix-up work for you. Ten days of labor. I promised them five dollars a day each."

"Five dollars!"

"If you need them longer, just say so. Here's enough to pay them." I fished out the five twenty-dollar bills Mr. John had advanced me and tucked them into her hand.

She crumpled them up and tossed the wad onto the coffee table. She leaned her head on my chest, and I felt her body go inward. Her words came out and echoed inside me. "Yazzie, are you remembering that you and Grandpa are my home? Home is not a place, it's my family. It's your family."

"I know, Mom."

No more words, her head still rested on my chest, and she started patting me.

Grandpa, Iris, and I said nothing.

Finally, she lifted her head, dignity renewed. Mom wiped her cheeks with her palms. At length she forced words out. "We're all tired. Let's go to bed. We'll eat a big breakfast."

"Mom, I'll be leaving at sunup."

"Then your breakfast will be ready before first light," she said.

I stood and walked slowly toward the room where I had slept for nearly two decades, turning once to look back at the three of them. Such a display of emotion, of loss, and of hopes gone crooked. My family looked stunned. I felt the same way.

I closed my bedroom door. I thought about my situation. I took a deep breath. I hadn't said that I got to escort a super-glamorous woman. That part could wait for later. Much later.

Soon it would be dawn, and I would be headed into a

bright unknown. And all of this other? It would have to wait, just for a little while.

❖❖❖❖

Home is not a place, it's family.

As the home lights went out, Zopilote stumbled into the darkness, his chest heaving.

Four

Linda Darnell waltzed down the aisle of the dining car, a waiter trailing behind her holding high a bucket of ice with a bottle in it. She smiled, and that smile of hers was a cut-crystal vase, lights bouncing off into rainbows. "Seaman Goldman," she said, holding out a hand like she expected me to kiss it.

I stood smartly, took the hand, which was surprisingly warm, and helped her into the window seat opposite me. "Miss Darnell." A bare-boned Southwest landscape whirled past the windows.

I looked quickly behind us and then sat. Since no one else was in the car, my performance was just that.

She nodded gaily to the waiter. The white-coated Negro set a champagne glass in front of her, popped the cork on the bottle, and poured. Bubbles floated up from the glass stem. Then he poured a glass for me. She held her glass up and sang aloud, "To you and all the men who won the war." Holding the elegant shape high above her head, she opened up and waterfalled champagne into her lovely mouth. Every drop.

I laughed. *She's going to be fun.*

I stood and came back with, "To the spirit that won the war." I sipped the bubbling wine and took my seat again. Theatrics were new to me.

The waiter poured Miss Darnell a second glass. I covered mine with one hand. She raised hers, drained it, and said, "Seaman Goldman, please step back, so I can see you."

I did.

"Well, aren't you the strapping specimen? How tall are you?"

"Six feet six inches."

She lifted the glass, held it out toward me, and said, "To handsome men in uniform." This time she let the champagne linger on her tongue before draining the glass.

I sat down, grinning. I was glad I'd worn my dress whites. Foolishly, I murmured my full name. "Yazzie Jacob Goldman. Please call me Yazzie. Seaman Goldman is in the past."

"To the present," she said. "Drink up! Champagne is to be consumed greedily, like life." She tossed down a third glass.

I offered another toast. "To the most stunning woman I have ever seen."

Her laugh was a glissando.

I wasn't kidding. Her beauty was dazzling—raven hair, flawless olive skin, and brilliant green eyes—plus I was entranced by her playfulness. Okay, yeah, maybe other movie stars were heavenly. But this one was a merry demon. When she turned her face to me fully, my skin flushed hot.

The waiter still stood at attention. "Miss Darnell, would you care for something to eat?"

"Yes," she said, "a margarita." A flash of that demonic smile. Then she gave exact specifications, tequila of a brand I'd never heard of, *añejo y commemorativo,* with fresh-squeezed lime juice, a brand of some liqueur I'd never heard of, and the glass rimmed with sea salt.

"You speak Spanish," I said. Hers sounded almost fluent.

She nodded. "In high school I got assigned to help a Mexican student with his English, and he taught me Spanish at the same time. We turned into chatter birds."

I waited. There was more to the story.

"Because of my complexion, people assume I'm Latino. In this movie I'm playing a Mexican dance-hall girl. Actually, I'm not one drop Mexican. My grandfather was Cherokee. My brothers and sisters are light-skinned."

She gave a *Who cares?* smile.

"So we're both Indians," I said.

She chuckled. I felt like she was opening a door, maybe to friendship. "It seems so." Down went some of that margarita. "You're an all-American Navajo, Seaman? With a last name like Goldman?"

"My grandfather, Mose Goldman, is a Spanish Jew from Santa Fe. We spoke Spanish, English, and Navajo at the dining table from the time I could walk."

That really got her laughing. She stopped, apologized, and said she'd just been surprised. "What a combination of ingredients!" And adios went more of her margarita.

I wanted to ask her questions. Where are you from? What's your family like? Did you grow up rich? How does it feel to be ticketed for superstardom? But I judged I'd better wait for her to volunteer.

When we ordered food, I asked for oysters Rockefeller. At home last night I'd used Grandpa's encyclopedia to find out the proper name and make sure what they were—oysters baked in a sauce of butter and a secret blend of green vegetables. I'd even memorized the name of the recommended white wine. I wanted to make the right impression.

I soon learned that the Rockefellers were good at making money but not appetizers, at least not to my tongue. Not to hers either. She actually spit the first bite out, right into her linen napkin. She waved the waiter over, and he took the plate away, apologizing as if he'd invented the dish himself.

I could barely keep a straight face as she ordered green chile salsa and tortilla chips instead.

Miss Darnell gave me a look that said, *Well, I'm glad you're not going to slow down my fun.*

No chance of that. Full steam ahead with this woman, whistle blasting.

Zipping the eighty miles toward Flagstaff, we laughed and cut up like old friends and told silly stories. She asked what my service in the war had been.

"A cop," I said. "Shore patrol. Navy."

I was afraid she'd think less of me, probably hoping I'd been at Guadalcanal or something. Instead she seemed excited. "Did you carry a gun!?"

I felt acutely conscious of the service .45 auto holstered on the left side under my blouse, which she hadn't spotted.

I answered, "Also a baton."

"Did you ever shoot anyone?"

"Not yet."

She hooted at that one. No shyness in this woman. If it was rowdy, she'd go for it.

Eventually, she tired. "I'm sorry, Seaman Goldman"— apparently she couldn't get to "Yazzie" yet—"but I must go to my compartment. I need to freshen up for our arrival at La Posada. You needn't cover my door. Let's be cautious, but not paranoid."

◈◈◈◈

I stood in the vestibule while the diesel engines bulled the train up the long climb to Flagstaff. I looked down at the wheels as they powered up the tracks and the steep grade, whipping gravity. I felt the diesel engines lift the cars and passengers, all of us spray on a sea-monster's back. The energy clacked and rattled through my feet, my legs, my ass, and my spirit with a thousand volts. The whole experience was an amplified drum and bugle corps rising and roaring through my body.

I loved it.

And then I saw the magic. Raising my eyes northward and high, so very high, we climbed the foothills of the San Francisco Peaks. These are the westernmost of the Four Sacred Mountains of Dinetah, which means Navajoland, and they stirred my heart. My spirit and blood were teased by the sacred stories of these mountains.

My mind, though, was dizzy with the vivid experience of my one hour spent with Linda Darnell. The awesome power of the train and the whirlwind experience of the woman blended together into a tidal wave of feelings. She had me transfixed. I was about to leap off a precipice into infatuation. Or lust. Something that was either trouble, ecstasy, or both.

With her crowding even the Super Chief out of my fantasy life, I barely noticed Flagstaff as we zipped through. Looking back at the San Francisco Peaks, I regretted how little attention I'd given them this time. Was I the man Grandpa had raised or someone horse-powered only by hormones?

❖❖❖❖

At Winslow, I helped Miss Darnell down the steps onto the platform. There Julius met us and made sure two porters toted her luggage. I followed her through the formal garden to the famous La Posada Hotel. *My privilege, ma'am.*

I thought I'd better own up. "I've never stayed in a hotel."

"Well, I know *all* about them."

I smiled to myself. Innuendos there?

We paraded along a brick wall toward a handsome fountain. "This must be one of the grand ones."

"For Arizona," she allowed.

La Posada was a castle-sized Spanish Colonial, with lots of Southwestern Indian touches. The gardens stunned me, like something you'd see surrounding an Italian palace in a movie. Painted pottery, bright with every color, splashed water into lower pots, down and down, until the water came together and formed a pool filled with large golden fish. Jacaranda and a showy kind of blooming cactus circled the garden, lush with banana plants and some sort of water system that kept everything moist. Rock roses, like the ones at home, were reflected in the pond. I was thinking how much Mom would love to have a garden like this. She fought every spring just to raise up her tomatoes and gourds.

Miss Darnell looked like she was somewhere else, and I decided to bring her back. "Mary Colter designed this hotel," I said, showing off my knowledge. "Nearly the only woman in a man's profession."

Linda nodded, with a hint of, *Another woman, who cares?*

"I've seen one other building she designed in this area. Grandpa took me there, the Watchtower, in the Grand Canyon. It's done in the Pueblo style and perched right on the edge of a cliff that juts out over the gorge. You feel as if that tower is a red-tailed hawk, about to launch into five thousand feet of bubbling air.

"Inside, the tower is covered with the paintings of a great Hopi artist, Fred Kabotie. My Grandfather is a trader. He sells that kind of art—he knows all the artists and everything about their work."

She gave my hand a little squeeze. I couldn't tell whether she was flirting with me, humoring me, or telling me she'd heard enough.

We walked past the reception desk, where Julius was taking care of registration. To our right stretched a pale turquoise hall, long and high. I'd never imagined such a display of Southwestern Indian art. It was king-size and absolutely terrific. I was at home here. I could tell her all about it.

I led her toward an eagle kachina made by a carver who Grandpa had taken me to meet down at Third Mesa, on the Hopi Reservation. "That—"

Miss Darnell took my hand and squeezed again. A big yawn told me this squeeze meant, *Enough for now.*

Julius sidled up and handed her a key. "Your room, Miss Darnell. And a letter for you." He handed me another key. "Our room," he said, "next door."

"I believe I'll go freshen up," she said, eyes tired. "Then maybe you'll give me a tour." She waved at the art and set off behind Julius and the bellman.

I took advantage of her two hours of getting fresh to check out the art thoroughly. Before the navy, I'd spent my life in a house jammed with Navajo and Pueblo art, selling it to the few tourists we got or toting it to traders in Flagstaff. Still, I had never seen anything like these pieces. They were bigger, more ambitious, and more imaginative than I'd dreamed possible. My first thought had been to sound like an expert to Miss Darnell. Now I didn't care if I sounded like what I was, awestruck. I found the manager and asked him about the artists, where they lived, what their clan was. He was glad to talk about them.

"Let's have a drink," she said from behind me.

After a quick introduction to the manager, I escorted her to the bar, and she went through the same routine with the ingredients of her margarita.

"The same for my friend," she told the barman.

"No," I spoke up, "I'm working. I'd better not." Maybe Mr. John sent me to guard Linda Darnell against a known threat. I ought to ask Julius, who'd spotted himself on a stool at the far end of the bar, where he had a wide range of vision and an open field of fire. Why did Mr. John send two bodyguards, instead of a bodyguard and a driver?

When her second margarita came, I saw her look at the fourth finger of her left hand. She tossed me a devilish smile and slipped the ring off and into her clutch purse.

"You're married," I said.

She licked the salt off the rim of her margarita glass and said, "Sort of. You?"

"I don't see that in my near future. And the way Navajos do it—"

"*It?* You do it differently?"

She knew what I meant. Or didn't mean. "The way we get married. Real traditional. My mother is set to choose my wife."

Her eyes danced. "Oh, I see. And how does she do that?"

"It's got to be someone I've never met. Some people are so squeamish about it, that if you drew pictures together when you were five years old, forget it. Plus, you're not allowed to see each other until the wedding day."

She whooped at that one. I wished it was a joke. "What happens if the two don't like each other?"

"That happened with an uncle of mine. One look, he and his new wife hated each other. The family tossed them in a hogan together, boarded up the door, and by the time three days went by? They liked each other very well."

"And who will your mother choose for you? Any guesses?"

"That custom, it's not for me. I intend to marry who I damned well please."

She glinted, she glowed, and I think she thought I was too funny—not in the good way—for words. After another drink, we went in to dinner.

Linda asked for a table where we could look out on the gardens. The maître d' bowed too deeply and said, "Anything for Miss Darnell." Again Julius took a table with command position.

She put her small purse on the table and pulled out her compact and dabbed powder under her eyes.

"Miss Darnell? I'm not trying to be nosy, but there is your purse, wide open, and there is an envelope jammed inside it."

She looked away from the mirror for a split second, glanced at me, and went back to studying herself.

Her tone didn't sound so merry all of a sudden. "You're very observant, aren't you?"

"My job, I—"

"Your job does not include rummaging through my purse."

"We both know I didn't do that."

"Good."

"But Julius handed you a letter when you checked in," I said. "Who knows you're here?"

"You mean other than the entire movie crew, Mr. Ford, his entourage, my manager, the people who take care of my home, the—"

"Your husband?"

"Of course," she said. "Look, I get lots of mail. Could we just have a nice dinner?"

I felt like an idiot, but it occurred to me I might feel like that plenty of times while I was taking care of this particular lady. I apologized, she accepted, but my job was still my job. I'd just have to learn to do it better. That was all.

With the menu in her hand, she came alive, and all was forgotten. All was a delight. "Posole," she said, dwelling on the syllables like she could taste the hominy, pork, and green chiles. "I love it."

"Where did you grow up?"

She looked into my face, took a pause, and made a choice. "Cherokee country. Then we moved to Dallas. It's Dallas that feels like home. The people there are real, not like those Hollywood phonies."

She tucked her face back into the menu. "I want some fry bread with honey to start."

Now I was looking at the ring on her right hand. It was a beaut. "May I see that?"

"Sir, you are an unusual man."

"Hey, you grow up in a trading post, you notice jewelry. Part of the deal."

She held her hand across the table. The stone was a brilliant emerald, like her eyes, and circled by small diamonds. Her hand was soft, sweet.

She took it back. "A gift," she said. Nothing about her husband or a boyfriend or . . .

"Your skin," I said, "smells like sagebrush right after rain."

"What an extraordinary thing to say. Thank you." She cocked her head, maybe reassessing me. Maybe just thinking about posole.

My sense of smell, all my senses, felt more acute. No doubt about it, the gleaming presence of Linda Darnell could wake a dead man.

Her eyes roamed around the dining room, which had viga and latilla construction, big horizontal beams supporting slender poles. "I think vigas are so manly," she said. "What a miracle. Mary Colter turned these common materials into something grand. That's courage. Not always easy to make yourself known."

Unless you're the most beautiful woman in Hollywood. This lady was a puzzle inside a puzzle. Which would make

my job, protecting her, trickier than I'd expected. Best to pre-
pare for the unexpected. Without, as she'd said, being paranoid. A fine tightrope.

For me, that dining room was an oasis of Southwest
color and design. The china was thick, same as they used
on the train. White dishes with deep red or black Hopi-style
rabbits, coyotes, storm patterns, and ancient people running
along the edges. They were hand-painted, so each piece was
a little different. The Navajo rugs hanging on the walls were
mostly eye-dazzlers with a few Two Grey Hills thrown in,
and all of them large. The placemats were train scenes, and
every one was a love song to the colors turquoise, yellow,
and orange. Mexican pavers on the floor caught our words
and held them. My grandfather would have said it was pure
grace. Nothing like Hollywood here. Nothing like any place
in the world. No wonder movie stars loved this hotel.

The waiter appeared. Miss Darnell ordered the fry
bread, followed by posole.

"Tell me all about yourself, please," she said. Miss Darnell placed her pretty chin in the palm of her hand and leaned
forward. "Other than who you are *not* going to marry."

I wanted to tell my story, because it would raise me in her
eyes. Of course, the story was mostly about my family. My
grandfather, and his devotion to the trading post, to his family, to the Navajo people, and especially to educating me. I
was a branch on Grandpa's tree. A branch growing thicker
and thicker, I implied.

As I talked, she gazed at me with those river-green eyes,
eyes that told me that what I was saying was the most interesting thing she'd ever heard. In her life? That wasn't possible.

The food came—mine the green chile stew, hers the spicy hominy soup. While we ate, I made a couple of attempts to turn the conversation to her, but she steered it back to me. "You're such a rare creature," she commented. I thought I liked that, though I wasn't sure.

When we finished eating, she led the way to the bar and sailed back into her margaritas. I studied out the room. It didn't look like there was anything or anyone to worry about. Which was a good thing, because she was tipsy for sure now. That made her smile more charming, her laugh more heady, and she begged more hungrily for my stories. She clasped my forearm every time she got excited or silly.

My first full-fledged dunk into star power. I was swimming her current just fine, but it was one whale of a ride.

Then, like pink sky breaking into deep blue, her whole attitude changed. She waved at Julius, got his attention, and beckoned him over. In an imperious tone she said, "Julius, thank you for everything today. I'll be all right now. I won't be needing you."

When he started to protest, she gave him a look that said, *Be gone, little man, and not a word.* And he was gone.

She gave me a long look of appraisal and eventually took a chance. "Yazzie," she said, the first time she'd called me that, "being a movie star is a lot of work. I'm always on. I can't be myself with movie people, and they're not themselves with me. It's playacting. All of it."

The bartender came to ask if we wanted another drink, but before he could speak, she shook her head no.

"I'm wondering if you and I could be friends."

I was stumped.

"I had good friends in Dallas, regular folks. I talked to

the girls about clothes and makeup and boys, and talked to the boys about hunting and baseball. Real stuff."

Another left turn. I couldn't get a word out.

She rescued me. "So, friends?"

"Sure," I said.

She sized me up. "I think you'd better see me to my room now."

I did.

At the door she said, "Don't stay up all night and stand next to my door, please. Studio protection, it's too much. As I told Julius, if anything happens, I'll scream loud enough to wake the dead." She gave me a peck on the cheek. "Enjoy your night with Julius," she said.

I didn't think leaving her alone in a room with a skeleton-key lock was such a hot idea, but I'd been given instructions, and I wasn't going to buck them. She wasn't the one paying me, but she was the boss. At least when it came to me.

My room was enough to calm me to the inside of my bones, despite the delicious Linda Darnell. Julius's wheeze was soft. The room was pretty. Black-and-white tiles, the two finest carved wooden headboards I had ever seen, and a claw-foot bathtub. I cleaned myself up and opened the windows. Some kind of tree with feathery leaves blew against the screen, just a gentle caress. La Posada truly was a paradise hidden in the middle of the desert, and, I have to say, a real surprise tucked inside a mostly ugly town. I fell asleep listening to the leaves and smelling sage in the garden below.

The next morning Julius was gone. I found him upright and standing opposite her door. Not to be outdone, I leaned on the wall next to him. I could hear Miss Darnell humming while she got ready, some Mexican love song.

She emerged, a vision of splendor. My breath caught for a moment. She gave Julius her imperious look. "Call my agent," she told him. "Tell him I have to stay in this lovely hotel another day. I need the rest. He can fix it with the studio."

Julius waggled his stogie up and down once and headed for the front desk, which seemed to mean yes.

She took my arm and let me escort her to the restaurant. When I gave my coffee order, I waited to see if she'd ask for a margarita for breakfast. "A Bloody Mary, please," she said, "with plenty of Tabasco."

She beamed at me. "Now that we're friends," she said, "tell me about a good time you had in Southern California."

I was tongue-tied. She waited. No help in sight. I dived in.

"Uh, two navy buddies and I went to The Pike in Long Beach." Everyone had heard of the place, an extravaganza of an amusement park made famous by the 1904 World's Fair. I spun out short tales, well embroidered as stories should be. The first was about the majestic rise and fall of the Ferris wheel. Gaining confidence, I flew into the wild ride on the roller coaster. I paraded out the laughs of the fun house, horsing around in the penny arcades, and the strangeness of the Laughing Lady. Finally I jumped into my excitement about the Diving Bell.

I stopped and waited.

She shrugged her shoulders and studied her placemat. Seemed like I'd just gotten a C on a test.

"My turn. My husband," she said, "is a good man. He photographed a couple of early movies of mine. We're friends. But that's all we are, friends. Well, more like father-daughter."

She let that one sit. It was uncomfortable.

"There's a man I'm dating, but he—"

She stopped short and changed direction. Talking to her was like watching a complicated bank shot on a pool table. Quick left, sharp angled right, straight back at you, and rolling to a stop nowhere in particular.

She launched. "Tell me, while you were in the navy, what was the best lay you had?"

I almost jumped out of my skin. I studied her eyes. Though they were playful, she wanted something real, and I didn't know what.

So, roll the dice and see.

I talked unsteady, like a drunk. "When you're shore patrol, you end up in bars, usually to break up fights. But what the sailors, and the women, go to bars for is—"

She mimed pulling with her hands, like, *Give. Out with it.*

"So, one time we straightened out a little ruckus and got the guys headed for the door, meaning we herded them to their ship.

"A pair of women sat at a round table toward the front, holding drinks. As I passed, baton swinging from my wrist, one of them said, 'What time are you off duty, sailor?'

"I said, 'After everyone else is asleep.'"

"Tell me what she looked like," said Linda. The cue ball banks again.

"She was attractive. Thirtyish, auburn hair cut short, nice, willowy figure."

I hesitated. "So she sticks out a piece of paper, and I take it. A phone number and also a name. Annie."

"She says, 'Call me between nine and ten in the morning.'"

I looked at Linda, carved the tablecloth with my finger-
nail. "I'd never even used a pay phone."

She laughed out loud.

"I wasn't used to women acting like that. After a minute
I nodded *yes*. And left."

I paused.

"Go on, get to the good part."

"At five after nine I called and said, 'It's your sailor. From
last night.'

" 'Come on over,' she said, and recited an address."

"Good, tell me what she was like. Exactly what she was
like."

"She opened the door wearing one of those fuzzy robes
that look like a towel. She took my hand, gave me one
glance, and led me around the house. When we got to the
kitchen, she actually asked me if I wanted an egg-salad
sandwich. I said I'd pass."

"Oddball thing to say."

"That's what I thought. Then she got all embarrassed,
covered her mouth with one hand, and with the other led
me to the bedroom. She looked like she was going to fall
backward on the bed, and then she said, 'You first.' "

Linda motioned with a cupped hand, "Come on, come
on," and she grinned.

"After I'd stripped completely, I laid down on the bed. She
took her time looking at my crotch, which was at full alert.
Then she dropped her robe, all at once, and was stark-
naked.

"It's hard to look shy when you're naked, but she did, and
she reached out to me. I took her hand, kissed her, rolled
her onto her back, which she seemed glad about in a way,

but she crossed her legs. Then she drew my mouth down to one breast. The rest you know."

"Details!" said Linda.

"What can I say? We did the usual things, I mean the basic thing, and she acted shy and girlish the whole time. Actually, she acted like she was ashamed and lapping up the adventure all at once. We finished pretty quick. Simple and straightforward."

"Missionary position."

"Yeah."

"Noisy."

"Never. It didn't take her long, or me."

"It doesn't really sound like a great lay," said Linda.

"Well, the great part was that she asked me back just about every weekday."

"Ever get beyond the basics?"

"Never. Our routine was do the deed and then eat egg salad at her kitchen table in the nude while she told me about her life. Her husband was a salesman, on the road five days a week. She said, 'I know he has honeys here and there, but I don't know how many.

" 'For a while now,' Annie said, 'I've wanted revenge. And, big boy, you are revenge on the half shell.' She tilted her head, pursed her lips, and said, 'I want you to screw me again, harder this time.' "

I couldn't believe I was telling anyone this stuff, much less a woman I'd just met, much less a movie star.

Linda gave me that *Get on with it* gesture again.

"And then . . ."

I had hit a brick wall.

"Yaz-*zie*?"

"She came up with some wild fantasies. She liked to pretend her husband set this up and was hiding in the closet, watching us through a hole drilled in the sliding doors."

"That excited you."

"Her too. Weird, isn't it?"

"No. How long did it last?"

"About a month. Then one day Annie just said, 'Sorry, it's lost its charge.' Her husband had gotten interested in her again, and she felt the same way. I was actually sorry to let her go."

"The thought of screwing the hell out of another man's wife fired you up."

I mulled. "Yeah, that must have been part of it. When I think about it now, the whole thing really wasn't a big deal."

"Liar."

Actually, I was. I'd made up the whole story.

Linda smiled and said, "How about screwing another man's wife right now?"

The words flashed neon in the air between us.

Linda said, "I'll do the things no one has done to you."

And in a blink it came out. "Yes."

She was already on her feet and walking. I hurried along behind. When Julius stood, she said, "I won't need you for a while." I trailed her up the winding stairs to the door of her room. There she turned straight to me, took both my hands, and said, "Midshipman, I'm glad you're six feet six inches. But I'm mostly interested in checking out those six inches."

When she closed the door behind us, Linda Darnell— Linda Darnell!—swept me into her storm.

She sat on the bed and undid my pants, took hold of me,

and smiled. Then she said, "Sailor, it is time to go on an adventure."

She was totally direct and over-the-top frisky. She led us both to the Long Beach Pike and took us on the Ferris wheel, the roller coaster, through the fun house and the penny arcades, and finally gave us the Diving Bell. Several times. She was the bandleader, and I loved dancing to her beat.

Neither of us gave a damn about lunch. We split the day between our play and long talks. I don't think I ever told anyone so much about myself in such a short time. And, by God, we did become friends.

When the sun started its soft purple fadeaway, I felt like I'd made a long journey, a river crossing from innocence to experience. I would never be the same man.

When we came out of her room for dinner, there was Julius, leaning against the opposite wall, waiting. He kept his face carefully blank, but the stogie corkscrewed, and he tried to get her attention. She ignored him. Julius had one hell of a job, and I didn't envy him.

After dinner we spent the night back in bed, blasting through the rides in the amusement park, all of the human male and female possibilities, with a couple of contortions tossed into the mix.

In the morning a paper was slipped under the door, the bill, Linda said. She flung it at Julius when we checked out, and said the front desk owed them an apology. It was not her job to be aware of the details.

Five

Driving north from Flagstaff, through the Painted Desert and then east into Navajoland, Linda was mesmerized by the mesas and buttes. I'd like to think I put that glow on her, and maybe that was partly so. But she loved the scenery of the desert Southwest so much she'd bought a little ranch in New Mexico some time before. I watched her while pretending not to.

I liked the car, a 1940 Cadillac 90 Town Car, with the driver's compartment separated from the passenger seats by a barrier of etched glass. Linda and I sat in back, hooting and howling at our own lines. Julius had to be my chauffeur as well as hers, and that didn't bother me one bit. Luxury tasted fine.

But the rockety-rock on a rutted road made for a long day, and after a while the glory of landscape fades.

For a minute I studied Julius's profile through the closed

glass. It struck me. "Linda, your two bodyguards are as different as day and night." I spoke softly, even though I knew he couldn't hear us.

"What do you mean?"

"My grandfather's Jewish, and he's the only father I ever had, but I grew up Navajo. I'm descended from Changing Woman, mistress of the cycles of the Earth. I was raised to be aware of sun and sky, mountain and river, plant and animal, and the human walk through all this Fourth World." I doubted that Linda wanted to hear the old myth, and so I moved on. In the rearview mirror I looked up at Julius's cynical eyes and the tough-guy stogie.

"But Julius wears his life like it's a pretty rough-worn road."

"It's his job to be suspicious," she said. "And don't be too critical. He's been on that road a long time."

I looked at Julius again. "I hope I don't turn into that."

"Everyone has their own path. Sometimes it rolls in front of us and it doesn't feel like a choice, Yazzie."

"I've chosen *hózhó*, harmony in living. It's hard to . . ." I turned the complicated meaning of *hózhó* over in my mind and left it twisting in the air like the last leaf on a tree.

She put her hand on my inner thigh. "I was raised mishmash, a practicing pagan. Maybe it has made me what I am."

I chuckled. "I like that."

She stared ahead, opened her purse—more powder. No words.

When at last the time came, at the end of a long day, I said, "Behold, Monument Valley."

My homeland opened her eyes wide.

"Wow," said Linda, "this is *something. . . .*"

I never had words for it, either.

By shooting *Stagecoach* here, Mr. John had made the valley a big deal, at least in the film community.

And this sunset was a supreme moment. The sun was disappearing in the west, right over our trading post. The light of what Mr. John called the "magic hour" was transfiguring Monument Valley into . . . Again, no describing it, just let it float.

"Magic time," I told her softly. "They're using the last of the light."

She perked right up and pressed the button that let her talk to the driver. "Julius, stop where I can see."

He eased the town car to fifty yards away from the false-front version of Tombstone, all the buildings on one side of the new temporary road and facing us. I had no idea what was going on—I hadn't seen a script—but there was a crowd of actors in the road in front of the saloon.

We stepped out of the car, and Linda glanced at the red-gold west. "That light is enough." She squeezed her lips together, thinking, just thinking. "Julius," she said, "go get Danny Borzage for me."

Julius moseyed off. Mosey seemed to be his top speed.

Danny Borzage was one of my favorite movie people. Like a few others, he worked with Mr. John on every picture, and he had a key role. He played accordion songs between shots. While Mr. John was considering the angle he wanted, how the shot would fit into the sequence, and just what its mood should be, Danny played a tune. Mr. John would drift on that melody into a mental picture that worked for him.

Danny did the same for the actors while Mr. John instructed them. He had a knack for supplementing Mr. John's words with just the right tune-feelings.

Danny also gave each major actor a treat when he or she arrived on location for a new film. He'd play a song that was a bit from a previous film the actor had done. On a John Ford set, there was always the feeling that something special was about to happen. A big part of that was Danny.

Linda said to me, "Open the trunk."

I did, and she pried one of her huge suitcases open. "Danny hasn't noticed us, and I have something in mind for my arrival."

Behind the town car, she started stripping off her traveling suit, a short jacket, frilly white blouse, and skirt with a kick pleat. Soon she was down to her bra and panties.

"Remember, formal with each other around the cast and crew," she said. "Miss Darnell and Seaman Goldman." Pretty funny words from a lady in her underwear.

Danny and Julius started walking in our direction. She saw them and scooted into her clothes before they could see her, a full Mexican skirt, ankle length, scarlet with bright white filigree, on top a white blouse, scoop necked. Perfect for her. She slipped into a pair of black ankle boots and stepped out from behind the car just in time to greet Danny like an old friend. She whispered something in his ear.

As the two chatted, the crew began to shut down. Clearly, Mr. John had called a wrap for the day. Some of the cast walked toward the food tent, where everyone ate.

"Watch this, boys," she said. Linda turned her head. "I rehearsed it for a tavern scene I have to shoot," she whispered to me, although it was a whisper anyone within earshot could hear.

Linda made a beeline for the food tent, Danny hustling after her. As soon as they got close, and the first diners were walking in, Danny struck up his one-man band.

I didn't know the tune, but it was a *zapateado,* a Mexican dance song. Linda flashed right into the footwork *zapateados* are known for, toes and heels beating out the rhythm.

The whole cast and crew gathered around her, jostling to get a better view. If she'd been on a stage, they might have heard sounds like the ones you do in tap dancing, but the desert dirt didn't allow that—Linda's dance was purely for the eye. And that was more than enough.

It was flamboyant. Her ankle boots flew. Her skirt flared into a wide hoop. Her arms swayed gracefully above her head. Her torso arched back, and her neck was as long and beautiful as a swan's.

When Danny swung into the chorus for the last time, he juiced it up. Faster, wilder, giddy. Linda gave it everything Danny called for and more. The dance whirled to frenzy. She ended in a hands-high pose and a dramatic chord of punctuation.

The crowd burst into applause and laughter. Over their noise Danny cried, "Ladies and gentlemen, Miss Linda Darnell!" His music and her dance were a brilliant duo that made you feel glad to be alive.

Mr. John stepped out, hands clapping in big strokes. When he reached her, he took one of her hands, lifted it high in triumph, and turned both of them to face the applauding audience.

She curtsied to Mr. John, he bowed to her, and then she curtsied to the crowd.

What a woman!

I chuckled. I would have bet anything that tomorrow Mr. John would gripe to me, *Talk about star ego!* But it would be good-humored.

And I say, Why not? I'm with Mom—if you got it, flaunt it.

◆◆◆◆

Linda asked to be shown to her quarters to rest. Danny walked the two of us up the driveway to a stone cabin perched on the sandstone bench near Goulding's Trading Post, Julius trailing with the car and her luggage.

"That one is Mr. Ford's cabin," Danny said to Linda, pointing to the end of the row, "that one for Henry Fonda, this one for you and Cathy Downs." I'd figured out from crew talk that Miss Downs was the good girl of the movie, a schoolmarm, and Linda was the bad girl, a dance-hall temptress. Miss Downs wasn't on the location yet, which gave me high hopes for more sport.

When Danny unlocked the door for her, we all saw one small square room, two day beds, and a closet with two ceramic chamber pots. Not exactly high style for movie stars.

We three men hefted her suitcases inside. She said, "Thank you, Danny, thank you, Julius," in a tone that dismissed them. They took the hint and walked off.

She pulled me inside by one hand, turned her face up to mine, and said softly, "I want you to stay close."

I felt obliged to say this, though it galled me. "I got paid to deliver you, and my job is done."

"No," she purred, and took a moment to think. "I guess Mr. John didn't tell you. Julius is Twentieth Century-Fox security, responsible for a lot of people. You are my personal bodyguard. I want you at my service." Her sultry tone hinted at more.

"I . . ."

"The money's not a problem. The studio head of my next picture thinks it's important that I arrive safely for his shoot, and they're paying for it. It's double Fox's daily rate."

I wondered how many studios took care of their stars with security before their filming started.

Regardless, what I could say?

"You're to stay close during the shooting, too. I think it's much ado about nothing." She put her hands on my chest. "Until Cathy Downs arrives, I want you with me day and night."

I could have debated with her, but why? I was in lust with a movie star who liked playing the bad girl. Mom wouldn't like it—more time away—but she'd come around. She'd like getting out of debt, and I relied on Grandpa to get that across to her.

Linda smiled in her special way, one of them, and said, "I want some privacy now."

I stepped outside and strode down the hill, full of juice, a bull turned out into a glorious field.

❈❈❈❈

The buzzard man was confused, and he hated the feeling.

Who was the woman at the center of attention? What was Yazzie so-called Goldman doing with her?

First his son disappeared for several days. Then this pair

cruised onto the location in the fanciest automobile Zopilote had ever seen, and she put on a big show for the cast and crew. So-called Goldman acted like her man. Zopilote had never seen a Navajo with a white woman, not in that way. Everything about his son made Buzzard's head writhe like snakes.

He needed to wait. He needed to watch. He needed to use his buzzard vision and buzzard nose, which could sense truth from far away.

See. Understand. Learn how to inflict the greatest possible pain.

He crept to the cabin that backed up against the sheer cliff. Peered in through the chinks between logs. The woman sat on her bed, no makeup, not looking like such a big somebody without that paint. Looking at a letter that she had taken from her dresser drawer, smoothing it out, reading it, tapping her teeth.

Something was on the woman's mind. He didn't really care what. She wasn't important. But a scavenger never knows what might be useful.

Six

Today was the vernal equinox, and I drove Linda in the town car through the purpling twilight to Oljato. I watched the light fade into shafts gleaming between gray clouds. Understanding my mood, she held my free hand and said nothing.

For my people the solstices and equinoxes are times the world turns. Spring is birth, and for sure my whatever-it-was with Linda was a birthing. Of what? I didn't know. Summer is growing to maturity, autumn aging, and winter dying. I hated the short days turning to the winter solstice, when dark would come earlier and then earlier and earlier.

Now I glanced sideways into Linda's green eyes and reminded myself, *This is the first day of spring.*

When the Dineh made their emergence from the Third World to this Fourth World, where we live now, they rose into a climate rough as a cob. This land between the Four

Sacred Mountains flips from frying your skin in the summer to freezing your ass in the winter. Such is our life.

Here's another "such is life": Tomorrow Cathy Downs would arrive. That meant this would be my last night with Linda. Mom was creating a kind of farewell, and a peace token to me, by inviting Miss Darnell to dinner.

Mose Goldman heard tires on gravel and pivoted his wheelchair to look out the window. The town car stopped in front of the hitching rails. Yazzie got out and looked around. He must have been relieved at what he saw. His clansmen Katso and Oltai had gotten a lot accomplished— corrals tightened, roofs repaired, and plenty more. That would raise his hopes that Mom was happy, and he was doing well by his family.

Yazzie handed Linda Darnell out and escorted her toward the front door of the family part of the rambling building. Mose couldn't see the lady clearly in the deep shadows of the cottonwoods. A movie star didn't make his heart go bumpety-bump. Except for taking Yazzie to Hopalong Cassidy shows in Flagstaff twice, he'd never seen a motion picture, nor laid eyes on a movie magazine.

He turned the chair again, and with his good left arm propelled himself to the heavy wooden door. As Yazzie pushed it open, Mose caught the last of what the lady was saying to his grandson, " . . . in your home we will be informal with each other, just plain Yazzie and Linda."

Hmmm. Mose smiled to himself.

He raised his good arm to offer his boy an embrace and made it a hearty one. He was getting stronger every day, right leg and arm improving. Unfortunately, his speech was still garbled.

Yazzie was saying, "Linda Darnell, this is my grandfather, Mose Goldman. Whatever that is good in me is a gift from him."

Nizhoni sailed out of the kitchen, crossing to the front door in her stately way. His daughter was a woman even more beautiful in her forties than her twenties, so her father thought.

"And this is my other great teacher, my mother, Nizhoni Goldman. Grandpa, Mother, this is Linda Darnell."

Nizhoni said, "Miss Darnell, welcome to our home. We've heard so much about you."

Mose lifted a hand in affirmation.

"*Gracias,*" Linda said in a demure tone. "I'm so glad—"

Just then Iris burst in the back door. Bursting was the way Iris did things, plus always being late and carrying the cat on her shoulder. Striding across the room, she inspected her hands, which meant she'd just been painting, had cleaned her hands with turpentine, and was making sure of not getting paint on anyone else.

"Miss Darnell," Yazzie said, "Iris Goldman, my aunt. Iris, Linda Darnell."

Iris stuck out a hand and Linda shook it. She looked at Iris peculiarly, then at Cockeyed, and at Iris again.

They both said, "Glad to meet you" at the same time.

"Yes, I know," Iris said, "I hate it when he calls me his aunt. I'm not old enough. Life is crazy like that sometimes."

In fact, thought Mose, Yazzie was twenty-four, Iris twenty-six, and the famous movie star looked younger than either of them.

"*Nuestra casa es su casa,*" said Nizhoni.

"In that case," said Miss Darnell, "will you call me Linda? Then I'll truly feel at home."

"We will all be on a first-name basis," said Nizhoni.

Mose nodded his assent. Damn, but he hated not being part of the conversation.

Over the first glass of wine at the coffee table, Linda was gracious. She turned herself from a star into the respectful guest of honored elders. Mose could see his grandson relaxing. They were lovers, of course, and Yazzie's lover wasn't going to usurp Nizhoni's role by playing the grand lady here.

"I want to tell you," said Linda, "it is a privilege to be in your home. I am eager to know the parents of so fine a man as Yazzie."

"Nuts to all this courtesy," said Iris. "You're stunning, you're gorgeous."

Linda said, "Aren't you kind?"

Mose could see Linda was puzzled by Iris, or maybe by the cat's aberrant eye.

Iris plunged straight ahead. "So who do you think is the best-looking man in Hollywood? I go for Clark Gable." Arms high like a touchdown had been scored. To keep from falling off, Cockeyed pinched her blouse with his claws.

Linda suppressed a laugh. "I'd say Tyrone Power. And he's great to work with."

Mose slapped his knee. He liked this conversation.

"Next to you," Iris went on, "who's the most beautiful woman?"

"I don't like competition," Linda answered.

Mose grinned. Iris gave a twisted smile that the old man read as, *I knew that.*

"Iris," said Linda, "you sound New Yorkish. Do you feel at home in Monument Valley?"

Iris gestured to Mose, who noticed everything. "In my family here Mose is my uncle, Nizhoni is my sister," a nod at Mose's daughter, "and I guess Yazzie is my nephew. Uncle Mose had a stroke, they needed my help, I came." Her smile turned coy. "And I fell in love."

"With Yazzie?" said Linda, arranging surprise on her face.

"Not hardly," said Iris. She stroked the head of Cockeyed.

Yazzie put in, "I never met my aunt until the night before I left to meet you at the train."

Iris gave Yazzie a funny look. Then she said to Linda, "I'm in love with painting this country."

"You mean . . . ?"

"I mean real painting."

That was a surprise. And a hint.

"May I see?" asked Linda.

"Sure. Let's go."

❖❖❖❖

Bouncing outside and up a gentle hill, Iris led them toward the old well. Mose still felt good about the way he'd dug that well out, then had it drilled deeper, then sluiced the water downhill to give the post running water.

When Yazzie took hold of the wheelchair, Mose growled at him and muscled himself up. He wanted to negotiate the slope of sand, stone, greasewood, and sagebrush on his own.

Just beyond the well stood a timeworn grain shed, and Mose saw from the doorway what a fine studio Iris had made of it. Endless energy, that young woman.

Gazing around the shed, Linda exclaimed, "Iris!"

Mose could see why. Huge charcoal drawings were pinned to the old wooden walls, and they were dazzling. He'd guided scores of white visitors as they tried to capture the canyon country in paint. They traveled thousands of miles to get the chance, but the landscape mocked their efforts. The scope, the grandeur, the magnificence of vistas like the Grand Canyon—such marvels could not be captured and straitjacketed on canvas and in paint, still less on paper and in watercolor. The scale of Mose's homeland spoke with the sky-booming voice of God, beyond man's ability to imitate.

So Iris had gone at things slantwise. She'd sketched the shed skin of a rattlesnake abandoned on slickrock. A branch of driftwood stranded on a sandbar. The bleached skull of a coyote. The head of an elderly Navajo man, his hair bound back traditionally in a white *chongo*. The figure of a Navajo woman weaving at a loom.

No vistas, no mesas, no canyons, no skies. His country seen, and treasured, in its details. His skin prickled with love for his niece.

"These are studies," said Iris. "Want to see the paintings?" Her body wriggled with excitement, but it didn't come off as bragging.

"Please," said Linda. She sounded genuinely impressed.

Iris lifted the paintings out of big portfolios, oils on canvas. They were even more impressive. Her colors were vibrant, audacious, almost outrageous. She was not so much painting Mose's homeland as her own amazement at it. His heart surged.

She held each one up for a long moment, set it down, and showed the next one, all without a word.

"Enough?" asked Iris, her fingers drumming on the last canvas.

Linda nodded. "Your work is extraordinary."

"I know," said Iris.

"Iris!" said Mom.

Cockeyed snapped his head toward Nizhoni, the crazy eye wayward.

Iris put her hand gently on his neck. "She wants me to be modest and demure," she told Cockeyed. "A real lady." Then to everyone, "My motto is 'Well-behaved women seldom make history.' "

Linda laughed merrily. Then she asked, "For sale?"

Iris considered, trying to hold still. "I don't know. I have a show in Santa Fe in July, and I need twenty paintings for that. You're welcome to come."

"How about a sale while I'm here?" said Linda.

Iris pursed her lips, thinking. She looked into Cockeyed's straight eye.

"Just two or three," said Linda. "Good to be able to say you're collected by a famous woman."

"Then sure," said Iris. "Pick two or three, any you want."

The walk back down the hill was quick and animated. Trailing, Mose saw that Iris had a bit of an *I won* swagger.

Zopilote watched the five of them come out the back door of the house single file, his son and the old Jew last. The young woman led the way, and Zopilote still didn't know who she was. She looked like the old man, and was probably family. She spoke English with a queer accent and punctuated it with hand gestures that would make Zopilote want to back away.

He thought, *She better leave soon, or she'll find herself buried here.* Why should he spare anyone from the Goldman family, except maybe his son? Very maybe.

He had no idea what they were doing now, walking uphill in the dark. He especially wondered what that movie star was doing there, at an old trading post.

They came up the path to the shed. Zopilote slid lower behind the rocks until he could see with only one eye. As the path got a little steeper, his son tried to push the old man's wheelchair, but Mose made a garbled sound, closer to a bark than a word, and his son backed off. But the old man couldn't do it alone, and he had to be helped.

Old Goldman can't get the chair up that easy grade with just one arm. Good.

They went into the shed, and he heard some exclamations and made out a word here and there, but he couldn't tell what they were talking about.

After a few minutes they pranced back down the hill. Zopilote heard some words about how wonderful the young relative was. Apparently her name was Iris.

He watched his son hold the old man's chair back so it wouldn't roll downhill too fast. *My enemy is helpless.*

He would wait until he saw the strange young woman—Iris, he reminded himself—until she left on one of her walks, and then slip into her shed.

We all four of us sat at the dining table, and Mom brought the good silver and napkins from the kitchen. I was glad

Grandpa had bought real silverware in Santa Fe and brought it to Oljato. It made my mother feel special, as if part of her lived in an oasis of the raw desert.

Straight to the point, as usual, Iris said to Linda, "You like misbehaving."

"When I can get away with it," said Linda.

"Are you misbehaving with Yazzie these days?"

Mom said, "Iris!" banged a plate down in front of her, then laid one at each of their places and steamed back into the kitchen.

Grandpa slapped his knees. Ordinarily he would have hee-hawed. I felt pretty uneasy about how that might come out.

I decided to take a risk. "I think we should find a movie star to misbehave with Grandpa."

All of them hooted. Grandpa rocked in his wheelchair un-til we were afraid it would fall over. Then he clapped me on the shoulder with his good hand. Cockeyed rested on Iris's shoulder in perfect calm.

"You are a fine figure of a man," Linda said to him. "How tall are you?"

That got Grandpa going. He whipped out his black-board and wrote: 6-8.

"Oh, my," said Linda. She threw me a mischievous look and glanced to make sure Mom was out of hearing in the kitchen. "Eight inches. I hope you're not like Fats Waller." She sang a few wordless notes and said, "And, I hope you're misbehavin'."

Grandpa gestured toward his lap and scratched on his blackboard, CAN'T!

We all laughed. Cockeyed raised both eyes to the ceiling, one behind the other.

Mom emerged from the kitchen, and we all straightened out our faces. She set a platter of steaks on the table. "Backstraps," she said. "Jake Charlie shot a deer."

She placed saucers and bowls in front of everyone, kneeldown bread, our Navajo version of tamales, and pinto beans spiced with chiles. They were grown in our backyard and watered with runoff from the roof. Green chiles weren't a bit Navajo, but Grandpa looked at them fondly. From his rearing in Santa Fe he loved them.

Mom sat down and said, "I hope you like green chiles, Linda."

"I have a home in New Mexico, and my cook has taught me to love them. It's practically addicting—almost as good as margaritas."

All set to it, Linda eating heartily. "I really like being here tonight," she said. "You're regular people, like the folks I'm most comfortable with."

Mom said, "Not so regular. My extraordinary father has read the classics in Spanish and English, and his family has a big house in Santa Fe."

Grandpa gave his lopsided grin.

"So how did he come to live here?"

"A story for the next time we see you," said Mom.

"Hmm," said Linda. That mischievous look came back. "A sophisticated city or a gorgeous hideaway. I wonder which Yazzie will go for."

Mom said, "That question scares me."

Silence. It scared me, too.

"Well, if everyone is finished," said Mom, "let's move back to the living room. The dessert needs to cool off a little. Yazzie, would you build us a fire?"

Three of them couldn't fill the oversize leather sofa, but they sat close, shoulders touching. I got a flame started with pinyon in the big lava-rock fireplace. I remembered watching Grandpa mason every stone of it himself. If home could take on a sensuous smell, I was sure it would wear pinyon.

Iris got up and stood on the hearth, her back to the fire. She must have liked the warmth, but Cockeyed jumped down and curled up on the coffee table. I could hardly remember Iris ever keeping her hands so still.

"Nothing smells as good as this fire," she said.

I took the chair flanking the sofa and breathed the pungent sweetness of the burning wood into my soul.

We passed five minutes in small talk. I wondered if Mom was going to broach a certain touchy subject, and Cockeyed's tail was twitching.

Soon she brought the fry bread, the honey jar, and a speckled pot of sweetened, fresh-brewed coffee on the table. Linda put a dollop of honey on the fry bread and wolfed it down.

Mom sat on the sofa next to Grandpa, wiped her hands on her apron, and said, "This is good, Linda. It's so good to have you here. Yazzie says you're very generous to him."

"Actually," Linda said, "he intends to pass that generosity on to you."

I fished in my Wranglers and brought out some bills. One by one I stacked twenties next to Mom's plate and topped them with a big grin.

She raised an eyebrow toward me.

"From Miss Linda Darnell and the studio for watching over her. Three hundred bucks out of the four hundred for a week. It's yours. Please," I said, "don't toss it in a wad. It means something to me."

Mom looked stumped. Grandpa started scribbling something on his blackboard.

Linda pitched in. "The next four weeks he'll be guarding me until I go to bed. But, because he is so diligent and so attentive, I've arranged for my next studio to pay him three hundred a week, to make sure I make it to the next set on time and safely. That's a total of twelve hundred more dollars."

My head jerked toward Linda's face. She smiled like a first dawn. She was trying not to look like she was gloating. I wondered who the head of her next studio was, thinking, *business or personal?*

I found my voice and tried to fill it out with gladness. "Mom, right now this is my way of taking care of the family. I'll give you two hundred of each week's money. You can pay medical bills or pay the Babbitt driver for plenty of stock to make a profit on."

Mom clasped her hands and her lips went into a line.

I was afraid Grandpa might be thinking, *The medical bills, my fault. I built this trading post, and now I'm busting it.* I wanted to say to him, *Grandpa, you gave us everything.* Instead, I leaned over and patted his leg. Gave him a reassuring smile.

"Look," I said, "I can hire Katso to watch the sheep, starting tomorrow. He's willing, and I'll pay him myself. When the shoot's done, and we have money and goods to trade, Grandpa can stock up on the finest rugs and baskets we've ever had. And we can sell them to the movie people, people with real money. There will be more movies made here."

Mom said, "It's not the same as having you home."

"From now on I'll be here every night."

"What I want is for you to be here, at home, all the time."
I looked at Grandpa and he nodded.

Awkward silence. Cockeyed's crazy eye peered intensely
into the shadows above the chandelier.

Never shy, Linda said, "Nizhoni, you're not pleased?"

Mom stood up. One of her hands scratched the other arm
like fingernailing ant bites. "Linda, I miss my son, and this
is where he belongs."

"The money doesn't make up for a short absence?"

"The money helps," Mom admitted, "but . . ." Longing
drained her face.

Iris jumped in. "Yazzie, what's your dream? I mean, Uncle
Mose's was to go on an adventure into the wilds and create
his own living, independent of his well-fixed family." Cockeyed turned his face straight into Iris's.

She looked at Grandpa. He nodded. Everyone looked
relieved.

"What is your dream, Yazzie? Say it."

Everyone waited. This felt dicey.

"Maybe I don't know. Part of me wants to go to L.A. and
New York and Paris and Rome and . . . I joined the navy to
see the world."

One tear held fast in the corner of Mom's eye.

Iris gave me an odd look and plunged straight ahead.
"Linda, we barely know each other, but can we talk about
this in front of you?"

Linda hesitated, and then she surprised us by saying, "Yes,
why not?"

Silence all around.

"Okay," said Iris. "We're going to talk about dreams."

◊◊◊◊

Dreams . . . How about nightmares? Zopilote felt like smashing the window.

Just then he heard something, a *snick,* and it was the second time—the first time he'd thought it had been his imagination. Had the rhythm of nature turned in on itself? He had not chosen the Navajo Witchery Way. It had called to him, made itself his home, had yanked him inside it. And inside that circle? Anything could happen.

He would have to be more careful. Perform some rituals, maybe.

◊◊◊◊

"Let's start easy," said Iris. "I'll tell you my mother's dream. She wouldn't mind."

"Easy" was hard to imagine with my Aunt Iris. I listened, but I sat on the edge of my seat, never sure where her words would take us.

Grandpa gave us his version of cheering. He loved his sister with all his heart.

"Frieda Goldman grew up in the same Santa Fe household with Uncle Mose. Everyone played music. But for my mom, it was her heart, part of who she was.

"When she was twelve, she was the violist in the family string quartet. Uncle Mose was busy then, learning about silver and turquoise and rugs. So she gets to be twenty, and she yearns for more. A touring violinist comes to town, and she gets infatuated with him. First he charms her out of her clothes, and then into touring around with him, and finally into moving with him to New York.

"It's a real dream come true. She gets into Juilliard, a new school for musicians. She gets a job in the viola section of the Metropolitan Opera, and she's still in love. A Cinderella story without the wicked stepsisters. And it happened because she had the guts to fling caution to the winds and run off with a man she hardly knew."

Mose held up one hand to say *stop* and scribbled with the other. At length he held up a sign: DAD + MOM = MAD.

"Right. That's what I hear. Your parents . . ." Iris shrugged. "What can I say?"

I hoped this story was going someplace where it came out supporting a person's right to have dreams.

"Anyway, after twelve years, my mother gets walloped with a big dose of the truth. It turns out the violinist is a bastard. They have an apartment in Greenwich Village, but he won't marry her, and he's mostly gone, supposedly on tour. Now, after all this time together, he comes to their apartment, to *her*, and he's begging. He has a babe in arms. He can't help it, he has to come clean. He has a wife in Chicago, always has. And the wife, she just bore a daughter and died doing it. Will Frieda take the child?

Here my grandfather made a growling sound that burbled at the base of his throat. Iris looked at him.

"I know, I know. She's heartbroken, stunned, but, yeah, she loves him, so she'll take the baby, even forgive the guy. Plus, she hadn't been able to have kids, and she felt that pain like a hole in her stomach. It was a piece of her that felt completely skewed. He goes on tour, he leaves the baby with her, and—guess what?—she never hears from him again."

Iris paused. "End of story? No. That kid was me.

"Fade out. Twenty years pass in New York while I grow up and Frieda plays her heart out in the opera orchestra. Fade in: Mom's father dies in Santa Fe, and we go home to New Mexico for the funeral. We never go back to New York. Six more years we're still in Santa Fe, living in the house where you all grew up, Uncle Mose.

"So I ask her—this is just a couple of years ago—'Mom, are you ever sorry that you ran off with that bum to New York?' I was hot to know.

"She looks at me like I'm crazy. 'What? I should be sorry?! Haven't I had everything? Stupid, but . . . Haven't I loved a man? Didn't I get a job I adored? And I found the love of my life, which is—guess who, Iris?—*you*."

Iris let that sink in. Everyone in the living room was perfectly still. "Now," Mom goes on. " 'You remember the prelude to *Tristan and Isold*?'—she never gets tired of playing that piece on the Victrola—'We did a lot of performances of *Tristan* at the Met, and I ended up feeling like it tells my story. That opening melodic phrase, so poignant, and ending on that chord of yearning—the one that cries for resolution, for fulfillment?'

"Sounds like a sad story, what with that piece of music? No. Mom says to me, 'If I'd stayed here? I'd never have heard the greatest singers in the world pour their hearts out in the world's most splendid melodies. I'd never have had any really large feelings, even if one of those feelings was longing. Most of all, I wouldn't have had you. You are my fulfillment.' "

Iris paused, maybe overemotional.

" '*Any* feeling is a great thing, Iris,' my mother tells me, 'as long as it's a grand one, a tidal wave that sweeps you away.' "

Linda said, her voice soft, "I'm on board with that. Any adventure is better than sitting around waiting for something to happen in your life."

Iris looked straight at me. "I know Mom would want you to hear that story."

I had nothing to say.

"I have a question, Iris." Surprise—this was my mother. "Why are you here? Why aren't you in New York painting and doing your shows in big-time galleries?"

Iris shrugged. "There's no explaining love, for a person or a place."

Grandpa held up his blackboard. I hadn't even noticed him writing, but he pointed it toward me. It said, FOLLOW YR DREAM.

Mesmerized by the flames of the pinyon fire, Buzzard wished he could smell it. Remembering that smell brought back the feeling of being in the hogan of his childhood.

Those five gathered around the fire beyond the window were talking about their dreams. He didn't pay attention to every word. He was sure, though, that he'd had dreams as a kid. He couldn't remember them anymore, but he knew bone-deep that he had them. All gone now.

Dreams as a young man, too. Winning the bareback competition at an Indian rodeo. Being named best all-around cowboy. Having the women crowd around him, admiring, eager to have a drink with him, ready to slip out into the cottonwoods for some adult fun. The rides, the drinks, the lays—those were his dreams, sort of, and sometimes he made them come true.

The taste of whiskey rose in his mouth. Funny, he didn't like it, not one bit, and he spat.

He watched his son and that Iris standing in front of the huge fireplace, warming their backsides. The old man, the movie star, and Buzzard's wife sat facing the blaze, their eyes lit and their conversation warmed by the flames.

Some part of him felt lost. He had to get some sleep. Pull himself together.

░▓░▓░▓░

My grandfather tucked his blackboard back into the pouch. Iris spoke up. "Uncle Mose, I'm sorry you can't tell us just how you made your dream happen." She opened her palms in Nizhoni's direction.

"You want me to do that, Dad?"

Mose gave an emphatic nod. *Yes.*

"Our family? Traders, always traders," Mom said. "In Santa Fe a lively business trading up and down the Chihuahua Trail.

"Lots of times the sons went out to set up smaller trading posts, and the family's power increased.

"Now picture my father, the grand engine who is Mose Goldman. This tall young man rides to the farthest corner of the rez, sets up at the spring—the heart of Oljato—and trades with local people from a tent. They're leery of him at first—these are the children of the Hoskinini, people who escaped the four years in a concentration camp for Navajos by hiding out. But he speaks their language and treats them with respect, so they gradually come to trust him a little. Maybe even like him.

"His thought is to build a bustling business over the years, sell it, and move back to Santa Fe in triumph.

"But he falls in love with a Navajo woman, and he comes to love the Navajo people and the country we live in. His dream changes—he wants to live among us, raise a family, and be happy. His family, unfortunately, turns out to be me, just me.

"Mose Goldman walks wherever the path of his dream leads. When the destination changes, he's still ready to ride on his spirit of adventure."

Grandpa gave Nizhoni a lopsided grin and shot his good fist upward in triumph. Cockeyed tensed, like he might jump off Iris's shoulder, but he didn't.

Iris pitched in. "Now, Uncle Mose claims he won't go back to Santa Fe, regardless. When he was doing rehab there after this stroke, he insisted on coming home. Mom and Aunt Nizhoni gave in to him. Silly."

Grandpa gave her a stern look.

Iris said, "I'm going to hog-tie him and take him back to finish that rehab."

Mose Goldman stuck out his tongue at her.

I looked at Linda. She was quiet. Maybe thinking of her options, her future. Weighing her own dreams.

꧁꧂꧁꧂

Far too late into the evening—a really fine evening—I escorted Linda back to the town car. As I turned the key in the ignition, I came right out with it. The question had been waiting for days. She said being a movie star made her feel like a phony. So why keep it up?

"Linda, I really want to know. You have what every young woman in America dreams of. Does being a rich, famous movie star satisfy you?"

"Sure."

"Okay." But, from her tone, I didn't believe her, not all the way.

We rode in silence for a couple of minutes.

"It was my mother who wanted it first," she said. "Even way out in Cherokee country, she got her hands on fashion magazines and such and dreamed of living the glamorous life.

"About the time I was born, the movies became gigantic, and she invested all her dreams in me and Hollywood.

"Dallas was our first step up. I was performing at twelve. I went to a Hollywood scout's audition the next year, and he liked me. I made my first Hollywood movie at the age of fifteen. I liked the clothes, the jewelry, the attention.

"And in the end . . . ?"

"In the end I guess I ate my mother's dreams and they turned into part of me."

"You're happy?"

She laughed. "Let's just say Beverly Hills is more appealing than a Texas feed lot."

Seven

The next morning I stepped out of Linda's cabin and got spanked in the face by a note on her door.

STAY AWAY FROM THE SAILOR
HE WILL GET YOU HURT

I stared at it. It was written in a child's printing. The culprit had fastened it with a thumbtack and had done it while Linda was asleep. While *we* were asleep. That gave me almost as many creeps as the scrawled words.

I yanked it off, shouldered the sticky door back open, padded to the bed, and handed it to Linda.

She read it, stuck it out to me, and said, "Forget it. I've had worse, far worse."

"Recently?"

She shrugged.

"Linda, listen to me. I can't protect you if I don't know everything."

She walked to her dresser and pulled out an envelope that had been folded and folded again. I recognized that envelope. Inside was a letter, worn thin with folding and refolding.

She gave it to me, and I sat heavy on her bed, reading. Plenty of details, but no signature. Then I read it again.

"You've had this since we got to the hotel in Winslow?" I said to her.

"Yes, yes, you were there when I got it."

"You may have put yourself in danger by ignoring it. Maybe all of us."

"It's not a big deal."

"Believe me, in the real world this is a big deal."

She turned her back to me.

"I have to show it to Mr. John," I said. "This is his shoot. And your life."

She shrugged. Acted like she didn't care, one way or the other.

"Get dressed," I said.

"I don't know if I like you like this."

"Get dressed."

※※※

Mr. John's face turned the color of a red onion. "Get Julius," he told a flunky.

Linda tried to say something.

Mr. John put his finger in the air. The message was clear—not one word yet.

Julius read the letter impassively. Then he read the scrawled note. When he finished, the cigar twisted, and I could almost hear the wheels grinding in his head.

Mr. John said, holding out the stationery, "This letter, this was waiting for you at La Posada?"

She nodded yes.

"This other letter, this note, you just found it on your door?"

Yes again.

"Julius," John Ford's voice boomed, "do we think it was written by the same person?"

"We are forming an opinion."

"God, Julius, you are infuriating. Everything we're doing—a private bodyguard, a studio bodyguard, go to the middle of nowhere—and we still can't keep crazy people at bay! I don't know whose head to have first."

Mr. John paced the floor, tapping the letter against his forehead.

"Very nice stationery." He looked into Linda's green eyes. "Who was the last boyfriend you dumped?"

"That's none of your business!"

She was on shaky ground there.

"Let me rephrase that," Mr. John said. "Do you remember the last boyfriend you jilted, and was there more than one?"

She turned her face up to him, an attempt at defiance. "Could we talk in private?"

"We cannot. Answer my question."

"Fine. Frank Cantonucci."

"Would you repeat that?"

"Frank Canto— You know exactly who I am talking about."

"Yes, I do. Oh, this is sweet. You dumped Frank Canto-nucci. Toss in Mickey Cohen," he said, "and we're really off to the races." Mr. John put his hands on his hips, looked out the window, and shook his head. "Zanuck will have a coronary if he hears about this."

"Don't tell him," Linda said.

"I have no intention of telling him," he said. "Julius, get over to Goulding's, make some calls, track this down. Do whatever you need to do to make it go away. To make him go away. Bribe him. Tell him I'll give his wife a small role in something. Threaten to get Mr. H. on his ass. Take care of it."

All of this sounded like very bad business.

Julius said to Ford, "Done." He was squinting at Linda when he said it. I didn't know their history—how could I?—but I had a feeling that this wasn't the first time she'd complicated his life.

"And be back ASAP." Julius was already out the door.

Then Mr. John turned to Linda. She shrank a little closer to me. Fortunately, I had remained off Mr. John's radar. So far.

"You! What do I do with you? I can hire extra security, but I can't keep tabs on your entire life, Linda. Frank . . ."

He paced, pulled his chin, and stuck his face in hers. "You have stepped into deep shit, and you're such a kid that you don't even know it."

For the first time, Linda looked scared.

"You know he has plenty of guys who could follow you

here, take care of you, and . . . Look out there. One very large desert. No one would ever find the body. Your body. Get that?"

"I can't—"

"Don't talk. I'm too angry, and I'm not finished. Getting involved with a mobster? Linda, they don't go away. And jilting a guy close to Mickey Cohen?"

"It was stupid, I understand."

"I could fix it so you didn't work again."

Her lip trembled.

"But, God help me, there is something so vulnerable about you. . . ."

Then Mr. John looked like the air had gone out of him. A spent balloon.

"What now?" she said.

"To hell with the message left on your door. I take threats seriously, but I will not be coerced. Since the guy making trouble wants Yazzie gone, he stays. And we need to beef up the security. I'll hire more, and we'll see what Julius wants when he gets back."

Mr. John looked at me. I was visible again. As long as that had happened, I stood straight and worked myself into looking tough.

"I trust Yazzie," Ford said to Linda. "He's a good man, although he has fallen for your charms like everyone else except for me, Julius, and the makeup man. Don't look at the floor, Yazzie."

Mr. John mused. "Today Cathy Downs will be here. I'm not letting her walk into this situation."

I was embarrassed beyond belief. Of course Julius would have told Mr. John about our goings-on. That was his job—security—and I should have figured that included being a spy.

Julius came in and shut the door too hard. "I did what I could for now. More later."

"What do you want for security?

"The Seaman goes. He's a magnet."

Mr. John barked, "Damn it. . . ."

Julius came back at him. "He goes. He's the problem."

"Who the hell do you think is in charge here? I say what's what."

"May I remind you that the note appeared while Yazzie was with her? At night? And no more afternoon naps."

Then Linda stepped in, for her in a gentle way.

"You don't want to lose those afternoon shots," said the star to Mr. John. "No nap, and I don't glow for the camera." She looked straight into Mr. John's eyes. "You don't want that." Her words fell on the floor and rolled around.

"That's bull," said Julius.

"Both of you shut up!" Mr. John snapped. "Here's what's going to happen. One armed man will be with Linda every minute. When the crew is around, when she's napping, when she's sleeping—all the time. And that armed man is Yazzie."

Ford glared at Julius, who then looked at his shoes.

"When Linda is on the set, or in the tent, or at the Porta-Potty, a second armed man will be within another dozen steps of her, his attention on no one else. Who do you want?"

"Colin," said Julius.

I breathed easier.

Mr. John leaned into Linda's face. "Even if it's your next studio that's paying for your protection," Mr. John said with pepper in his voice, "right now you're working for me."

She studied the ceiling.

"I am waiting," he said.

"I understand."

"And you'll do as I say?"

She nodded.

"That's not bad," said Julius. "I'll get Colin on it right now."

"Yazzie, there's no way in or out of the cabin but the front door?" Ford said.

"None."

"All right. While she's inside, you will be her protection. Yazzie, you're here in the afternoon and at night, with Colin outside the cabin. You're right with Linda on the set, and Colin's her shadow. Got it?"

"Yes, sir."

"Linda," he said, "take no chances. Never be without two armed men. Never."

He started out the door and turned back. "And don't tell anyone—cast, crew, anyone—about the note on the door or about that letter."

Eight

After a few days, things settled down some. Whatever had happened, and whoever had tacked that note up and sent that letter, the incident seemed faded. Maybe a twisted jab. A wicked one, but . . .

One lunchtime, when Linda was finished being a bad girl with me for an hour or so, I stepped out of the cabin and into a surprise.

"Hi, Yazzie," said Iris with verve. "I came down to, you know, see what's going on. Raphael here has been very nice to me, and— Is Linda inside there?"

"Uh, yeah."

"I just want to say hi to her."

Iris slipped past me through the cabin door. Automatically, I looked for Linda's guard, Colin. He was sitting in front of Raphael Garibaldi, fifty feet away. Colin had a ruff of Woody Woodpecker red hair, a flock of freckles, a short burly frame, and the eyes of a rooster ready to fight. His amiable Irish looks were a mask. Perfect view of the door, and plenty of attitude that was well-disguised.

Raphael was the makeup man who worked on Linda every day, just before the costume woman finished her up for the next shot. I sat behind the guard and next to Raphael, which I knew would irk him a little. He didn't like all the lunch-break time Linda spent with me. He often nudged her to get down to her dressing room faster so he could do her makeup, get things moving for the costume person, and get her in front of the camera.

From inside the cabin I heard the enthusiastic greetings of two young women who sounded like old friends.

Raphael got up and followed Iris inside. I leaned against a cedar tree, waiting. The tree trunk curved back. Good smell. It was comfortable.

Out they came in about two minutes. Iris and Linda made a beeline for the cedar. Iris gave the guard a *What's-going-on-here?* glance along the way, and she plucked her sketchpad from behind the tree.

"I'll introduce you to Mr. John and tell him you're a great artist," said Linda. "Mr. John loves artists."

"Meanwhile," Iris said, looking at Colin, "this gentleman and I haven't been introduced."

"Oh, sorry," I said, embarrassed. "Iris Goldman, this is Colin Murphy. Colin, Iris Goldman, my aunt."

Politely, Colin stood and nodded. "Seldom seen so young and beautiful an aunt," he said.

Iris was plainly embarrassed. Her right forefinger went to her mouth in her habit of touching the crooked tooth, but she kept her upper lip over it. "You're pretty husky for an Irishman," she said. Then she turned kind of red. It was about the first time I'd seen Iris with a lame comeback, more like something I would say.

"Let's go," Linda said. We walked down the hill.

Linda wasn't giving me a choice about Iris being around, and I wasn't sure how that would work out on all fronts. As we approached the mob of crew around the shot, Iris almost danced with excitement.

Careful not to stammer, I said, "Mr. John won't want you sketching the stars."

Iris looked at me with a tickled expression. "Jeez, Yazzie, I won't embarrass you. I'm only going to put a few up for sale to the highest bidder. Maybe sell them to a gallery in Santa Fe . . ."

Oh, boy, there went my job.

"I'm kidding. God, you look whiter than a white guy right now."

Linda put her head back and laughed. Those two women could be a dangerous pair. At least to any shred of dignity I imagined I had, or might have, someday.

Colin was silent, his eyes flicking everywhere.

Linda led us through the crowd around the camera and introduced Iris to Mr. John. He said, "What about you, Yazzie? You vouch for this young woman?"

"Sure, she's my aunt."

Iris fidgeted again. I got it. She was uncomfortable with "aunt."

Mr. John said, "Welcome to the movies, Miss Goldman."

Iris saw his right eye flick down to her sketchpad. She said quickly, "Don't worry. I won't do people."

"People in general would be fine," he said. "Stars, no.

Stick with Yazzie and Colin. They'll show you the ropes."
He took another look at her. "Plenty around here to fire up
an artist."

He turned and walked away, his focus already in three
other places at once.

Linda was front and center, Mr. John was taking care of
business, and that left me and Iris looking at the light set-
tling to the earth and the glow on the bluffs. She was right.
You could get delirious over this place. I was so used to it,
I didn't see it sometimes. The quiet between us was easy.
She turned to me, looking puzzled.

She gave Colin a stealthy glance and said to me softly,
"You understand that I'm not really your aunt, don't you?"

"Navajo way, yes, you are."

"Maybe Navajo way, but I'm not your blood relative.
You know that, right?"

"Uh . . ." Sometimes it wasn't easy living in two worlds. At
least two worlds.

"Never mind. So what are these ropes I need to learn?"
she said to both of us.

Colin spoke up. "Aside from 'Shhh, don't make a breath of
sound during a shot' and 'Don't get in front of the camera
during a shot,' not so very much."

We were standing in the street of the false-front town, with
an angle into a window of the tavern. Crew members were
busily doing stuff I only half understood.

"What do you do all day?" she said, giving me her look.
"I already know what you do during lunch break—I mean
the rest of the time."

I felt myself flush. "Basically, my job is to stick tight to Linda, be on guard, listen to stories, guard Linda, tell old stories, repeat bad jokes, and guard Linda."

"Same as I," said Colin, "except I'm studio and Yazzie's personal."

"Whoo-ee!"

"Iris, it's an education," I said. "I like to watch people's postures, their gestures, their expressions, and especially their strange little habits. That story is a lot closer to the truth than whatever they're saying."

"An artist knows that, too."

"All but movie stars," Colin said. "They're different kinds of artists. Don't even know if that's exactly the right word for them."

"Are you interested in the truths that are in gesture and expression? You see it in all the great portrait painters."

Colin and I stumbled over each other saying, "Cops know. . . ." We smiled sheepishly and stopped.

"Caravaggio is my favorite for that," Iris went on. "There is the soul, stark-naked, in the bodies and the faces. They're fully alive, telling all their secrets."

I was really stuck. I'd never been to any big museums, didn't know any art but Navajo and Pueblo. I loved those, but human expressions and body language weren't part of that art.

Colin smiled—it was a fine, quirky smile—and shrugged. Evidently he was as out to sea as I was.

Mr. John saved us by calling, "Lights."

I put a finger to my lips and pointed to Victor Mature and Cathy Downs. Iris wandered off with her sketchpad, despite the fact that we had told her, in no uncertain terms, that it was a foolhardy idea to go anywhere. But there was no stopping Iris.

❧❧❧❧

Colin was intense, watching them setting up the shoot, and Iris's exploration was starting to ramble farther away from us. That made me anxious. Very. I asked Colin, in a muted whisper, to double up on his guard-duty for a few minutes. While Linda was shooting a scene, or with the crew and cast, the situation felt fairly safe.

"Unless, of course," said Colin, "someone substitutes a real bullet for a blank."

"I just want to make sure Iris is okay. I don't want her wandering off too far on her own."

He put his arm on my shoulder and whispered to me, "You're a good nephew. I'll keep double watch, and you take care of that spectacular woman."

There she was, engrossed in the cedars on top of the hill. I hung back and watched her. My holster felt like a warm friend and fiend at the same time. Iris had spotted a bone, a big one. It was the leg of a horse. I had no idea what she thought it was—probably a dinosaur bone. She tucked it under an arm and walked on. The steepness of the hillside and the loose rocks made her clumsy.

She spotted a piece of Navajo sandstone, probably millions of years old. She picked it up, spat on it, rubbed the spittle around, and put it in a pocket.

Another rock, this one shaped like a fist with a finger. Then another, like the wing of a dove. Each she held up to the light, and the shaped shadows fell around her.

She walked another twenty yards, and that was as far away

as my nerves would allow. I ran and scrambled to keep up with her, and loose rocks scattered behind me.

She turned. "What are you doing here?"

"Keeping an eye on you. Iris, anyone or anything could be here."

"I have spent a few months alone, eating Spam and camping with the sheep. This is nothing."

"And there wasn't a possible crazed ex-boyfriend on the loose."

I shouldn't have said anything, and I couldn't believe I had.

"Or a jealous husband . . . Why hasn't anyone thought about him?" She barreled on. "And don't worry, Linda told me about the mess when I got here today. My lips are sealed."

Oh, great . . . And about the husband, I didn't have an answer. Maybe he had become too much of a nothing in Linda's life to take him seriously. On the other hand, sometimes a man will take just so much, and then he breaks. A dry reed sucking on a dry pond.

"I don't know about the husband, Iris. I only know one thing. You're coming back down this hill with me."

"Okay, okay. Relax, would you?"

We made it down to the edge of the flat between the hill and the false-front street.

Iris looked at the sky. She liked the wing shapes of the ravens. She took out a piece of charcoal and sketched the shape and light quickly. I was amazed. One look, and she had the feel in under two minutes. My guess is that she used those shapes as clues to what a painting might become. She took a last look up into the cedars.

Then she stood very still. "Yazzie?"

"Yes?"

"Look at that tree trunk, that one, just to the left of the pinyons."

Odd. Uncanny. One spot on a tree trunk had gnarled itself almost into the shape of a human head. Nature is a true wonder. I liked seeing the world through Iris's eyes.

She fished a piece of charcoal out of one pocket, shifted her sketchbook to the other arm, and took a couple of steps toward the tree. For some reason she stopped, fingered her angled tooth, and decided against it.

"What?" I asked her when she got back to me.

"Another awkward uphill walk for something spooky? I don't think so. Spooky isn't my cup of tea. It's the light I love."

We walked back down to the set, and Colin smiled up at both of us as we cleared the rise. All was well with Linda.

❖❖❖❖

Buzzard let himself breathe, and then breathe again. *I'm getting out of here.*

And as he walked away, close call with Iris, he heard it again, the *snick*. He surveyed the horizon. Nothing. He looked to the place where the sound had come from. Nothing but a slight trickle of water dropping into an ancient Indian step carved in the stone. That is what he told himself.

❖❖❖❖

"Lights."

Iris slipped between me and Colin, and they traded looks that were sort of flirty. Linda caught my eye, jiggled her hips, and smiled at me.

I passed a script to Iris. No sound anywhere. Cathy

Downs was leaning against a wall, Victor Mature sitting on the hitching post. They'd been there, doing nothing, for several minutes. Now they jumped up and stood so that it looked like they were talking, and not peaceably.

"Camera."

"Action."

They spoke a couple of lines—Cathy Downs was trying to put the Doc Holliday character on the straight and narrow. He got rid of her and her idea of how he should live his life.

"Cut and print."

Lots of happy faces.

Linda trotted to Mr. John, shadowed by Colin. I checked the circumference of the set. Nothing unusual.

Linda had been transformed by costume into a Mexican whore, and now her name was Chihuahua. She nodded to Mr. John and strode into the tavern, easily visible to us and the camera through the big false window. She sidled up to Doc at the bar, bringing news about the Cathy Downs character. For Iris, I pointed out the script lines they were speaking.

CHIHUAHUA

She's packing, Doc. She's leaving town.

DOC

Happy, aren't you?

CHIHUAHUA

I ain't sad.

DOC

Chihuahua, I'm going to Mexico for a week or ten days. And while I am gone—

CHIHUAHUA

Take me, Doc, will you?

DOC

Why not? Why not? Tell François to fix a bridal breakfast, flowers, champagne. You get your prettiest dress. Tell him the queen is dead. Long live the queen!

CHIHUAHUA

Oh, oh, Doc.

"Cut!" barked Mr. John.

I whispered to Iris, "Notice, not 'Cut and print.' Meaning what he saw and heard wasn't what he wants. Maybe the way the actors stood or moved wasn't the right body language. Maybe a line reading wasn't good. Maybe the sound man didn't get what he needed. No telling."

"So they'll do it again."

"And again. Sometimes they wait until the light is just so."

"Light," said Iris, "is everything." She held up the bone of the horse leg against the sky, and I scratched my head.

"Anyway . . ." I said, "when the shot actually rolls, only a small part of the crew and a few actors are involved. Mr. John is always next to the camera and the guys who operate it. He talks over and again to the lighting man and his helpers, and then to the one, two, or three actors, typically, in a shot. Danny Borzage makes that accordion sing to set the mood.

"Mr. John works the actors like a slave driver until he says every actor's favorite words, 'Cut and print!' "

"You think Linda's good?"

"She doesn't seem to give much thought to what she's going to do in front of the camera. But at least half of the time," I said, "she surprises everyone by getting it just right."

"I sure don't envy Linda," Iris said.

"You may be one of the few women in America who doesn't."

"Please. Bodyguards! And apparently she needs two, and right out here in the middle of nowhere, a country populated mainly by ravens and buzzards. Freedom," Iris said, "is a pretty steep price to pay for what she's got—expensive stuff and only a few people she can count on."

"Mr. John says she's naughty, and you never know when that's going to cause trouble.

"Naughty? Well, you know that firsthand," Iris said. "At least you can be trusted."

Best to let that one pass. "I hear the studio head of her next picture is concerned about her and wants to make sure she arrives in one piece. That's why I still have a job."

It was Iris's turn to shrug. "If he's the possessive type, he sure didn't hire the right bodyguard, did he?" She slapped me on the ass, sat down on a boulder, and opened her sketchpad. She studied the cedars on the hill, made a face of frustration, and started positioning the bone just the way she wanted it.

Talk about an infuriating woman.

I stepped forward to watch the next take. Always, I kept one eye on Linda and one on the crowd. When she was in front of the camera, or being touched up by the makeup man, or having a cameraman take a light reading off her face, I talked with whoever was handy, but I was always eyeballing everyone around her. My job.

What mattered to me right then was her safety. Also what mattered was that the time we spent together was good, and not just the sex. When we were alone, she was a different person and a lot more likable, a country woman, full of laughs, plenty of fun, and not a bit taken in by all the fancy people who ran the show. Linda was real with me, and we both liked that.

※※※

Zopilote could find his way around that place he had once called home in the dark. He had done just that many times. In broad daylight? Easy.

He picked the padlock on the door of Iris's shed. Also easy. Inside he found nothing. Well, two huge books that were like folders with loose drawings, plus a box with paintings stretched on wood frames. Silly things on decent canvas. No trinkets or personal things that belonged to Iris. And really, who gave a damn, other than she seemed pretty uppity and could use a lesson? His idea was already set in place.

He slipped back outside and ran low from boulder to boulder to his hiding place.

He studied the trading post again. Nizhoni must have hidden all that cash somewhere inside, but where? She rarely left home, and the old man sure didn't go anywhere, so he couldn't search the house without getting caught. *Just details. I'll steal a gun. Some binoculars, too. Need to see better.* The money his son gave his wife and the crippled old man? *I'll have plenty of time to look around for it when they're gone.*

Mr. John got two shots in that afternoon. During the second, Iris stood between me and Colin, holding out her pad. The sketch was of the Clanton and Earp boys playing liar's poker, a favorite way of killing time on the set. The drawing was terrific. Faces and postures were a little exaggerated, but for a reason. What Iris had done made their moods clear. Each one was individualized in a way that's hard to put words to. It was like she knew them better than they knew themselves. Also, the lines of the drawing were vigorous, confident, and suggested the camaraderie and competitive spirit of the players.

Mr. John called, "Cut and print," and the assistant director added, "That's a wrap today."

Linda walked toward us, taking time to trade pleasantries with people she passed.

Watching her, Iris said to me, "Her career is . . . she's streaking up like a comet. But something behind the way she holds herself . . . it's like she's not comfortable in her skin. I hope things change for her."

I said nothing. Too many thoughts. Colin watched us curiously as Linda approached.

Iris said softly, "I don't know. I suppose anyone would get a kick out of being a movie star, if only for a day."

"Did you like watching the shoot?" Linda said to Iris.

"I enjoyed this part," said Iris, and handed her the sketch.

Linda took a long look. "You are a true talent," she said. "Sensational."

"A gift to you," said Iris.

"Oh, thank you. Thank you." She tucked it under an arm. "Would you do some sketches of me?" Linda said.

"Glad to," said Iris. "Also gifts."

Linda took a deep breath in and out.

"Iris Goldman, you are a friend."

She turned to me. "Seaman, you said you'd stay and have supper with all of us in the food tent."

"Sure."

"Iris, why don't you join us?"

Iris hesitated. "I promised Nizhoni I'd—"

Colin pitched in. "Oh, come on, it's fun. We'll be sitting at Mr. John's table with Henry Fonda and Victor Mature and—"

Iris held up a hand. "You're right. I want to stay. Just let me walk up to Goulding's and radio her to say I'm not coming."

"Tell Mom I'll be late tonight," I said.

She gave me one of her teasing looks. It asked, *How late?* And, *Why are you staying?* Then, *Don't bother, I know.* All that at once. She ran off toward the Goulding's office.

❧❧❧❧

Danny Borzage stood at one of the entrances to the food tent, playing "Bringing in the Sheaves" on his accordion. Linda, Colin, and I started toward him. I chuckled.

"Sheaves for the supper song," she said. "Jack's idea of humor."

We walked through the crowd and wound between tables. Everywhere, we were Miss Darnell, Seaman Goldman, and Colin. They knew what Linda and I did alone in her cabin. But as long as she didn't parade it, everyone would keep up the pretense. Reality was a created mirage.

She led the way to Mr. John's table, which was mostly full. He sat at the head, sunglasses on, patch covering the left eye, the eternal white handkerchief in his mouth. I hoped he took it out to eat. Several seats down the table was Victor Mature. Linda paused to give Mature a touch on the shoulder. He reached for her hand, and she slapped his fingers lightly and giggled.

I wondered how many love scenes started when Mr. John called "Action" and didn't end when he called "Cut," but were consummated in a cabin or behind a bush. Victor Mature shone with dazzling good looks and was a threat to lift every skirt. He also seemed natural enough playing a learned doctor who had come to hate himself and was half-consciously looking for death at the bottom of a bottle. By pulling away from his hand, the dance-hall girl was setting boundaries. I liked that.

Linda said hello to each of the others seated at this table. Flanking Mr. John were his wife, Mary, on one side, her brother, Wingate Smith, on the other, next, Henry Fonda and an actor people said Mr. John always found a part for, Ward Bond, then the producer across the table, and Victor Mature.

Danny Borzage waddled up carrying his big accordion,

slid it underneath a chair, and sat next to Mature. Mr. John gave him a big grin.

Linda tiptoed forward to her director, gave him a buss on the forehead, took a seat well down the table, and nodded me and Colin in next to her. Colin put his broad-brimmed hat on the chair next to him, saving it for Iris. Cathy Downs and Janey, the first-aid lady, filled the end of the table. Julius and a couple of others eyeballed the director's table and went somewhere else.

One thing was odd. Walter Brennan, one of the stars who would get a big credit, was at the head of the next table behind me and Linda. The second tier of actors, those playing the nasty Clanton brothers and the good-hearted Earp brothers, sat down-table from Brennan.

It was easy to see the pecking order. One table was those who called Mr. John "Pappy" or "Jack." The second table was the people who called him "Mr. John"—the Clanton family and the Earp brothers, whose real names I couldn't keep straight.

Brennan, the evil Clanton patriarch, was the odd man out. He called the director "Mr. Ford." Something about Brennan made Mr. John's hackles rise, and anyone could see that the feeling was mutual. When the two did a shot, the air itself seemed ready to burst into flame.

One afternoon Mr. John had said irritably to Brennan, "Can't you even mount a horse right?"

"No," said Brennan, "but I got three Oscars for acting."

So the performer with the most Oscars of any actor in the world was relegated to the second tier. I suspected that, no matter how long his career would be, he and Mr. John probably wouldn't work together again. Too much tension.

Standing and watching, Colin waved Iris to join us. When she sat down, she took his elbow for a moment. I wondered who she'd be flirting with next.

Mature set out to entertaining the table with wisecracks and bits of song and hijinks. Though he didn't seem like much of an actor—and Ford clearly didn't think he was—he had those good looks, he wasn't a bit self-important, and he was a barrel of fun. He and Danny Borzage were Mr. John's tonics.

I heard Iris say, "So who are you, Colin Murphy, and how did you end up in this desert?"

Inviting myself in, I said, "I've been wanting to know that, too."

"My family came across the sea near the end of the Irish War of Independence. Sick of it all, they were—the spying, the betrayals, the jailings, the killings, the whole lot of it— but mostly sick of the English. Besides, Pap was a man marked for death by the Brits."

One beer, and he sounded a lot more Irish now than he had earlier.

"I was the first of our crew born in this country. I dropped into a heritage of fighting and honorable bloodshed, and when I was twenty years old Pearl Harbor set off World War Two. On December eighth, I was at the front of the line to sign up for the big brawl."

"Colin was one hell of a fighter," Ford called from the head of the table. "Drove one of the landing craft onto Omaha Beach. Got his troops safely there when a lot of landing craft were going down."

"Omaha, yes, sir. While you were there filming, and made your landing in the middle of that awful killing ground, determined to show the truth about it. And got wounded and won a commendation."

Mr. John waved that aside. "Don't insult the brave men who died there by bringing up a guy who only fought with a camera." Then Mr. John turned back to talking to his brother-in-law about something or other.

"Did you meet Mr. John at Normandy?" said Iris. I wondered whether she hated war because it was war or because it had killed so many of her tribe. Well, my tribe, too.

"Not at all. I come to him later in Hollywood, and he got me war record on his own."

"Why did you go to Hollywood?"

"In love with the movies. *The Wizard of Oz* to *Wuthering Heights* and even to that silly *Gone with the Wind*. Foolish about 'em I was."

Iris, Linda, and I waited. Listening to his voice was like hearing music, and the words barely mattered.

"So when the killing was over, and I got demobilized, I went out to Fox and wrangled my way close enough to tell Mr. John we'd both been on Omaha Beach on the same day. Didn't need to say I was Irish, had me name to tell him that."

"And you wanted to be a security guy?" said Iris, disbelieving.

"No, I wanted to write movies. I do yet. But I judged the way to start out was to get a job, watch 'em being made, and figure it out from there."

"And meet people who'd read your script when you got one written," said Linda.

"There's that," said Colin.

Mr. John called down the table, "Hey, Yazzie! Tell the

story about the shot in *Stagecoach* with fifty Indians riding hard and . . . You know, the one. Tell it!"

At the time I'd got a big kick out of this screwup. Mr. John motioned me up with his hand, so I stood to tell it. "One afternoon, well, like Mr. John says, about fifty Navajo extras were supposed to ride hard behind the stagecoach and fire off rifles and arrows. The guard and John Wayne were supposed to shoot back.

"Mr. John wants to offer the riders a deal. I'm the translator. I say, 'When Mr. Wayne starts shooting that gun, one or two of you fall off your horse, and Mr. John will give you a bonus of one dollar on top of your day's pay.'

"They nod and lead their horses off.

" 'It's dangerous,' Mr. John says to me aside, 'taking a fall in the middle of all those flying hooves. Think anyone will do it?'

" 'Yeah.'

" 'Maybe I should have said two dollars.'

" 'No.'

"So we do the shot, and all fifty Navajos fly backward, and go *kerplunk* onto the sand. Pretty good shooting with just six bullets, even for the Duke."

The whole table laughed, including those who knew the story.

"Mr. John yells, 'Cut!', gathers the extras and has me explain bit by bit. 'I'll give every one of you the dollar I promised for the stunt you just did. But I need just *three* of you to fall off your horses, and you three will get another dollar.'

"This time he lets me pick the ones who take a dive. Naturally, I choose three of my clansmen, and I tell them to ride out in front and fall off in order: 'You fall the first time that Mr. Wayne shoots, you the second, you the third.' Worked just dandy."

The whole table laughed. Mr. John said, "Can't beat that. Second take went fine. Cut and print! Thanks, Yazzie."

"Sure thing, Mr. John." I sat down next to Linda again and glanced sideways to see if Iris was smiling.

"Yazzie—our bridge between red and white," Mr. John said.

"Traffic runs both ways," I said, grinning over a shoulder at him.

That was my personal highlight of the evening. After that, I sat through white-man food I didn't like and a bunch of phony conversation that didn't interest me.

Mr. John came to the rescue again. He clapped his hands once. "Let's have a dance tune."

Danny rose and dived right into a popular swing song of the time, "Call of the Jitterbug."

Linda and Iris jumped up as one. Iris pulled Colin up by the hand and started swing-dancing, her face turned up to his. Linda pranced straight over to Henry Fonda, held out both hands, and she got a big grin, in return, maybe the only one I ever saw from Fonda. Then I saw why. Brother, could that man dance. He was long and lanky and brought off some real tricky steps. A natural.

He and Linda made a terrific pair and stayed right with it when Danny switched to another hot swing tune, "Minnie the Moocher." By now half the cast and crew were following their star's example and hopping away. Linda looked like she was having a great time.

Iris either adored dancing or Colin, I couldn't tell which.

At the end of the second tune Victor Mature cut in on Fonda, which I guessed only he could do. Linda got a dubious look on her face but went along with it, and soon those two seemed to be having fun. But she stopped after one more dance.

She said to her roommate, "Are you ready, Cathy?"

"Sure."

"Seaman Goldman, will you see us to our cabin?"

"Yes, ma'am."

"Colin," said Linda.

He dropped Iris's hands and turned into a shadow that would flicker behind us up the road, armed and watchful.

Iris looked downcast.

Linda said to her, "The Seaman will be back in five minutes." She looked at Julius.

He nodded and mumbled around his cigar, "I'll wait at the town car."

We all played our parts. Linda and I said a proper goodnight at the cabin door, no touch of any kind, and I headed down the hill to Iris, Julius, and our ride home.

In the backseat I asked Iris, "You like Colin?"

She shrugged. She looked out at the night and wondered aloud, "What is it like to live in so much unreality? An art that is passing images on a screen. Fake relationships with other people. Conversations about things that aren't real."

I followed her eyes out and up. I had an impulse to tell her one of my people's old stories about how the night sky was created.

But she pushed on. "I don't see, for instance, who Julius really is."

"A guy who's always looking for something to be grouchy about."

"No one starts out like that. I wonder if he *remembers* who he is."

I thought back to Julius at La Posada. Being treated as if he was invisible. Papers flung at him, being dismissed, watching others become lovers. Driving people around. I was no fan of his, but I didn't understand how he got it done every day, and I was glad I didn't live inside his sour skin. I also wondered if living like that could make you twist into something very different than how you'd started out.

Other people's lives . . . It was time to turn the subject to something different. Since Iris was looking at the stars, I said, "Do you know how Coyote created the Milky Way?"

"No."

Her mind was still elsewhere. Julius? Colin? Lots of big questions. I understood.

"Coyote," I said, "is tricky and a troublemaker. Before the Holy People created the sun and moon, they were planning the arrangement of the stars. But they left Coyote out of the planning. Annoyed, he grabbed the buckskin where the stars were laid out and tossed them into the sky. They're scattered up there, sometimes very chaotic, because Coyote is chaotic.

"He got a good talking to, but he was still mad about being left out. So he added extra days to the year, which made the months uneven, and he arranged for the moon to fly in a way that made thirteen moon periods, not just twelve. *Dajinóo*."

"What does that last word mean?"

" 'So they say.' "

I gave her my starriest smile.

"So Coyote is a troublemaker."

"Yes, and not really. He loves mischief. He shakes things up, he throws things into disorder. But he also destroys conformity and brings change, which is good."

I hesitated. I thought about me having a romance with a movie star. Me riding the Super Chief to a different life. Me not marrying whatever woman Mom had picked out for me.

She said, "You have some of Coyote in you."

"Yes." I wondered if she liked that. Wondered maybe if I liked it, too.

She laid her head against my shoulder and was quiet the rest of way. I liked the feeling. And I was glad she wasn't resting on Colin's shoulder.

◆◆◆◆

Night turned into dawn, dawn became day, and the sun rose high in its arc. Noon. A harsh and tortured time.

Zopilote lay still, facedown. In prison a man learned great patience. Now he felt calm enough to watch an occasional speck of dust drift down. Nothing else was disturbed by his presence.

What a roost he had found to see, to smell, to learn. The great weapons of the *zopilote,* his eyes and nose. Even at mountaintop height a buzzard's eyes could see a final mortal quiver, its nose could smell the last gasp of life and the entry of death. Long live the king. The king is death.

The woman came into the cabin first, as usual. She sat on the small stool in front of the dresser, adjusted the mirror on its handles, and studied her face and hair. She looked as she ever did—had she not just finished showing off in front of the camera? He had gathered that she playacted an unmarried woman who traded sex for dollars. Zopilote had seen her facial expressions, and they suited a degraded woman.

Not touching a woman felt like going twenty-five years without a taste of water.

The temptress stood, ran her fingers through her hair until it looked wild, and shook it out hard. Did that make her feel prepared for what was coming? She unbuttoned her blouse and slipped it off. Then she unfastened the waist of her full skirt and stepped out of it. She readjusted the mirror to a lower angle and looked at herself full length. She wore something called a slip, which Zopilote had seen only in advertisements in newspapers and sometimes in color photos in glossy magazines. Beneath the slip, he knew, were the halter called a brassiere and a flimsy pair of underpants. He hoped that Navajo women had not started wearing such things. They had better sense.

A rap on the door. His heart beat faster, and a few specks of dust fell.

She cracked the door open, peeked out, and let Zopilote's son in. *This misbegotten man gets what has been ripped away from me. The man whose name, people say, is Yazzie Goldman. Born for Jew, so they say. So they say.*

As the two sat on the bed and ate the sandwiches his son had brought from the movie people's tent, Zopilote began to smell desire, arousal.

He believed this was the daily ritual of the temptress and his son, and he was eager to see every detail of what surely came next. They rolled back on the bed, and the temptress slowly took his son's uniform off, piece by piece. When he was completely naked, she did something to him for a short while that only a whore would do to any man. Then she jumped on top of him with a fury, still in her slip, and with her hips attacked him—there was no other word for it. After a while he moaned and she cried out. Then she collapsed on his naked body and seemed to doze.

The ripeness of the swirling lust dizzied Zopilote. It made him feel drained dry.

He didn't yet know what to do about his wife. *But now I know my first revenge upon my son.* It felt good. He would take what he wanted.

He lay very still. He thought he was completely quiet, but in this position he could not be sure.

After a little while the temptress did the whore thing again. And then she rolled him on top of her.

Zopilote squirmed as this Yazzie Goldman mounted her and stifled a gasp as his son thrust into her cave. Soon Yazzie rolled her over, and then they did things Zopilote had never pictured, like they were circus acrobats.

He watched, feeling jolted by every motion, his own body lifting and dropping on the waves of their rutting. The smell made him writhe with lust and envy and fury and in came the Darkness Rolling, filling his bones and his lungs. Becoming him. Yes, the rituals were making him feel more at ease.

❧❧❧❧

My days were routine.

I watched, horsed around with Linda and others, and waited for lunch. She ordered sandwiches brought up, and we ate them naked in bed. After the loving, she sent me outside so she could take a nap. If she didn't have a shoot to do that afternoon, she wanted a repeat of our noon recreation. She had a libido that wouldn't quit, hinted at in public, and in private displayed in big headlines.

Cathy Downs acted sheepish about spending the nights with Linda. I personally didn't take to Cathy, an upbeat, outdoorsy, cheery creature who was exactly what she seemed to be, pretty and boring, like the sweatered girl with the sweatered guy on a package of stale breakfast cereal.

Iris came down several times and drew people, anyone but the stars. She hung around with Colin a lot and gave the chunky Irishman some sketches of himself to send to his parents. I wondered if something was developing there. Whatever, it was fine by me.

Bottom line: Linda and I were limited to afternoon trysts, but what afternoons. What a job.

Until it wasn't. (And I didn't receive my send-off on a fancy piece of stationery.)

Nine

Linda's big scenes in the movie were a series of shots where she butted heads with the white hats, Wyatt Earp and Cathy Downs's schoolmarm. Earp tried to push Doc toward the marm, who wanted marriage. Chihuahua schemed to get both of them to back off—*she* was Doc's girl and he was marrying her. Trapped, Doc ignored his teasing promise to Chihuahua and skipped town to escape both women.

In the course of making a living, Chihuahua dallied with Billy Clanton. Doc came back and caught them together in her room. Clanton shot at Doc and accidentally hit Chihuahua.

So here came the crux for Doc Holliday. Chihuahua bleeding, needing surgery, and him the only physician in miles and miles. Fear and self-disgust.

He gave it a go with the scalpel, thought he'd succeeded, and felt good about himself for a change. A glimmer of triumph in view.

Then Chihuahua died.

But that was still to come. Linda was nervous about her scenes with Henry Fonda, I could see that. She was comfortable with everyone in the cast but him. In front of the camera, she had fun teasing out the wild man in the Victor Mature character and pushing away the Fonda character, who tried to turn Doc righteous. Off camera, Fonda's flinty reserve made her edgy.

It turned out that I underestimated her, and maybe she underestimated herself. She bristled at the marm just right, and Mr. John printed the third take. She was just huffy enough when she stood up to Fonda's character. Take after take, I admired her more.

And noon hour after noon hour I liked her more.

The dying was Linda's big moment, and my sad one. It would be the end of her work on the picture. When she left, my job disappeared with her. Probably our friendship—and all else we had together—too.

On the morning of her last day of shooting, when I picked her up, she squeezed my hand once at the cabin door. Then I walked her down the hill, Colin trailing. She didn't look at me, and I couldn't sense what was going on inside her mind.

In her role as the wounded Chihuahua, she was down and fading out. Her part in the first shot was simple. For some reason, evidently Mature battling himself as he did the cutting, Mr. John asked for another take and another and another. What he was looking for I couldn't tell, but he got sharp with everyone, and we were going to be late for lunch. Mr. John kept calling Mature over for quiet talks. Linda was tired of playing the suffering and expiring beauty. That wasn't her. She was vibrant and full of life. Make-believe dying was getting old.

When Mr. John finally called out "Print," she sat up from her deathbed, looked straight at me, and snapped her head to the side, meaning, *Get your tail up to the cabin.*

I did, expecting her to be drained.

What a woman. In the cabin she threw off her clothes and came at me on fire. I'd never experienced anything like it, so wild, so much of herself, but even more so. It was a little odd. She still wore the makeup that made her look like she was taking her last breath. The contrast was macabre. Not that I didn't get a kick out of everything she did.

And suddenly it was over. She said, "I have to sleep now," closed her eyes, and turned her death-mask face away from me.

Outside sat Colin, alert as always, and the makeup guy, Raphael, who was folded into what he called "the lotus position" on the ground under the usual cedar. He was an odd duck, about sixty, toilet-seat bald, with long stringy gray hair from the ears down, a monklike appearance. He was what we Navajos call a *nadle*, a guy who likes other guys. To us such men are special. They have the powers of men and women, and are often the creators of beautiful sand paintings, ceremonial baskets, and the like. But white people have names for these men that are nasty.

"She ready yet?" Raphael asked.

Though Mr. John's shooting with Linda was over, the stills-photo guy wasn't satisfied with what he had of her, so he wanted to get some more shots, her dancing and swirling her skirts in the tavern and such as that. Some of the pictures would be turned into posters to be plastered in movie theaters around the country. He planned to shoot them this afternoon, while Mr. John was filming elsewhere, and the stills would go out to the press as publicity material. I assumed that tomorrow morning, driven by Julius, Linda and I would head for La Posada.

I plopped down next to Raphael. "She's taking a nap, and she needs it." Pause. "And she needs you too."

He shrugged. "I made her look like death twice-over this morning, and I'll make her look more gorgeous than ever this afternoon." He checked his watch, ever dissatisfied with the amount of time Linda and I left him to do his job. He sighed, and said, "*Wait. Wait. Wait.* It certainly makes this part of my job tedious."

Eyes front, Colin said, "Miss Downs isn't coming up to the cabin this afternoon." The Irishman stayed ready, like expecting bad times ahead made up his very core.

Some days Cathy came to the cabin after lunch, whenever she saw I'd left, and got her own nap. While Linda was with Cathy, I usually sat under this cedar, Colin and I covering both actresses.

"Enough. I'm going to meditate," Raphael said, "while the princess recovers her glow." He closed his eyes and was gone.

I propped myself against the tree and tried to feel easy. Waiting was tough, no arguments there. I couldn't stop thinking about the finality of what was coming. Losing Linda and probably never seeing her again, or hearing from her. Being back home at the trading post? Not much consolation in that.

I thought of being daring and asking her to stay a couple of nights with me at La Posada and catch the Super Chief on its run to Los Angeles. I didn't. She might be wild about the idea, but it would go pretty hard on me if she said no.

Still, I yearned for more time and a romantic good-bye. I dreaded the moment of handing her on board, bound for Los Angeles, her home in Bel-Air, and her husband—a universe beyond my reach, beyond even my imaginings. Yes, I belonged here. I might not be crazy about it, but I knew it. But I could already feel the hole Linda Darnell would leave in my life. Grandpa had lived his dream. Frieda lived hers to the hilt, and Iris was living hers. Mine was to *make a big life*. Like Linda's. Like the rest of them. Come what may.

Soon Raphael opened his eyes. He claimed he could nail thirty minutes of meditation right on, no need for a watch.

"Oh, please!" he said. "No sign of her yet?"

"None." Amazing how our conversation didn't distract Colin one inch.

"Why don't you let me get you started meditating?" he said. "God knows that trying to get her moving, when she isn't in the mood, is impossible."

"I can't close my eyes," I said. "I'm on the job, watching out for Linda."

"Blah, blah, blah," he said. "Try twenty minutes. I'll sit right here and help Colin keep watch."

Colin looked at Raphael and let out a loud laugh. Then he apologized.

"No problem," Raphael said. "I wouldn't want me for a guard dog, either."

This was the third or fourth time he'd asked to teach me meditation. He must have thought I was a real wreck. Whenever I said I'd pass, I got a lecture about how meditating didn't belong to one religion but fit with all, and then a rambling talk about metaphysics, and I never figured out what that is.

Sometimes white people are funny. A few, including the Hollywood types, think Indians are noble savages who bear a special spiritual wisdom, but they feel obligated to tell us about their own beliefs. I think our *hózhó* is as fine as anything they know about. So why do they always want to teach us, not learn from us? They don't see the irony of that.

On the other hand, most white people think we're dirty, drunken savages.

Noble savages or drunken savages, either way we're savages. For them, there is no way out of the corral inside their minds. Maybe we all have corrals, and rodeo arenas too, in our minds. Places that we go to rest, places we go all out and test ourselves to the limit. And they are not known to other people.

"Meditating will change your life," he said. "It—"

I held up a hand. "Okay, okay." I'd heard his talk until I could have given it. Colin was in charge right now, and this was the last time I'd see Raphael. I figured it couldn't hurt to give it a try.

"You watch that cabin sharp?" I said to Colin.

"Damn sharp."

"Now," Raphael said, "let's get you in the lotus position."

"That's not going to work," I said. "I've tried it. My legs aren't bread dough."

"Just find a comfortable position to sit. That will be fine to start with." He ticked off instructions, most of which I'd already heard. He also gave me a mantra to say over and over, a magic word that is supposed to stay secret.

I sat beneath the sheltering pine, relaxed, and let a good feeling of calm settle inside.

"Now," he said, "close your eyes, say your mantra in your mind, and feel each breath, the spirit of life, come in and out, in and out."

I did it. Actually? I think I slept through it. But that was okay.

❖❖❖❖

In twenty minutes, presumably, Raphael tapped me on the knee. "Can't wait any longer," he said. "Even a star can only push it so far."

He padded up to the cabin door and knocked. No answer. Knocked again. Again no answer. A third time.

Finally, he tried the door. It was locked.

He turned toward me and Colin, his shadow filling the doorway. Raphael said, "I'm going to find Cathy Downs and get her key." He trotted off.

I wondered *What the hell?* but there was no way Linda wasn't safe. Three of us, and two had their eyes on the front of that cabin every moment. No doors or windows except in front.

Pretty quick Raphael came back with a key, went in, and just as quick came back out, leaving the door open. He gave me a peculiar look. "Back in a minute," he said.

I hoisted myself up and walked groggy-like to the cabin door to see what was happening. The sight woke me up like being thrown into a fire.

Linda was huddled in the bed on her side, still stark-naked. She was whimpering. Her face was swelling up and going multicolored fast. It would be a patchwork of eggplants and lemons, mixed hideously with her pallid makeup.

I pulled a sheet over her, sat down on the edge of the bed, and took her hand. There were no words I could say that would be a bandage large enough to fix her hurts. "Sweetheart, what happened?" I'd never used such a word with her before.

"Don't touch me," she said, pulling her hand away. "Just don't touch me." Her bruised eyes were swollen shut, and I couldn't tell if she knew it was me.

I quieted the hurt and shock I felt and tried to be a center of peace for her. I lowered my voice to a whisper. "What happened, sweetheart?"

"Don't touch me. Do not touch me."

I shook her hand a little. "It's me, Yazzie. Who did this to you?"

I was rocking on a boat that had tilted from despair to anger. I wanted to catch the person who did this and make them pay for it in every possible way. I thought about the note on her door, about the letter she'd received. Mr. John and his anger and his worry. The way she had brushed it off. His fears had been absolutely right.

I looked around the room, my focus made bright, and I wondered how the person who did this had gotten in. The whole situation felt, and looked, impossible.

She snatched her hand away from me and got loud. "I said, DON'T TOUCH ME!"

At that moment Julius barged through the door, followed

by Colin and Raphael. Julius clicked his eyes deliberately from one of us to the other, collecting details.

Now she ramped up to a scream, propping up in her bed and hurling words at the walls. Her voice went down to a growl that sent shivers down the back of my legs: "Get . . . away . . . from . . . me."

Then I turned my focus to a different reality—I knew exactly how this looked to Julius.

Suddenly the barrel of his .38 revolver was in my face. Colin jerked both my arms high behind me.

"Goldman, hold still for the cuffs."

Knowing the drill, I did it without one word.

Linda was still raving. Loud voice, blind eyes. My heart twisted like a wet rag being wrung hard.

I couldn't imagine what had happened to her, how she felt, who had done this terrible thing. I wanted to hold her. To comfort her. To wrap her in blankets and kiss her. To kill the person responsible. All of those things.

I felt the clamp of Colin's handcuffs and heard the *snick*. At that moment I hated him. He whispered to me, "Sorry, Yazzie."

"Raphael," snapped Julius, "go tell Mike Goulding to radio Kayenta for the cops. Then send Janey up here. Tell her we need everything she's got." Janey treated aches and pains for the cast and crew.

"Goldman, get out the door and away from Miss Darnell. Now."

I did.

Julius and Colin marched me to the pine where I'd been dumb enough to close my eyes and doze. He cuffed me to a branch just above my head.

"I'm staying right here," Julius said, "and I'd be glad to use this on you." He held his .38 up. "Don't try anything."

The stogie was out of his mouth, and he was speaking distinctly.

"We've been idiots. I'm going to see that your ass is in jail for the assault, battery, and rape of Linda Darnell."

Life turns on a dime, which is a very slim coin.

Ten

The tribal cops were sent, and they were Hugh Cly and Melvin Etcitty. Everything was desperate, turned upside down. Painful. But all was not entirely lost.

When they freed me from the tree and recuffed my hands, I turned and saw a small crowd around Linda's cabin.

"Eyes front," said Hugh, making himself sound tough. He marched me, with his baton poking my back, to the cop car. It was a pickup truck with paint so faded that the police insignia was almost invisible. We got into the front seat, me in the middle. The jail was in Kayenta, an hour's dirt-road drive. We spoke in Navajo.

"Hugh, I don't have a lot of time."

"We know that, and we seen what they said you done." He added, "And we're not supposed to talk together. You know that."

"I didn't do it."

"We called it in, and the Loot ordered us to arrest you."
Then Melvin added, "And we're to keep you away from the
crime scene."

"Loot's sending some guys who are smarter'n us to do
the actual investigating," Hugh said with a twist.

"Until the really smart guys get here," Melvin said. "The
Fibbies."

Hugh got the cop car rolling.

I didn't need any explanation. The FBI would be on the
job as quick as they could get here. A crime by a Navajo
against a white woman was federal jurisdiction, not Navajo.
Would be anyway because the Gouldings' little stretch of
land wasn't rez but what was called an "inholding"—they
owned it, not the tribe. And a crime against a movie star, a
celebrity, was the sort of case J. Edgar Hoover loved. The
feds would be all over it.

"You know how it goes, Yazzie," Hugh said. "We've got
to move fast if we want to find anything out, because as soon
as they all get in here—"

"You're out, I said."

"Yep. We're not supposed to be smart enough to figure
out crimes on our own. No more talking now."

I had to watch out for my chance.

After about fifteen minutes I saw a decent place. Time to
act.

"I need to relieve myself." I'd picked a spot just before a
sharp curve in the road.

Hugh braked to a stop. He knew what was up. He pointed
with his lips, Navajo-style. "Over behind those rocks,
maybe?"

I held out my cuffed hands. "To do this, uh, you know, I need . . ." Melvin shook his head, freed me, and kept the cuffs.

I clomped up a sandy gully, slipped behind the rocks, and waited. As soon as I was well hidden, Hugh and Melvin drove on.

I hoofed it up the gully in the opposite direction. Over one rise, then down the next canyon, up and across a mesa high above. A long walk ahead of me.

Since none of the big law-enforcement agencies paid much attention to Melvin, Hugh, or any of the other Navajo cops, it didn't matter much what they decided or ordered. Melvin and Hugh were my clansmen, and I was going to walk free. Same story with a jury or a judge—clan came first.

Maybe it's not a perfect system. For sure it isn't. But in some ways it creates balance.

It was going to be a cold night, but I'd make it home before dawn.

◆◆◆◆

I scraped the heavy front door open an hour before first light. Mom was up waiting for me. She gave me a wrapping-up hug.

"I'm out of a job," I said. "And Linda has been hurt so bad . . . I can't even talk about it. Not all the way."

"Mike radioed us. She said that you're also wanted by the police."

She gave me a kiss on the cheek, leaned back holding my shoulders, and burst into tears. She'd been a-jangle emotionally, unusual for her, ever since I got home. Each night I came in late for a reheated supper and took off for work right after sunup. But arrested? In the company of an important woman who had been beaten? That was the last straw.

She said, "Gone for six years, and now?"

I felt as if I'd become a plague on her life. She loved me, but the effect was the same.

I heard Grandpa's wheelchair. He was a light sleeper in his old age. He was going, "Ow, ow, ow . . ."

"Out of a job," I repeated for his benefit, "and the cops are after me. Worst of all is Linda. What happened to her, and the shape she is in? It rips me up inside."

Mom pulled me over to the couch, and I sat down. "I have coffee made," she said. "Let me get you a mug."

I sat, numb, willing to be led anywhere.

"Now," she said, "tell us what happened."

I told the story. "The most terrible part is that I didn't hurt her, I don't know who did, the person is still out there.

"Yes," said Iris. "And if there's a jealous boyfriend . . ."

" . . . Or husband," I added.

"She is still in lots of trouble."

"And we may be, too."

Mom shot a look at me. She didn't know about the husband part, but it was very minor right now.

From just behind me, I heard Grandpa, a sea of turmoil rising and falling in his nonsense words. Iris said, "I think he wants the details."

I gave them to him. He nodded in his lopsided fashion.

Iris said, "And what are the charges, exactly? Hugh came

by, but he didn't tell us much. He didn't want to be seen around our house."

I couldn't look her in the eye, so I looked at Cockeyed's screwy one. "The assault, battery, and rape of the movie star Linda Darnell."

"That's what I figured. What idiots. She's your girlfriend, or paramour, or consensual fling. Something like that. How can a man rape his own girlfriend?"

"Iris," I said, "it's a rough world, and it happens all the time."

"But not by you."

"Absolutely not."

Grandpa pulled out his chalkboard.

Iris said, her words falling like flaking paint, "This is too damn real, isn't it? Paradise, dreams . . . they've been shattered. I can't imagine what Linda is going through. She believes in those things."

She turned quick to my mother and said, "Loan me the truck. I have to get to the hospital to see her. She doesn't have any other friends around here."

"I'm not sure she has many real friends in the world," Mom said.

Grandpa scrawled crazily, shaking his head: IRIS + LINDA—NO!

"Grandpa, she needs someone."

He waved his chalkboard.

"Iris," I said, "I agree with Grandpa. You stay close to home. Whoever did this, Linda is his target, and you shouldn't get too close."

"But—"

"Iris, I agree with Yazzie and Grandpa on this, too" said Mom. "You have a big heart, but this is a world we know nothing about. Best to stay clear."

I had turned it over on my walk home, all night, trying to find the truth of the matter. "I can't figure out how the guy got in. I stayed right there, guarding the only way in or out, and the other guard—your Colin, Iris—and the makeup fellow were right with me. When the makeup man went in to take her down to her dressing room, he found her battered."

I played it through my head again. "Since no one went in or out of that cabin but me, I have to be the bad guy. That's how it would look to me. Someone figured just how to set me up. I was the perfect fall guy."

"Yazzie," said Mom, "we are all attached to Linda. She is a good woman who has lost her way, and somehow you got in the way of a road she started down long before you came into her life. Sometimes we have to be careful who we draw close to us."

That rubbed me the wrong way. I thought, *Your mating choice wasn't so great . . . whoever he was.* And then I brushed that aside. I hated to think so, but part of my mother's words were right because they came from experience.

Six eyes on me, plus Cockeyed's straight one, waiting to see if I had more to say. Grandpa wore a face that was terrible even for him. And I was bone tired and buzzed up at the same time.

"They assigned Hugh Cly and Melvin Etcitty to take me to jail," I said, "So, you know—"

Mom explained to Iris how I got away.

"That was a piece of luck, anyway," Iris said.

Mom stepped in front of Iris, took me by the upper arm, and led me toward my bedroom. "You sleep," she said. "Some *biligaana* lawyer will get here plenty soon."

I wanted to shut my eyes, to turn off my mind. I couldn't stand looking across the landscape of my future. It was a badlands. Finally sleep, that great healer, found me.

❖❖❖❖

About noon Mom rousted me out to meet the tribal lawyer.

"Martin Green," he said, offering his hand. The tribal lawyers' being *biligaanas* made things sticky. I wasn't sure how they could help people they didn't understand. Our home may as well be in a different country.

Green was a timid-looking fellow with round, gold-rimmed spectacles, and his thin hair parted right in the middle. He was disheveled, and the knees of his pants were sandy. Turned out he'd gotten his tribal car stuck in the sand twice between Kayenta and Oljato.

Grandpa came wheeling out, and I smiled sideways at him. He didn't send back his lopsided smile—he was feeling pissy. He held his board behind the lawyer to show what he'd already written: SHUT MOUTH. I nodded.

Iris came in from the back door, and she and Mom sat thigh-to-thigh with me on the eight-foot sofa. Female guardians. Mom gave me a pat of confidence on the knee.

"I'm here on official business," said Green. "I need to talk to Mr. Goldman in private."

"We're a family," Mom said.

"I—"

"Don't take any risks," Iris said, "with your welcome in this house."

He should have known his position from the fact that Mom offered him nothing to eat or drink. With Navajos, no hospitality means not welcome.

Green sighed and sat down without invitation. "I have to ask Mr. Goldman a few questions."

"Which he may or may not answer," said Iris.

Grandpa shook his fist, like *Way to go.*

"I'm a cop," I said to everyone. "I know what not to say."

Iris got on me. "People who think they can't incriminate themselves—"

I put a hand on her arm. She stopped. I finished gently. "Right. I haven't done anything wrong, so that protects me. Dumb. Anything can be twisted to work against you."

"Could we back up here? "I'm *your* lawyer," Green reminded us. "Whatever you say to me is privileged. I can't repeat it to the authorities."

"Let's get going," I prodded.

He nodded, uncertain. "You know something about the law governing arrests and criminal charges."

"Damn straight," I said.

"The FBI is on the way. The jurisdiction—"

I held up a hand to stop him. "I know. Anglo and Indian, felony. It's the feds."

"Right."

"So some feds are coming by train from Albuquerque and driving the dirt road up here."

"Actually, one of them stayed in Flagstaff to get a statement from Miss Darnell, and the other two are on the long drive. But the evidence looks strong. You're guilty."

He waited.

"By now Miss Darnell has told them it wasn't me."

"We're in contact by shortwave. The agent asked her who did it, but she just babbled and cried. Now she's under heavy sedation again. He's hoping she can give a statement tonight or tomorrow."

"I didn't do it. Take my word for it."

"To them your word is a fart in the wind."

"At least you have some juice in you," Iris said.

Green blinked several times. "All right. You, the other guard, and the makeup man were stationed in front of her cabin with an excellent view of the only entrances and exits, right?"

"No questions yet. Tell me what they think. Then I may correct something."

"Okay, here's the picture. You took your usual lunch break with Miss Darnell, maybe an hour."

He waited, but I said nothing.

"You came out. Miss Darnell customarily takes a nap at that point. Colin Murphy, the other guard, and the makeup man, Raphael Garibaldi, were sitting under a tree. Garibaldi meditated while he waited for the chance to take her down to her dressing room."

Green looked at me, paused, and without hearing anything from me, he went on.

"When Garibaldi finished meditating, he talked you into meditating while he and Murphy watched the cabin."

I nodded. Grandpa gave me a sour look.

"Garibaldi's under the impression that you actually fell asleep instead of meditating. Yes, Murphy was on duty, but . . . When he woke you up, Garibaldi was out of patience.

He knocked on Miss Darnell's door and got no response. So he went down the hill to get a key from Miss Downs."

Green thought I might confirm some little thing, but I didn't. I wanted to get information, not give it.

"When he got back, he opened the door, looked inside, excused himself, and went back down the hill in a hurry."

"While he was gone, you went inside. Miss Darnell had been beaten. Garibaldi, Murphy, and Julius Roth arrived a couple of minutes later."

Green went on quickly. "Here's the difficult part. All three say Miss Darnell was crying out at you, telling you to get away."

"The words weren't to me. Her eyes were vacant and swollen shut."

Iris put a hand on my arm and looked a reprimand at me. Grandpa said "Da-a-a . . ." but couldn't get out whatever it was.

Green went on, "I don't want you to tell the police anything about that. When they ask what she said, just don't answer."

I stopped myself from protesting. It was like jamming a log down my throat.

"Unfortunately, Garibaldi, Murphy, and Roth were there and heard her. But do not confirm that. Roth pointed his gun at you."

"Actually, he held it in my face."

Grandpa snorted like a bull.

Green lurched on. "Garibaldi's hands and Murphy's show no signs of abrasions or bruising. Neither do yours, but that doesn't mean anything. Any of you could have worn heavy gloves."

I couldn't stand this. "I didn't do it. Neither did they. Garibaldi doesn't even go for women. Someone," I said, "is still out there, still enraged. Probably still gunning for Linda and possibly me. Even my family."

Green looked into my face a long while in that prying, white-man way. Then he let his breath out in a gush. "I understand, but it looks bad," he said. "You were in the cabin with her long enough to do anything."

I nodded.

"I warn you," said Green. "Don't take Murphy or Garibaldi lightly. Their stories match, they both fit the facts and time at the scene, and their recall of detail is excellent. They will make powerful witnesses for the prosecution."

Iris and Mom stood up at the same time, and I thought they were about to throw Green out. With a gentle hand I pulled Mom down next to me.

Grandpa made a coughing sound. *Okay,* I nodded, *I get it, he's on my side.*

"When Julius Roth alerted him," Green went on, "Mr. Ford got Mrs. Goulding to shortwave Kayenta and send the police. Then he had Mr. Roth drive Miss Darnell to the hospital in Flagstaff. They're worried about a concussion. They probably won't be able to tell, even with examination, if she was raped."

I glanced sideways at Mom. Her face was set hard, her lips pursed. I could feel the familiar lecture coming later—this-is-what-you-get-when-you-stray-too-far-from-your-roots.

"So, Mr. Goldman, you tell me—how could anyone but you have beaten Miss Darnell?"

"I have no answer for that. And we're done here."

"I represent you. You can tell me everything. If you confess to murder, I wouldn't be allowed to reveal that."

"I know the rules. But I'm done talking."

"Tell me why."

"I'm a cop."

"What does that have to do with anything?"

"Watch and see."

"If you—"

"Mr. Green, 'done here' means 'done here.' Next time I see you, I hope you'll have evidence for me. For now we're finished."

I went to the front door and held it open. I was not impressed with my legal representation. It seemed clear to me that he thought I did it, and until that changed, he was useless.

Green got up and started out. Then he stopped. He set his jaw, gave me a long look, and came out with it: "If you interfere with the investigation, you'll go to jail for obstruction. You know that."

I stared him down.

"I advise you in the strongest terms to stay away from that cabin and away from Miss Darnell. As of today you are not guilty, or may not be. If you insert yourself into their investigation, you will be guilty of obstruction, beyond any possible defense."

I looked at him, gave him no words.

"I beg you not to try to solve this yourself."

I said, "I agree. Trying wouldn't be enough."

After I closed the door on him, I turned to my family. "I'm sorry . . ." I began.

I put my arms around my mother. Over her head I saw Grandpa writing on his blackboard. Iris watched the three of us, her face sorrowful.

After a while Mom turned an anguished face up to mine. "You have no idea," she said again.

She wasn't making any sense.

Mom jerked herself away and ran to her bedroom.

I looked at Iris. "Looks like Raphael is against me now. Also Colin Murphy."

Iris said, "Then he's against me. You want me to go to Flagstaff with you?"

"No."

"She may want a woman there. A friend."

"I'll handle it."

Grandpa held up his slate. TAKE JAKE C.

Eleven

I scouted the hospital, just four long halls in the shape of an X. I told Jake Charlie, "Drop me on the east side and wait there." The main entrance was on the west, exactly the wrong direction for any entrance door by Navajo ways.

I got out and looked up at the sky. According to the Big Dipper, we were square in the middle of the night. "You need to sleep," I said to Jake Charlie. He answered with his customary silence. "Stretch across the front seat and leave the keys in the ignition. If you hear me get into the truck, drive out of here. Fast."

Jake Charlie was probably snoring before I opened the east-facing door.

I wondered what the hell I was getting into.

I'd never been in a hospital, and was traditional enough to be wary. Hospitals are packed full of *chindi*. If a person dies in a hogan, no Navajo will go in there again. Going into a place where people die every day—that *really* doesn't work.

When I got home, finally and truly back home, without one foot in the glamorous world of movies, this hospital would be another reason I'd need an Enemy Way ceremony. The Navajo word for "hospital" means "place where white people go to die." Dying is something you can do on your own.

I was nervous, but I damn well meant to find Linda. I needed to make up for my failure in my duty. I liked her, to understate the case, and I was beyond worried about her. It wasn't me who hurt her, and the one who did could be anywhere, even walking the halls, dressed as a doctor or nurse. My imagination was on the loose, but considering the situation, I was giving it as much room as possible.

The halls were an eerie quiet. They smelled like alcohol and anguish. The lights were at half-mast, and the flooring caught the glow, bouncing it off curling edges. Impossible to imagine that people came onto the earth almost every day in such a place. That people died here? That seemed very real. This was a railway station gone crazy with no particular schedule, a place no one wanted to be, hauling in new people and hauling out the dead on her linoleum tracks.

I slipped down a twilit hall toward the bright center area, wondering which room she was in. Flagstaff only had this one country hospital, no security, but I didn't want to attract attention. Didn't want to cause the slightest stir.

When I got farther from the door, I could see a rectangular counter at the junction of the four halls, like the brain of the four legs. A nurses' station.

One nurse was standing, facing slightly away from me in three-quarter profile, looking at manila folders. She'd flip through one, put it down, and page through another. She wore the uniform, a starched white dress and one of those odd white caps with wings.

Then I noticed. Hard to see, in the half-dark beyond the brightly lit station, but midway down the hall opposite a slouchy man leaned against a wall next to a room door. I knew his shape very well.

Hoping the nurse wouldn't look up, I padded back down the hall outside into the crisp night air and trotted around the building to the opposite door.

Big risk, but facing it head-on, that's the best way I knew. From the west entrance I walked openly toward the slumping Julius. I didn't want to look like I was sneaking around.

I eased up close without attracting his attention. Looked like he was dozing on his feet.

In a flash, his piece was in my face.

I breathed deep. I wasn't surprised and it didn't matter. He was doing his job. He thought I'd attacked her, and he wasn't taking any chances.

I held up my palms so he could see my hands were empty.

"Give me your gun," he muttered.

I pulled out my .45 auto, popped the magazine, jerked the slide back to eject the cartridge in the chamber, held it by the barrel, and stuck it out handle first. He slipped it into his suit-coat pocket.

He lowered his .38 snub nose.

"I've gotta make sure," he said.

I nodded.

He patted me down, and then waved me through to her room. He said, "She's sleeping now, but she was asking for you all afternoon."

◇◆◇◆◇

One look, and I almost felt like it was me who got hit in the face. Over and over and *all* over, brutally. My stomach went tight and terrible. Her face was ravaged—purple, yellow, misshapen. I didn't want to do anything to wake her up, but she was so sound asleep . . . probably drugged. I stepped into the bathroom and flushed the toilet. I tiptoed back to her bedside. She didn't even blink.

I knelt by the bed and looked at her, my eyes locked. I can't tell you what my feelings were, because I only half knew myself. Large, beyond all words in any language.

The room had no heart, no soul. Like sitting inside a huge icebox. The furnishings were her bed, with the head cranked up, a stool on rollers that doctors use, and a hard-backed visitor's chair. I took the chair and slid it close to her. I knew one of my feelings—a fierce desire to protect her. I would watch and wait and not sleep. Julius was out there, sure, but I'd seen what happened when it seemed like she was being guarded. From then on out, having failed her once, and seeing how she'd paid the price? I wasn't leaving her.

◇◆◇◆◇

"Yazzie."

"Yazzie."

The words crept into my sluggard mind, like the half-light from the window. I opened my eyes and looked at her.

Linda was holding her arms out to me.

I slid into them like a ship into home port and held her, careful not to touch her face.

She pushed her battered cheek against mine. It must have hurt, but she needed holding and knew it.

She put her soft palms on my chest and moved me back a few inches. She looked into my face. Something had opened inside her, and the way she held my eyes now felt more intimate than anything we had done in the heat of sex.

Linda said, "Let's get out of here."

"Rest," I said. "You need it."

"It's impossible to rest in a hospital, and get that expression off your face—I know what I look like. They said there's no permanent damage. They're going to release me this morning, but Yazzie, I want to get out of here right now."

I went to the window and looked out. Sunup in a few minutes. When I turned back, she was at the closet, stark-naked, about to step into her underwear.

I started to turn her around by the shoulders, hold her, that's it, but she brushed my hands away. "No touching, not yet. Sorry, I—"

"Linda, I'm the one who needs to apologize. I let you down in the most terrible way. I don't know how it happened, but I do know you counted on me, and then . . ."

She started over. "The only place he hit me was in the face."

"Over and over, Linda. Anything else?"

"We'll talk in the car."

We were leaving, and that was fine with me.

I opened the door carefully, but Julius was already facing me with his hand on his weapon.

Linda said, "We're getting out of here, Julius."

"I'll have to let the studio know."

"Do that and I'll get you fired," she said.

"You need the hospital's permission."

"Permission," she said with a curl of disgust. "Just walk me to the nurses' station, I'll sign their goddamned paperwork, and we're out of here."

He accepted the words as immovable.

I pointed to my empty holster, on the cross-draw side.

He pulled out my automatic and raised an eyebrow at Linda.

"Of course," she said. "Give it to him. You think this is a game of charades?"

He handed it to me. "Goldman, this is one hell of a mess."

"Believe me, I understand that."

"I hope you do. She said it was you."

Linda said, "I'm not saying that!"

"You did," he said to her, "and now you say he didn't. Leaving us with several possibilities. You have either gone completely nuts and can't be trusted to know what's real and what's not, or you've pissed off someone so dangerous they can practically make themselves invisible. I don't like either scenario."

She pointed to her face. "I'm not wild about it, either. Look at me!"

Julius stood there, looking. "I'm going with *not crazy*. Your attitude is still in place."

"I damn well need attitude right now, don't you think?" she said. "Julius, walk me down there."

She held me back with a palm. "I don't want you to get close enough for the nurse to make an ID."

She led Julius down the hall, her head held high.

I couldn't hear anything, but what I saw was that the nurse

had a dilemma. She worked in a hierarchy and was used to following orders. "Doctor's orders," in fact, was a phrase regularly chirped on the radio in a way that sounded like pronouncements from Mount Sinai.

On the other hand, the nurse had a movie star standing in front of her. If you think a doctor can carry on like a five-star general, you should have watched Linda Darnell. The nurse's posture went from assured to subdued to meek. Papers were put on the counter. Linda flourished some writing on them, presumably a signature, and off she marched. The only words I heard were the nurse's last ones, to Linda's back. "This is AMA."

I asked Linda what it meant.

" 'Against medical advice,' " she said. "They mistake advice for leg irons. Julius, bring my suitcase."

When he came out of the room with it, he made a face, miffed that I shepherded the woman while he was playing porter, once again. We would have to come to some kind of truce.

Jake Charlie was outside the pickup, leaning against the front door. Linda said, "Julius, bring the car around."

When the Cadillac town car nosed up, she spoke her will hard and fast.

"Julius, put my suitcase in the trunk. You will ride in the pickup with Jake Charlie."

"At that I draw the line, Miss Darnell. I'd lose my job."

"You'll lose it if you don't," she said. "I swear on my mother's grave."

Julius hesitated.

"Seaman Goldman will drive me in the Cadillac."

"Miss Darnell."

"You will go to the police station and tell them Seaman Goldman is escorting me back to the location."

"What?"

"I'm not breaking any law. You will tell the police to radio Mr. Ford that we're on the way."

"I . . ."

She thrust her hand out. "Give me the car keys."

Julius did.

She handed them to me, strutted toward the passenger door of the Caddy, and waited for me to open it for her.

I handed Jake Charlie the shopping list Mom had tucked into my pocket and a wad of bills and whispered into his ear.

When I got in, she scooted all the way across the big front seat and sat real close to me. I couldn't imagine how her face felt. An atrocity.

"The last two days I wanted so much for you to be next to me."

"I was arrested."

"I know. Nothing to worry about now. I told them it wasn't you. Definitely not you."

I started the Caddy. There was plenty for Linda to worry about, but it seems like it had escaped her.

"What did you give Jake Charlie?" She missed nothing.

"Cash and a shopping list."

She looked at me with questions in her eyes.

"Mom's spending my pay on supplies for the trading post. They're cheaper here than from the truck company that delivers to the posts. Jake Charlie will do the shopping." And Julius would have to spend the whole day in Flagstaff, traipsing around from store to store behind Jake Charlie. Tonight he'd probably sleep in the seat of the truck. Not a plum assignment, and it wasn't going to make coming up with a way to work together any easier.

Linda put her head back on the seat, and she smiled a little. "Free. I hate hospitals."

"Linda, everyone does."

We rolled. And then she started to talk.

Twelve

"He raped me."

She barely gave it time to soak in. "I'd just had sex that was as good as it gets, and then the bastard violated me."

The storm clouds of those words hung between us. She stared out the V-shaped windshield, eyes dull and blank. I kept my eyes forward, which felt like respect.

"I didn't tell the cops, I didn't tell the FBI. I won't tell anyone but you." She fixed me with her eyes to make sure I understood. "If I act like a victim, the public will feel sorry for me. And when they feel sorry for me, I'm not a movie star anymore."

I thought and then nodded.

"I was asleep, and heavy steps woke me up. He jumped me before I could get out a squeal. Right off, he stuffed a gag down my throat. Then . . .

Her eyes sketched the outline of bluffs and buttes.

"When he finished, I didn't act beaten down. That was

what he wanted. I was mad. I grabbed for his balls, but he was too quick for me. I kicked and hit, which only egged him on." She peeked into the shadows of her memory.

"That's when he hit me with his fist. And hit me and hit me. The son of a bitch meant to pound me into submission."
Pause.

"I didn't give him an inch. I fought all the way."
Pause.

"The more I fought, the harder he hit."
Pause.

"Until I passed out. The bastard beat me unconscious."
She swam around in her darkness for a moment.

"I remember screaming, I didn't know where you were, and then Janey gave me some kind of shot. I didn't come to until I was bumping along the road—Jack made them take me to that shithole of a hospital back there. I didn't need it. But his mind wasn't on what I needed. It was on protecting the studio's investment. And keeping me from suing their ass off."

I didn't blame her, but I thought that was a little harsh. I was sure Mr. John was plenty worried about her. We turned off the pavement and onto the dirt that stretched 160 more miles to Monument Valley. On any other morning I would have enjoyed the comfort of driving the luxury car, but I didn't notice much except our words hanging in the air like bruised fruit on a tree.

"If my face was messed up permanently, if my looks were gone, I damn well would sue them, and for millions. But I'm not suing anybody. Who would hire me then?"

Suddenly she grabbed me by both shoulders and put her

face where it half blocked my view of the road. I stopped the car.

"I want you to find that guy and stomp his ass into the ground. I don't want him to fuck anybody again, ever, not even a sheep. I want you to make him look like a rattlesnake your truck flattened in a rut."

I didn't say anything for a while. My throat was jammed up. I lifted her hand off my shoulders and brought it toward my lips.

She pulled it away. "Sorry," she said softly, "I told you, I'm not ready. Not ready for you to start touching me. And I don't want to hear you say *you're* sorry about anything, not again, Yazzie. This was not your fault."

After a moment I used the only way I could bring myself to speak to her, cop mode. Direct. "Describe him."

"I never saw his face. He wore a black cloth mask with holes cut in it. Tall and skinny the way Navajos are. Not as tall as you, not by about half of a foot, and not hunky, but real wiry. *Real* strong. I thought he was going to rip my arm right out of its socket."

"Anything distinctive? 'Tall, skinny, and strong' describes a lot of men."

She thought. "That's all I remember."

"Describe the backs of his hands."

"Oh. Wrinkled. Brown. The skin of an old guy, fiftyish."

"Did he say anything?"

"Right when he jumped me." She shrugged. "But I didn't understand what he said."

"Do you remember what it sounded like?"

"What *what* sounded like?"

"What he said."

"Oh. 'Gesso,' like the stuff you put on a canvas before you paint. And it was a kind of war cry, like some Japanese soldier yelling *'Banzai!'* "

" 'Jaysho?' "

"Yeah, I guess. Maybe."

"If that's what you heard, it means 'buzzard' in Navajo. Why that, I wonder?"

She shrugged. "How would I know?"

That one word led me down a new road. Maybe opened up more possibilities for suspects than we'd been thinking about. Maybe.

We rode in silence. I was careful to avoid ruts and potholes and sandy spots. Sometimes I looked at her face, with the Painted Desert sliding by in the background. It wasn't half as colorful as her cheeks, which twisted my guts.

She wouldn't have to urge me to pummel this guy. She wouldn't have to pay me, either. *My* mission now, not a studio's.

After a while she said, "I feel safe with you, and I can sleep." A beat went by. "I'm going to lay my head on your thigh, okay? But don't touch me."

❖❖❖❖

I wanted to take Linda to my house. I thought Mom would fuss over her and Iris would sit with her and talk. She needed some women around her, that was my opinion. Linda refused. We were headed to the set, and she wouldn't hear anything else about it. God, she was stubborn.

When we got to the location, the entire cast and crew were in the big tent, eating supper.

She said hard and fast, "Drive right on up to the cabins."

I swung left uphill, wondering what she had in mind. I parked in front of the place where we'd spent so much time together, the place that now held so much ugliness. We got out and she looked at the door. I checked it first. Locked. She gave me her key and I opened it.

"I can't go in alone," she said. "I can't do it." She thought. "From now on you'll be with me every minute, night and day."

I nodded. *My* mission. I didn't think it was going to sit so well with Mr. John.

"Let's get back in the Cadillac and lock the car doors."

We did. I was still in the dark about what she was up to, and for a moment I hoped that getting her out of that hospital was the right thing to do. Her head might not have been straight yet. On the other hand, I couldn't imagine how anyone could keep her in that place, keep her anywhere that she didn't want to be.

I waited for whatever came next.

"I want you to go to the door of the tent and get Julia. See her?"

I looked a question at Linda.

"Julia Wasserman, the wardrobe woman. Tell her to come here to the car and bring a fright wig and a Gypsy skirt for me. Keep the car locked tight, then get right back here."

I did it fast, no questions.

When we sat in front of the cabin again, locked inside the car, she said, "I can't go back in there. Not yet. Give me a few minutes."

"Take all the time you need," I said. "I still think that you being here is a bad idea for more reasons than I can name."

Julia walked up and leaned her face against the car window. "Linda, are you . . . ?" Julia's face painted a picture of shock. "Oh."

The word ached with sympathetic pain.

"I'm fine. Put the wig on me."

Linda got out, tilted her head for the wig, dropped her jeans, and pulled on the Gypsy skirt. She shrugged into a white blouse, tied it in front to show a little midriff, and it was perfect with the full, many-colored skirt.

Linda said to Julia, "Why didn't Jack come right on your heels?"

"He doesn't know. He's eating in his cabin."

"And the A.D.?" Meaning assistant director.

"He's batting his eyelashes at the continuity girl again. With his wife on the location, no less."

"Scurry on down ahead of us. Tell everyone I'm back. Holler it out." Julia took a step, but Linda grabbed her elbow.

"Get Danny and his accordion out in front. Tell him I want that tarantella, Chopin . . . can't remember the title. The one he played for me in that James Whale horror picture. He knows the piece."

Julia trotted downhill.

Linda said to me, purling, "Will you escort me, sailor?"

I offered her my arm, and down we strode.

Julia had done her job. The entire crew was scrambling out the tent doors.

Closer, closer. They didn't know quite what to think yet.

"When I start dancing," she said, "burst out laughing. Make it really loud. Uproarious."

"Okay."

"I mean it. All out."

Danny stood out front on our left. We walked to maybe a dozen steps from the crowd.

She dropped my arm, and I slid behind her.

She strutted back and forth, glaring at them, daring them to really look at her face—one very terrible close-up, literally a horror show. And the fright wig? Half of them started backing away, wanting to run like hell.

Finally she nodded at Danny. With a huge grin he plunged in.

It was a wild, devilish piece of music, a dark fantasy of melody leaping and plunging, rhythms going mad. It was probably meant to show off swirling skirts and on-the-edge femininity.

Linda turned the dance on its head. Her feet flew recklessly through the steps, but her fingernails clawed the air and her voice screeched with fury.

Though I was scared of sounding like a fool, I did as I was asked and busted out laughing. It worked. Her audience of colleagues and coworkers saw a lady's dance of virtuosic grace turned into a parody, a grotesque display starring a spider woman. She pranced straight at them, creepy fingers grasping, her face a Halloween monster.

They backpedaled, tripping over each other and laughing about it.

Diving into the spirit of the moment, Danny added more frenzy to the tempo, and Linda soared right with him, faster and faster, wilder and wilder. The crazier she danced, the crazier they laughed.

Danny spiked the final chord. The spider woman raised her arms slowly and artfully over her head, fingers touching.

Utter silence. She lowered her arms gracefully in two arcs, one in front and one in back, and bent into a deep curtsy.

The applause and cheering were probably the most genuine she'd ever gotten.

Ever the star, she fluttered to my arm, used it as support for another low bow, and led me on a statement strut up the hill.

"You think that did it?"

"The queen of all—you pulled it off."

She nearly stumbled, caught herself on my arm, and grinned up at me. She said, "Let's just hope I get up the hill before you have to carry me."

Thirteen

Mr. John glared down at us from the summit near the cabin. He didn't say a thing about her face, or the dance, but you could see him adding it up in his head.

"You are really something," he said, making it half praise and half mockery.

She said, "Yippee ki-yay, cowboy."

"My cabin," he said, and strode off.

She hesitated, shrugged, and followed the boss.

"I'll wait in your cabin," I said.

I started looking around inside. Like the rest of us out on the rez, Harry Goulding improvised everything. Without materials, the basics of living required creativity. We found uses for empty cans and cardboard boxes you wouldn't believe.

So Harry made these cabins catch-as-catch-can. There was no timber for twenty miles, all the way to San Juan River, so Harry made the cabins from stone, which was free and available underfoot. He traded some Navajos cans of Mr. Coffee, what the Navajos call Hosteen Cofay, and Bluebird flour to mason the walls. They put the buildings up fast and went to a little trouble only for the roofs, like Indians and whites did all over this country. They hauled some thick poles from the river, ran them parallel up to a dense ridgepole, and sealed the whole thing with mud, pretty much like pueblo construction—viga and latilla. The roofs were angled enough to shed snow in the winter and sturdy enough to bear its weight. From inside you could see the light poles and roof beam, making an upside-down V for a ceiling.

But that's not all I saw, and it gave me an idea. I studied the ceiling light over my head. When the movie people arrived in '38, their carpenters spent a few studio dollars to make the cabins look less rough and to insulate them against the cool evenings. They studded up walls on the inside with rough lumber and stuffed newspaper down behind it. Then they replaced the oil lantern that hung in the middle of the room with a ceiling light. For power, they ran an electrical wire behind the lumber. Last, they installed a flat ceiling of four-by-eight-foot slabs of one-inch plywood, and supported that with two-by-fours.

Flat ceiling. A crawl space then, for sure, low at the sides but about four feet high at the ridge pole. Room enough.

I knocked on the door at Mr. John's cabin and told Linda and him I'd be right back. Then I trotted to Goulding's Trading Post and greeted Harry's wife, Mike. Perky, smart, altogether one of my favorite people, and she and I hadn't had a good talk in six years. If I hadn't been a Navajo—outside the family we don't do touching—she would have given me a hug, and I half wished she would.

I asked to borrow a flashlight. She was out of batteries—that's rez life—but she lent me a Coleman lantern.

I walked to Mr. John's cabin, and those two were wrapping up a pretty good argument. Neither one of them paid me any attention when I knocked and went inside.

"And now you've gotten Yazzie into trouble with your hijinks. I'll get him out of it, but I'm not sure how."

"I—"

"Goldman, stay out of this."

"Don't talk to him that way."

I didn't care how either of them talked to me. I pretty much wished I could fade into the walls.

"We check on the ex-boyfriend in L.A. His time is accounted for, which means nothing because he wouldn't come himself anyway. For good measure we called Mr. H, had him do a little surveillance, all of that. Your knight in shining armor telephoned Cantonucci and made a few threats. He suggested coming here, and I said that was not acceptable, in no uncertain terms."

"Why is that?" she said.

"Because, I'm not having his ego all over my shoot. We're just about done."

I wondered who the devil this Mr. H. was.

Ford brushed her words away like a fly. "I'm not going into details, but he is irrelevant."

Then he turned to Linda. "I've talked to Mike Goulding and asked her if you could stay with her for a few days while we wrap and I clean up things with the various law-enforcement agencies. She is happy to have you. And, she is a damned good shot."

"I'm going back to the cabin."

"You have got to be kidding me."

"What happened is done. It's over."

"Until we catch the guy, it's not over. And how can you think of going back to that place? Linda, I swear to God, you need a shrink."

That did it.

"You—you are not allowed to speak to me like that. No one is. I am not running my life on fear. Understood?"

"No. I do not understand one damned thing."

"Fine. Yazzie, will you please walk me back to my cabin?"

"Linda, I think Mr. John's right," I said. "Staying with Mike Goulding is a good idea."

"I'll go to the cabin by myself then."

Mr. John *whapped* his hand against his forehead. "Linda, just go then. Yazzie, do what she wants."

Seemed to me that was pretty much what I had been doing for a little while.

We walked up the hill and the moon spilled on her shoulders. She looked beyond exhaustion, and she had plenty of reason to. I didn't blame Mr. John for being angry. She was infuriating. She also had more guts than most people I'd ever met. Maybe it was pride. Maybe a combination of all that.

I turned the key and checked inside. All clear. She staggered forward and flopped onto the bed, her eyes open and unblinking. I locked the door behind us. Checked it twice. Just then, lying on the bed, she looked like a little kid who needed a doll to hug or a thumb to suck. She was all in. I told her to give me a minute. She nodded her head yes.

I stepped into the water closet. It was literally that, a closet the movie carpenters had built so the bigwigs could use the chamber pots in privacy.

And sure enough, above was exactly what had to be there with the way that place was built—a panel opening into the crawl space.

I came out of the closet and sat down on the bed. Linda took my hand. I told her where I was going.

"I'm scared," she whispered.

"I'll be right above you," I said. "I'll be able to see you." Part of me was afraid of what I would see and what could be seen. Everything.

Back in the closet I turned one of the two chamber pots upside down, stood on it, pushed the panel out of the way, and muscled myself up. Here, next to the wall, the crawl space was so small I had to slither in. Newspapers were spread flat everywhere, an inch or so thick.

I saw prints in the dust right off. I went over to one side on hands and knees to avoid scuffing them, but I still had to get to the exact spot where the four-by-eights of plywood met, square in the middle of the room, where the light fixture dangled.

The wire slithered out from beneath the newspaper there, and a small hole let it through to follow a slender chain one foot or so down to the clear fixture.

I held the Coleman lantern toward each corner of the crawl space from that spot. The newspaper showed a clear pattern. Most of the paper was covered with years of dust and sand, but a path angling from the panel to the hole for the light was almost dust free, and a wiped-off spot had a human shape, chest to knees.

Unfortunately, the hole for the wire and chain was not so small. Someone had scraped it wider open, maybe with a knife. I leaned over with a push-up that let me down, touching as little of the newspaper as possible, and put my eye to the hole. The fixture blocked sight of the floor straight down, but it gave a clear and unobstructed view of the beds and everything else. I was gazing down on Linda, her eyes fixed open.

Painful clarity: The bastard had to have been in the cabin when we got there, and he'd laid right here and watched us make love. When I left and she'd started napping, he crept to the water closet, lowered himself, dropped the few inches—that was the heavy step she heard—and jumped her. Afterward, he hoisted himself back up and watched, laughing silently while she was discovered, people scurried around, the cops came, and Linda got stretchered away. After nightfall he slipped off.

My gullet was hot coals.

I crawled back the way I came and let myself down.

"Let's not talk now," I said.

She nodded, bleary with oncoming sleep.

I sat with her until she dozed off. I breathed with her and felt awash in tenderness for her.

But I had to take care of business. I locked the door, sprinted to Mr. John's cabin, brought him back with Colin, and pointed out in a whisper what I'd discovered.

Colin sat with Linda, and Mr. John called me outside with one crooked finger and gave me a good clap on the shoulder. "You out-detected the feds," he said. "We don't know who, or why, but we know how. That's huge."

He looked around. Complete darkness. He said, "Linda must be exhausted. I came down on her too hard. I'm on edge and I took it out on her."

"She's already asleep, and you know Linda—probably a squabble with you perked her up a little."

I wasn't so sure that was true, but he needed some kind of ease.

"I'll send the agents up in the morning." He shook his head and threw his white handkerchief away. "Will you watch Linda tonight?"

"Absolutely."

"You're back on studio payroll, too. Show the agents what you found, and don't let them screw anything up."

He called Colin out and started to walk away with him, and then he turned back to me. "No hanky-panky tonight. Got that?"

I got it, and it was about the last thing on my mind, anyway.

Fourteen

Rap-rap.

The federal agents were right up and at it the next morning. Which was a shame, because Linda, still sound asleep, could have used more rest. I'd slept badly on the floor next to her, tossing and turning on the wood planks. When the feds pounded on the door, I was sitting with my back against it, dozing.

Rap-rap again. "Goldman!"

Sounded like an order—"Snap to!"

I cracked the door open. "Yes."

They introduced themselves with a swagger, like *I am power, you are shit.* Special Agent Tuckerman had thick hair that would have been gray had he not blackened it with liquid shoe polish. Special Agent Mize was a generation younger than his partner, as tall as me but wider, and had the face of a choirboy. First suits and ties I'd seen in this desert, and the first official titles I'd heard. Out of place.

"Mr. Ford said you figured something out. What?" They were playing roles, Shoe Polish in front as the spokesman, Choirboy backing him up with the cop stare.

I was figuring out how to play this, but apparently thought wasn't allowed.

"I asked you a question," Shoe Polish said.

I decided to tread softly. The way they stood reminded me of what I learned in the navy—that a lot of jerks like to throw their rank around. They were trouble. By doing their job better than they did, I had made them look bad. Made J. Edgar Hoover look bad. Time for some tail-saving.

"Sir, I think I know how the perpetrator got to her."

"You *what*?"

I held a finger to my lips. "Miss Darnell needs to rest. Can't this wait a few minutes?"

"Nobody gets to sleep through an FBI investigation."

"Excuse her," I said in a soft voice, stepped outside, and closed the door behind me. Then I explained to them what I had suspected, why, what I did, and what I found. I concluded, "So I know how it was done. Don't know who or why."

"You don't know squat," said Shoe Polish.

I waited for the good cop part of the routine. Instead I got from Choirboy Mize, in a sharp tone, "Goldman, what makes you think you're entitled to stick your nose into our investigation?"

"Sir, I do not believe I am intruding. First, an accused man has the right to try to prove his innocence." Not that I expected an appeal to common sense to work. "Second, sir, Miss Darnell is paying me to protect her. I let something terrible happen. I'm doing my job double-time now."

A look at their faces told me I was pissing into the wind, but I soldiered on.

"Third and last, sir, I was a cop in the navy. Shore patrol, stationed in San Diego, and trained in NCIS investigative techniques."

And I figured out the "how" when you couldn't, you asses.

They emitted trained-seal barks intended to sound like mocking laughter.

"Fart one, fart two, and fart three," said Shoe Polish Hair. He had a rear-end fixation.

"Let me give you one, two, and three, Goldman," said Choirboy. "One, Keep your nose out of our investigation. Two, Keep your nose out of our investigation. Three, Keep your nose out of our investigation."

What a clever guy. I waited quietly. Finally, they came around to the present reality.

"Show us what you think you got," ordered Shoe Polish.

Finger to my lips, I ushered them inside to the water closet. Their clumping woke Linda up. She switched on the light and stared at us.

I helped them get their creased trousers and shiny shoes through the hole without getting nicked or scuffed. They duckwalked, one to each side, saving their dry-cleaning bills. I stuck my head through the panel opening to point out the prints. They had government-issue flashlights that could have been chandeliers. You could read the prints in the dust like a newspaper headline.

"These are what you consider to be the old prints?" Shoe Polish said.

"Yes, sir."

"And these hand and knee prints are where you crawled?" Choirboy said.

"Yes, sir."

"Enough," said Shoe Polish. "Let's get back down."

They did, and brushed hints of dust off their sleeves and cuffs.

"So, Goldman, what do we have here?" said Shoe Polish. I shrugged. "You just saw for yourself."

"What do you think?" Shoe Polish asked Choirboy.

"I think Goldman is conning us. He made *all* of those prints," Choirboy said.

Linda bumped in with, "I told you, he didn't do this," and pointed to her bruised face.

"Begging your pardon, Miss Darnell," said Shoe Polish, "please let us do our jobs."

She jumped in again. "He didn't need to sneak into my bed. I gave him full access."

Choirboy's lips curled with disapproval, but a junior agent couldn't talk back, especially not to a movie star.

"It-was-not-Yazzie," Linda repeated, each word like a hammer whacking a nail.

Shoe Polish said to Choirboy, "Go get the camera. We need pictures of the prints."

I was dealing with a government agency, and everybody knows what SNAFU stands for.

Shoe Polish said in a supplicating tone, "Sorry to intrude, Miss Darnell. We'll have to ask you some questions later."

He took my elbow and steered me outside. He stood on a step so he was tall enough to get right in my face. "Right now is the last time you get to open your mouth or do one damned thing about this investigation. Understood?"

"Yes, sir." *And screw you, sir.*

"You got any thoughts about who did it?"

I considered. Didn't matter whether I tried to be helpful or avoided inflaming these jerks. Best just to tell the simple truth.

"I don't know a thing but what she told me, which is what she told your man in Flagstaff. You'll want to get it from her."

"After I hear it from you."

"Well, sir, she says a wiry, strong middle-aged man, at least half a foot shorter than me, brown-skinned."

I stopped. Like any interrogator worth his salt, he waited.

I went on, "But that age is based only on seeing the backs of his hands and hearing his voice. I believe it was a Navajo."

"Why is that?"

"Because of a word he said to her."

"What did he say?"

"A possible Navajo word. She didn't know it." I wasn't going to lie, but I didn't have to volunteer anything.

"Mr. Ford thinks it's a boyfriend who went off the deep end."

"Could be."

He waited. Mize slid by me with the camera and, judging from the clumping noises, boosted himself up into the crawl space.

I waited, thought, and decided they needed a little more. "Why would a Navajo do this? Nobody local makes sense. This shoot is a bonanza for the whole region, which is very, very poor. Mr. Ford pays the Navajo extras and laborers eighteen dollars a day. He says he's coming back next year, and that other shoots will come here. For a Navajo to cause trouble . . ."

I shut up. It was all true, except that the word *Jēsho* or *Joshay* just didn't fit. Words heard while you're being beaten? Hard to count as hard evidence. Still, it was a distinctive word, and the one word like it in English that sounded anything like it, "gesso," made no sense.

Since I was standing there, not speaking, the agent assumed I didn't have a thought in my head. I recognized the way he looked at me. Only his training kept him from snickering, or saying, "Red nigger." I'd heard it before.

As Choirboy came back with the photo gear, Shoe Polish said, "Set it down. I need your help for a moment."

He looked at me like a scientist curious about an insect. I heard Choirboy setting the gear next to the chamber pot. "Okay, Goldman, that's all for now. You're through here."

The tone, the attitude? My stomach went right to the bottom of my feet. Before I could turn, Choirboy levered my hands up high behind my back. The sneaky son of a bitch clamped on cuffs.

"And I," Choirboy said sweetly sick, "am personally going to escort you to jail."

Tuckerman said what I least wanted to hear. "Yazzie Goldman, you are under arrest for obstruction of justice."

Damn it. No Navajo has a clansman in the FBI. I doubted that my grandfather had any relatives there, either.

❧❧❧❧❧

We walked over to the Fibbie rental car. I knew exactly where I was headed. Albuquerque, brick jail, door with bars slamming shut with a metallic clang.

Worse, much worse, Linda was being left with less protection right when she was in deep shit.

Mary Ford stepped out of her cabin and started downhill toward the shoot. "Mrs. Ford," I called, "I need help. Would you please get Mr. John?"

"Shut up." Mize jacked my cuffed wrists up higher behind my back.

I'll remember that, Choirboy.

Mary walked toward us, fast. "Is Seaman Goldman being arrested, Agent . . . ?"

"Special Agent Tuckerman. He's being charged with obstruction of justice."

Mary Ford nodded to herself. She knew cop-speak. "We'll see what we can do about that, Yazzie." Down the hill she went. No telling what would happen. Mr. John was damnably stubborn about having his filming interrupted.

I said calmly to Tuckerman, "Mr. Ford needs to know you're leaving Miss Darnell without a bodyguard."

He tilted his head sideways. "So what's that?"

Colin squatted underneath the cedar.

"It's what did her no good before. Mr. Ford needs—"

Shoe Polish said, "He needs to know what we want to tell him. Period. Get in the car."

Maybe they'll buy themselves some trouble. Hard on the heels of that thought came, *If their actions get Linda hurt, I will wipe the floor with them. Just for starters.*

As Shoe Polish was about to stuff me into the backseat of the rental car, Julius Roth came striding toward us, moving faster than I thought he could manage. I was damn glad to see him.

He introduced himself, and Tuckerman gave his name, emphasizing the words "Special Agent."

"Commander Ford would like a moment with you before you go anywhere," said Julius.

"Commander?" said Shoe Polish.

"Commander, U.S. Navy, retired. Wounded and commended for bravery at Normandy. He wants a word."

Nice surprise, Julius, I thought.

Choirboy started stowing his photo equipment in the trunk.

"I repeat," Julius said, "Commander Ford is on his way."

There was too much power on parade here, a major outbreak of I-am-a-big-deal stuff. White people. I hoped not to spend the rest of the day in the back of the car, hands pinioned, while they worked it out.

Mr. John stalked up the hill like he was stomping scorpions. Behind him was . . . ? Then I remembered—Roy Pease, the unit publicist. Every shoot had a man on the spot who made radio calls and wrote copy and mailed out photos to generate as many stories as he could for the press and the radio. Never too soon to start marketing. I had no idea why Mr. John brought him along now.

"Seaman Goldman"—more of that BS—"is anyone inside watching after Miss Darnell?"

"No, sir."

Mr. John jerked his head toward the cabin, and Julius hustled.

I watched Ford suppress an angry look and replace it with formal courtesy. "What's going on here?" Mr. John said to Tuckerman.

"Goldman is being charged with obstruction of justice," said Shoe Polish.

Mr. John glared at him. "Seaman Goldman? Because he did some investigating and made some discoveries on his own?"

"That's not how I'd put it, sir."

"Commander Ford, I showed them what I found. They—"

Mr. John held up a finger, and I stopped talking. This was his location, and he was boss. He considered for a moment, turned his head, and spoke inaudibly to Pease. Sometimes the patch on his left eye helped him shut out people like Shoe Polish and Choirboy.

Pease scurried along the dirt road toward the trading post.

"Special Agent Tuckerman, Special Agent Mize, please tell me everything about the situation here."

They recited all of it, what I said I'd found, what they'd seen, what Linda said. Using their notes, they showed off what meticulous care they had taken in observing and listening. Shoe Polish nailed it down with, "The Bureau regards his activity as obstruction of justice."

Mr. John had chewed this morning's white handkerchief to death. He spat it on the ground. Then, unpredictably, he broke into a great big smile. Charm was one of his modes. "Gentlemen, I have nothing but admiration for the FBI, and I certainly respect regulations and the chain of command. You may know that I have some experience with such matters.

"Right now my orders are to get one job done—direct a

motion picture. And Seaman Goldman's arrest would present me with obstacles."

Shoe Polish started to speak, but Mr. John held up a finger.

"May I make a suggestion, Special Agent Tuckerman? Please come to Mr. and Mrs. Goulding's office with me, bring your prisoner, and let's make a couple of calls."

Tuckerman considered. "All right, sir, with one understanding. A federal investigation of a violent felony takes precedence over making a movie."

Mr. John inclined his head courteously. "A felony comes first with me as well, gentlemen, and my studio. Especially an assault on one of our stars."

Up at the trading post Mr. John solicited the help of Mike Goulding. She led us all to the office, and we stood around for a moment while Pease finished a conversation on the two-way radio. Then we all walked in and Mr. John sat down at the radio. Pease sat at Mike's typewriter and started pecking.

"What's the name of the SAC at Albuquerque?" Meaning the special agent in charge, head of the Albuquerque office, and these agents' boss. Mr. John understood chain of command, all right. Also the power of going over someone's head.

"Thompson," said Tuckerman.

Some radio-speak followed—"Come in, affirmative, negative," that sort of thing. Then Mr. John introduced himself to SAC Thompson, complete with his own titles and commendations. He also mentioned that he'd won six Oscars. It was weird to hear Mr. John brag, but I supposed he'd learned in the navy how to push the power buttons.

Pease handed Mr. John a sheet half full of typewriting. "I'm informed," Mr. John told Thompson, "that the attack on Linda Darnell was the lead story in the two biggest motion-picture dailies yesterday, *Variety* and *The Hollywood Reporter*. It's also prominent news in the *Los Angeles Times*, *The New York Times*, and other newspapers across the country."

"That's right," said Thompson, his voice too loud on the radio. He sounded glad about the ink the crime was getting. "And *Photoplay* will be all over it, et cetera."

"Thank you. Now give me a moment, please."

"Roy," he said to Pease, "were the stories accurate?"

"They ran with what I telegraphed them," said Pease. "What other choice did they have?"

Mr. John allowed no one from the press on his location. He said softly to Pease, "Now write your headlines and the lead."

He spoke into the radio again. "SAC Thompson, there has been an important discovery in this case. I'm going to ask Special Agent Tuckerman to explain it to you."

Tuckerman slapped the sides of his own head with both hands. But he was trapped. Mr. John and I would hear every bit of whatever he said. So he told the truth pretty straight, except for adding that he suspected that I might have made the prints myself, instead of discovering them. As soon as he could, he stepped away from the radio.

Thompson had the nerve to say to him, "Good work."

Mr. John plunged right back in. "Now, SAC Thompson, the newspapers and industry journals ran what we told them yesterday. They have no source but us, so they'll do the same again tomorrow and next week and so on. Let me discuss the implications of that with you. The implications *for* you."

Tuckerman and Mize leaned close to Mr. John, like they were scared of missing something. Maybe they were scared.

"You may not know, SAC Thompson, that my last year of military service was with the OSS." The Office of Strategic Services, the U.S. government intelligence agency. "We at the OSS did our best to keep our operations secret and out of the public eye."

Pease *rat-a-tatted* away.

"Come to the point, Mr. Ford."

Mr. John ignored this impertinence. "Your agency, as you know, SAC Thompson, operates the opposite way. Your director loves publicity."

I gulped. J. Edgar Hoover damn well did. But to mention it?

"He will eat up a story about a woman movie star courageously going deep into Indian country to create a work of art and in the course of her duties being brutally assaulted, perhaps even sexually assaulted. Especially with implications that an Indian may be the perpetrator. And your director will be watching you most carefully. You may have heard from him already."

Thompson said nothing.

"So you want to tread carefully here," said Mr. John, "and in particular you do not want the Bureau embarrassed by what the newspapers and movie magazines say. They are available on every street corner, in every drugstore, dime store, and grocery store. They are the most widely read publications in this great country. They *are* public opinion."

Silence. I wondered if Tuckerman and Mize could still draw breath.

"Now I call your attention to this fact: We are in a very remote location here, a full day's drive from the nearest town, in an area where local people don't speak English. The magazines are hungry, in fact desperate, for news about Miss Darnell. We get dozens of requests every day to interview her. I will allow no one in the press or the radio to speak to her. Absolutely no one. If any of their representatives show up here, I will have his ass kicked unceremoniously two hundred miles to the railroad station."

Pease jerked a sheet out of his typewriter and handed it to Mr. John.

Mr. John glanced at the writing and nodded to himself. "Bottom line. The press is entirely dependent on the version of the news that we choose to telegraph to them each day. Now, SAC Thompson, I assure you, the press is important to us as well. We want all the inches of coverage, and all the photos, we can get. But we let the public know only what we want to tell them."

The Fibbies sure as hell could see the head of the hammer falling, and they knew whose skulls it was going to hit.

"So let me read what our publicist has written for them today. I'm just seeing it for the first time, and I will go over it carefully with him to make sure it's what I have in mind."

Mr. John crinkled the sheet audibly.

"Headline: MAJOR BREAK IN DARNELL CASE
"Subhead: NAVAJO SHORE PATROLMAN SPOTS WHAT
    FBI AGENTS MISSED."

"Next subhead: FBI ARRESTS HERO WHO SHOWED THEM UP."

Mr. John paused, stuck a handkerchief in his mouth for confidence, and said, "So, SAC Thompson, would you like me to read you the rest of the story? Or perhaps I should have someone at the studio telegraph it to you and to the director himself."

"I think I get the point, Mr. Ford."

"Commander Ford," Mr. John corrected him. "Let's make this simple. I request that you tell your agents to release Seaman Goldman. That's what you give me. Here's what I give you: I instruct the seaman to work with your agents, tell them everything he knows and everything he thinks, and cooperate with them completely. He's Navajo and can provide knowledge they don't have, and can translate during their interviews with the Navajos."

"Let me speak to Special Agent Tuckerman," said Thompson. "In private."

Mr. John grinned at Tuckerman. Then he, Pease, and I left the office and walked across to Linda's cabin. I leaned against the Fibbies' car. None of us had any doubt about what was getting said on that radio.

I was super-animated. Mr. John had not only gotten me out of a trip to jail, but inside the investigation. It was a beautiful thing. Pure justice.

Shoe Polish and Choirboy came down to us, their body language all draggy, and Mize uncuffed me. I rubbed my wrists.

Tuckerman looked at Julius and Colin, propped against

the front of Linda's cabin. "We'll wait until after lunch to talk further with Miss Darnell."

Mr. John, Pease, and I strolled off into a midday that sported the most glorious sunlight I'd ever seen.

"Mr. John," I said, "that was a masterful performance."

He grinned up at me. "Call me Jack."

Fifteen

Linda plumped up her pillow, pulled the covers above her shoulders, and turned her back to me. After the two days we'd had—the long drive yesterday, her dazzler of a performance for the movie folks, my arrest, Jack to the rescue— she was worlds beyond exhausted and universes beyond tired. Me, too.

"I'm sorry, Yazzie, I'm not ready to be touched yet."

"Linda, that is not what's on my mind."

She laughed a little bit. "Liar."

"It's sort of a lie, but Linda? I can like you for more than what we do in bed. Anyone could."

"Oh. That's . . . that's sweet."

We came from different worlds, all right, and I thought that she could use some of my world. Feeling good, nurtured, standing on your own two feet, feeling love from the earth and her cycles. I wished I could tie that up in a box with a ribbon and give it to her. That night I slept in Cathy Downs's bed, doing what I was supposed to do. Protect Linda. Who might have been safer where Cathy was, in the tent.

❖❖❖❖

Do I need to tell you that Tuckerman and Mize didn't let me anywhere near the investigation? That they hired Harry Goulding to do their translating? Or that they came and went in the cabin as they damn well pleased?

One time they came in so fast, and without a knock or word, that they embarrassed Linda in the water closet using the chamber pot.

I got right in Tuckerman's face. "You guys not only have the manners of goats," I said, "you're stupid. My job is—"

"We know how to investigate a felony," said Tuckerman.

"Does that count with you?" barked Mize. He was holding a crate they'd brought to make getting in and out of the crawl space easier.

"My job is guarding Miss Darnell," I said. "I'm armed, I'm trained, and anyone who comes in without knocking and asking permission is taking his chances." Pause. "Fair warning."

Mize shouldered me from the side.

I shoved him hard against the door facing. "I'd love to mix it up with you," I said, my voice a growl. Shore patrolmen are used to brawls, and I was spoiling for one.

"You're on the edge of assaulting a federal officer," said Tuckerman in a sharp tone.

I backed off. "You started down this road," I said, "and you're both out of line. Enjoy reading about yourselves in the newspapers. Does Roy Pease have your first names?"

"The investigation comes first," Tuckerman said. *"First."*

"I believe Commander Ford will want to know whether it comes ahead of common courtesy." I nodded toward the water closet.

Silence.

Linda came out of the closet. Mize emptied the pee outside—trying to be polite or to embarrass her more?

Tuckerman glared at me. Then he stepped onto the crate and disappeared into the darkness above.

Fortunately, Linda slept most of that day. I got a gofer to drive up to Oljato and bring back an F. Scott Fitzgerald novel for me. If I couldn't be rich, I could at least read about it.

From above I heard the word "prints" more than once. I gave thought to where fingerprints might be. On the rubber sheath of the electric cord going to the lightbulb? On the bulb itself? And I saw black fingerprint dust on the transparent fixture that kept the bulb from glaring at us naked.

As they left, I said, "Get any prints you can use?"

Mute shoulder blades, a door slowly closing.

I liked the idea of prints. Solid procedure. But if her attacker hadn't been in the army or in prison, or if he was a very careful criminal, his prints probably wouldn't be on file.

Whatever prints they got would be photographed meticulously, then sent to Flagstaff by car and to Albuquerque by train, be photographed again in a lab, and those photos sent to the Arizona and Utah state police and to Washington, D.C., while the originals were filed. It would take a couple of weeks to get word on the person. By then Linda would be back in Hollywood, the shoot would be over, everybody gone, and the whole thing out of my life, nothing to do with me. Which felt . . . odd. Cold.

I pulled a chair up by the bed and studied her face. The doctor in Flagstaff had told her that it would be fine, and it seemed to be true enough. She had a paint palette of bruises and some scratches, but no cuts that would leave scars. She had a mild concussion, according to the doc, and I could see signs of that. Back and forth from clearheaded, sometimes fuzzy, sometimes dizzy for a moment. Then back to piss and vinegar.

She had nothing more to do here than those still shots for publicity. With Raphael's magic, and the right lighting, the bruises wouldn't show. Every now and then, she slipped into a haunted look, like putting on a gray silk gown. If the camera caught that in its lens, the photos would be more art than publicity.

A few more days and my life would slow down again. Having been arrested and cuffed and then going through that drill all over again wasn't a particular highlight. But it was the flip side of being in the heat of this amazing woman. She was living large. Terrible and extraordinary things happen in a large life. I understood that. I still wanted a big life, but a life that depends upon the admiration of others? No. That's dangerous to the body and the spirit. All I had to do was look at the F. Scott Fitzgerald books we had on our shelves at home to understand that.

Sixteen

Linda was excited, fidgety, almost dithery. She'd prettied up in one of her Mexican dance dresses this morning, for no reason I could figure. Yesterday she'd finished her stills, and we were set to leave by town car for La Posada and the Super Chief tomorrow, driven by Julius. She had no work to do today.

She hung around the entrance to the food tent and made silly conversation with people she'd hardly spoken to during the entire shoot. She was absolutely delighted to see everyone, very impressed by whatever they were wearing, and thought that anything anyone said was either brilliant or hilarious.

While the cast and crew got into the food line and found seats, she stayed outside and paced, looking at the sky.

"Linda, you ready to go up?"

"Pardon?"

"To your cabin."

"Not now, Seaman."

"Seaman," no less. That didn't sit well.

I stood by, my job now. My mind was very much on private time together. Though we hadn't touched each other since the attack, we still spent her lunch breaks and every night together in her cabin. I think her mind was on nothing but safety. I knew our time together had a limit, and we had less than forty-eight hours left. I wanted it to end memorably, peacefully, happily. Margaritas in the garden at La Posada. A fine meal. We knew each other well—no awkwardness. Conversations and laughter. Good time together before saying good-bye.

She was antsy about something, and I was completely in the dark about what.

"Linda, what's going on?"

"Seaman, I'm fine."

"You don't seem fine."

She gave me a look over her shoulder, distant, but friendly and smiley. Maybe her concussion was still acting up.

"Get the keys to the town car from Julius," she said.

I ducked into the tent and obeyed orders.

"Let's drive down to the main road and back," she said. "I'll show you where."

Her giving me directions around Navajoland? That was odd, but we motored along the Oljato Road past the fake street of Tombstone to the wide dirt road, the one that led to Flagstaff. I turned the car around and stopped where she asked me to.

She leaned over and eyeballed the odometer. "Point

two," she said. "All right, now drive to that place where the road curves for the first time. You know where."

Of course I knew where. Oh, what the hell. I did it.

She studied the odometer again. "Point six," she said. "Four tenths of a mile. How many thousand feet is that?"

Points. Who cared? "About two thousand," I said.

She got out of the car and stared east again. "Straight as a string," she said.

"What's going on?"

"Oh . . ." She waved a hand in the air, dismissing me.

I was starting to get annoyed. I was not her Julius Roth. I stepped out and joined her next to the car.

Mike Goulding trotted down to us. I hadn't seen her coming. "He's in radio contact," she said, "and he's got us visually."

What on earth?

"There he is!" Linda exclaimed. Her heels bounced up and down.

I followed her eyes and saw the approaching mystery. It was a speck in the sky, maybe an airplane. Yes, definitely an airplane. It made a wide circle to the east, arced back west, and headed straight toward us.

"Go get Mr. Ford," she said to me. "Quick."

I ran, as she asked, back to the food tent, and was more puzzled by the moment.

Jack (but I still thought of him as Mr. John) hurried along with me, followed by the regulars at his table. Even he looked excited. He must have given permission for an outsider to visit the set. Now I was getting more interested and less ticked off.

All eyes focused east, and Linda took the director's hand as if he was her boyfriend. Jack looked a little uncomfortable, gave her hand a squeeze, and let it go. "I told him that this strip was long enough," he said, appraising the road.

The airplane was coming in for a landing, and damn if it wasn't going to use Oljato Road for a runway. I studied it out. "Well," I said, "if he goes off track, he won't do anything but give the greasewood a wing-shave."

"He never goes off track," Linda said.

Sure enough, whoever was piloting didn't. He set down on the main road within ten feet of the greasewood on the far side of the Flagstaff Road, bumped her steady along Oljato Road, reversed his engines to slow down, used his brakes, and came to a stop well before his runway curved.

The pilot's door opened and down climbed God.

Linda ran to him, jumped into his arms, and he swung her like a child.

I followed close, my stomach aching.

Dapper mustache, neatly trimmed hair, wiry figure. A handsome man—the world knew his face. This was Mr. H., Howard Hughes, holder of a dozen world airspeed records, including several circumnavigations of the earth, designer of airplanes, a man of fabulous daring and fabulous wealth. And the owner of her next studio, RKO.

He was also one of the most eligible bachelors in America. He liked to date movie stars, starting with Katharine Hepburn and on to Bette Davis, Ava Gardner, and now, apparently, Linda Darnell.

A hulking young man climbed down from the passenger side and took a position a couple of steps behind Hughes.

His suit hung open to make his sidearm visible. The rich man liked security. Needed security.

Linda turned to Jack and his cronies. "Howard, this is John Ford, our director. John, Howard Hughes." They shook hands.

"Six Oscars," said Hughes. "Very impressive."

Jack was trying to look nonchalant, but he couldn't quite pull it off.

"America's best director," Hughes went on, "in my opinion. Even more impressive."

Linda introduced Hughes to Fonda, Mature, and the others, getting to me last. "This is Seaman Yazzie Goldman, the man you've been paying to take care of me. He's become a good friend."

"Very glad to meet you," he said.

The lunch crowd was gathering. Linda paused, stepped away, lifted a hand high, like a circus barker, and announced, "Hello, friends. Howard Hughes!"

Everyone already knew who he was and why he was there. Probably only one of them was boiling like hot oil ready to cook fry bread. Me.

We went in to lunch, Hughes on one side of Linda and me on the other. He didn't introduce his security guy, but he addressed him as Rulon.

"Howard," said Linda, "before you start in—I know you, please don't interrupt—what happened to me was not Seaman Goldman's fault. His performance has been impeccable. He'll show you how it was done. Very clever, very dastardly. I owe him everything."

Hughes eyed me. I suspected he didn't tolerate mistakes and did not accept explanations.

I wasn't going to give him a damn thing.

Then I remembered that he already had everything, including Linda.

I wobbled behind them toward Jack's table. I felt like I'd been head-conked with my own baton.

❧❧❧❧

It was satisfying that Hughes acted like a smart, well-mannered, considerate, steel-rod-up-the-spine, first-class ass.

Jack had another table pushed up to his usual one so that Hughes, Rulon, and others could join his crowd. As we ate, it got even easier to dislike Hughes. He poked at his food daintily, said very little, listened well, and was impeccably polite. Every one of the movie folk around him was a little different than normal, putting on a show in some way. There was not one of them who might not want to work for him sooner or later, and actors were always afraid they'd never get another job. Even Jack had recently formed his own production company. He intended *My Darling Clementine* to be his last picture for the intrusive Darryl Zanuck at Fox. RKO could be among his future employers.

The only thing I liked about Hughes was that he kept his hands off Linda. She couldn't keep hers off him.

As Jack led us out of the food tent, Hughes asked me to show him what I'd discovered at the cabin.

I nodded.

Linda said, "Yazzie" in a low tone that I understood. I was to give no hints about our relationship. No problem.

The three of us walked up the hill, my mind popping with pictures of the two of them romping around the bed I knew so well, Hughes enjoying the body I knew so well. But he spoke to me courteously, followed me up the access hole without hesitation, and wasn't afraid to get his pants dusty as I showed him what had happened. He caught on quickly.

I took a last look down past the light to the bed. First my head had played and replayed pictures of a brutal rapist having his way with her. Soon it would be pictures of the fabulous Howard Hughes topping her. Living large wasn't always what it was cracked up to be.

When we got back down through the water closet, he said, "Good work, Seaman Goldman." Linda gave me a big smile and a nod. I embarrassed myself by feeling flattered.

"May I speak with you outside?" Hughes said to me.

Linda looked startled.

"You won't be alone, Linda. I want to clear up a few things with Goldman."

I didn't think she was worried about being alone. She was worried about Mr. H. and me being out of her earshot. Too far away for her to divert our conversation.

"First, let me give you your last week's wages." So this was my sign-off on Linda. He handed me an envelope full of bills, and said, "Hold on a minute." He counted off five crisp hundred-dollar bills on top of that. "A bonus," he said. "You earned it.

"I made a few calls on Linda's behalf. It turns out that Frank Cantonucci was the fellow who sent her the letter she received at La Posada."

"Is he . . . ?" Burning in my belly. "What can I do?"

"Frank sent a man up here, one of his employees, and his assignment was to follow Linda around. Scare her a little. No rough stuff. Your standard intimidation mode."

"A *no-broad-treats me-like-that* mode?"

"Exactly so."

"Mr. Hughes, what happened to Miss Darnell was a lot more than intimidation."

"Yes," Hughes said. "Cantonucci's goon obviously got out of hand. He even set his rifle sight on Linda twice, no bullets, pretended to fire. As it turned out, the person he ended up intimidating was an old Indian, probably someone simply curious or looking for work, who took off running when he heard the *snick* of the hammer."

"But the assault on Linda—"

"Frank's man went too far."

We both waited. The other shoe had to drop.

"The fact is, he went berserk. I don't know if it was the glamor, or her beauty, or jealousy, or what."

So Hughes probably did know about me and Linda.

"Where is he now?"

"He's been taken care of. To my complete satisfaction. No more problems for Linda."

"Mr. Hughes—"

"Frank's man was paid to be a menace, and the menace is out of our lives." He clapped me on the shoulder. "Simple as that."

My stomach didn't like it. *Only because I wasn't the one who took care of it,* I said to myself.

I walked with Hughes to the cabin door, and he opened it wide. She waved a girlish little wave. Very pert, very friendly.

Then she suddenly said, "Don't forget me, Yazzie Goldman." I felt like she'd also said *I won't forget you.*

I wouldn't forget—how could I? And I knew that she wouldn't, either. But we wouldn't see each other alone again.

I walked down the hill and left Linda Darnell with the man she liked better than me. God is a hard act to follow.

Seventeen

I spiffed up in my dress whites and walked into our living room. Mom was decked out to beat the band in a traditional Navajo velveteen dress and showy turquoise jewelry. Looking at herself in the mirror beside the front door, she said with a tune in her voice, "I never get to go anywhere. This is quite a treat!"

"You're just giddy to meet Howard Hughes," I said.

"Maybe a little," Mom allowed. "So is Iris, but . . ."

Iris was wrapped in a blanket and stretched out on the sofa, looking at a magazine. Grandpa had parked his wheelchair next to the couch and was fiddling with something in his good left hand. I saw that his other hand was helping a bit. Both hands working? I was witnessing a small miracle.

"Grandpa?"

He held it up proudly. His old, two-barreled derringer.

"What are you doing with that?"

"Oh," Mom said, "pay no attention. He carries it all the time, always has. You know he likes guns." She said that just like things were all back to normal. She really *was* in a good mood.

I remembered now, and saw that he was oiling it—clumsily, but getting the job done.

I looked over Iris's shoulder. She was flipping through photos of Howard Hughes wearing an airman's helmet standing in front of some monster aircraft. Half the women in America were infatuated with the guy, and 100 percent of the women in my own home were.

"Why aren't you dressed?" I said.

"I'm sick—not going farther than the outhouse."

It was the first time I'd heard her dejected, and one of the few times I'd seen her without Cockeyed.

"You'll get cheated out of dancing with Hughes," I said. "And Henry Fonda. And Colin."

"Actually, I wanted to dance with you."

I heard wheels on gravel, peeked out the window, and saw the town car.

"Come here," said Iris.

She pulled me to her by the hand, I held back, and then she pulled my head down to her face. "I promise not to throw up on you," she said.

She kissed me. Though it was light, it wasn't sisterly.

"Rise and shine," said Mom, and tugged at my elbow. She was primed and ready for the road.

I said, "I'm sorry you won't be there, Iris. You'll be okay while we're gone?"

"Yes. Go have a ball for both of us."

I bent down, hugged Grandpa, and turned his derringer over in my hand. "Take care of Iris," I told him, "and don't get too carried away with your old friend there."

"Bye!" Mom fluttered her fingers at both of them.

We strolled out the front door of the trading post and toward Julius. "We sure have a fancy chariot," I said.

"And a night on the town!" Mom exclaimed.

I chuckled and asked myself, *What town?* But I wasn't about to dampen her spirits.

The Gouldings were giving a dinner party, which they did every time Monument Valley hosted a movie shoot. And this time the guests of honor were even more special than usual.

Hughes was definitely the Gouldings' focus. He owned a movie studio, and if he felt like it, he could send half a dozen crews a year to the valley.

Julius put the car in gear. I looked back, saw Grandpa at the front door, rolled down the window, and waved to him.

"Time!" he called, probably expecting us to understand he meant *Have a good time.* His speech was getting better. Arm and leg better, too. With us getting him back, bit by bit, my world had started feeling firmer on its axis.

Julius rolled down the road.

"I hear Mike Goulding has champagne shipped in for every wrap party," said Mom.

"It's true," I said.

"If they play some good music, I'm going to dance with Mr. Hughes," she went on, "if I have to ask him myself. Time to let it all out!"

"Poor Henry Fonda, playing second fiddle."

Mom said, "Then you dance with him."

Julius pressed the accelerator harder, and we both laughed. Our laughter circled into the night, a sky full of stars, and started to heal something large. Something like time itself.

From the rocks behind the well, Zopilote watched the trading post, almost in shadow now. His wait was nearing an end. Only enemies were in the house—a weak woman and a crippled old man. Tonight Zopilote would let it roll, that darkness within. He was ready.

He turned over and raised his stolen binoculars to the front porch. He was proud of them. Buzzard's eyesight, super-powered. It was easy to steal from the movie people.

He saw the old Jew in his fool wheelchair. What was he doing?

Oh! Zopilote chuckled. Mose Goldman was thumbing a cartridge into a derringer. Good to know.

He watched the old man slip the gun into a pouch that hung from the arm of his wheelchair. Also good to know.

Shadows from the west lengthened and blanketed the barn. After a while they swallowed the trading post whole. Buzzard waited.

The young woman, the one they called Iris, went to the outhouse, which she'd done three or four times already. The runs—the fresh smell was rank. Maybe in there for a while, like before. Not that it mattered.

Zopilote picked up his little surprise and slipped down the hill.

It was time for Buzzard to sail earthward and attack.

※※※※

Iris came out of the outhouse feeling wan. She wobbled on the walk back. The living room was dark. Uncle Mose must have gone to bed. That was where she was going. Worn out, *all* the way.

She felt her way to her bedroom and opened the door with only a slight squeak. She put a knee on the mattress, reached high for the string that hung from the light, and put her hand on something . . . furry.

She made a suck-in whine and wondered where the noise came from. She reached higher, got hold of the string itself, and pulled the light cord.

Hanging on the end of the string was the corpse of Cockeyed.

Iris screamed.

※※※※

Zopilote thrilled to that sound.

He waited, standing in the closet by the front door of the living room. In one hand was the double-barrel, which had stood there for a quarter century. Zopilote made sure, several days ago, that the old Jew was still a person who held on to his habits, and that he still kept the shotgun loaded.

Iris came bawling out of her bedroom, down the hall, and right behind her came Goldman in his iron chariot. He yelled something at her, but no human being could have understood it. He turned on the living room light. At the door to the bullpen, the woman turned around, held up the body of her pervert cat, and boohooed louder.

The old man left-handed his rolling chair to her and

drew her onto his lap. She sobbed on his shoulder. Zopilote would have bet she was more scared than aggrieved.

Time for more fear. Plenty of it.

He stepped quietly out of the closet and leveled the shotgun at the two of them.

The old man tried to rise and croaked out a throttled sound, like "odd." Zopilote smiled. He understood that utterance, what it meant. The old man understood it. Iris didn't, but she would find out.

Zopilote raised the two barrels high and swung them downward at the old man's skull. A hard hit, but it glanced off.

Iris shrieked.

Sweet music to his ears.

Zopilote knelt in front of the old man, looked into his eyes, and saw that he was stunned but more or less conscious. Fine.

Zopilote reached into the wheelchair pouch, got the derringer, and slid it into his pocket. Two weapons now.

"Who the hell are you?" said Iris.

He pointed the barrels straight at the woman's head. He snapped in English, "Shut up. Facedown on the floor."

She gave him a sharp look but did as ordered, no fighting, no bargaining. He would have hated that.

Zopilote walked casually into the bullpen, went behind the main counter, pointed the shotgun at the radio from six inches away, and blew it to smithereens.

Then he walked back and tore down a curtain. He gagged and bound Iris, ignoring the hatred in her eyes. He set the shotgun on the floor and bound the Jew to his rigid chair.

"Let's go, old man. Time to chase your pot of gold."

He rolled the old son of a bitch into the night and to the family pickup, opened the hood, ripped off the distributor cap, and stomped it into pieces.

Then he wheeled his half-conscious enemy down the road and into the sandy crossing of the wash. Thirty feet around a slight curve, he saw the pickup he'd stolen from a neighbor. He drove the truck back to the old man, untied him, lifted him out the chair, and with a huge effort heaved the big bastard onto the tailgate. Then he slid the chair next to the old rummy, its wheels facing up, and drove into the wilderness to the west, buzzard-wing black.

Now dark energies rule the world.

True to his spirit, his smile was yellow teeth and a black, gaping maw.

Eighteen

The dirt road to the west was an old packhorse track called the Rainbow Bridge Trail. At a place chosen with care, Buzzard made a right turn onto slickrock. He wove between boulders, some the size of chairs, others as big as cars, over a crest and down a long slope. At the bottom was a huge rock shaped like a loaf of bread, with a cleft in the middle, as if the bread was sliced.

Zopilote steered the pickup into the cleft. He was safe here. No tracks on rock. A rise blocked the view from the road, so hidden from anyone who might come hunting. But the only hunter within miles was Zopilote.

His old enemy was fully conscious now. He slid the cripple chair to the tailgate and off. He dragged the man's useless body to the tailgate and rolled it off.

Wait! What if the old man hit his skull and died? The delights of torture, ruined.

Zopilote switched on a flashlight, jumped down, and shined his light into the old man's one visible eye.

The eye was electric with malice. The Jew's face was badly scraped, perhaps something broken, but he was very much alive.

Zopilote laughed. The geezer's expression said he could also hear.

Buzzard righted the chair and set the hand brake. He hefted Goldman into the chair. Why did the bastard have to be so big? Slowly and carefully, he used strips of torn curtain to bind the old man's arms and legs to the wood and iron of the chair. Then he got in the truck, drove it a hundred yards down the slickrock, stopped, and killed the engine.

Buzzard smoked a cigarette. He looked at the stars and admired the infinite blackness between them. He wondered how high a buzzard could fly into that blackness, how long it would take to join those inky forces. He hand-rolled another cigarette and smoked it. Surely the old man's bowels were watery with terror by now.

He walked back and squatted in front of his prisoner.

"You know me."

It was not a question.

The old man spat toward Zopilote's face, but his lips and tongue failed, and the spittle drooped to dry ground.

"Say my name!" Zopilote said, his voice lilting with mockery.

His captive spat again and this time hit Zopilote's knee.

Buzzard pulled out the derringer and showed it to the old man with a grin. Then he cocked one barrel, put the muzzle against the old man's temple, and barked, "Say my name!"

The sounds "odd" and "dick" garbled out of the ancient mouth. For sure Zopilote was recognized.

"Say how much you hate me."

More garbage words rat-a-tatted out. Zopilote thought he heard "hate" and "evil."

"No matter how violent your feelings are, I hate you more. I had twenty-five years to do nothing but water and fertilize my hatred for you and your daughter—my *wife*, who betrayed me."

He grinned again.

"In court you said I was a murderer. That I was not a man gravely offended. Not a man justly angered. Plain and simple, a murderer.

"I have just begun to kill. You, Father of the Betrayal Clan, will start dying first. And then?" He licked his lips.

"Except for that movie whore, I have not fucked a woman in more than twenty-five years. Before I shed my wife's blood, I will fuck your daughter every way possible. Then I will cut out her lying tongue and keep it for a souvenir."

He got out a hunting knife and made a honing motion with it on the palm of his hand. "As she watches in horror, I will cut her throat with this blade, enjoy seeing it pump out all her blood, and catch it in a bowl. In front of her, whether her eyes still see or not, I will cover myself with her evil spirit."

He cackled. It echoed against the bluffs, and the sound twisted between sand and stone for an eternity.

"But back to you. What about the captured one, the helpless one, the one useless even to himself? Do you want to know how you will die?"

No answer.

"You boil with curiosity. I will supply the details.

"And if you don't want details? Hmmm. How can you stop your ears? How can you keep your mind from seeing the pictures my words will draw?"

Zopilote stood. "Before we start, I think I will go for a little walk. While I am gone, enjoy your imaginings."

He was unable to stay away as long as he would have liked. He felt too greedy for the pain he was about to inflict. He leaned against the big boulder half a dozen feet away.

"You will die, of course. Much simpler than Nizhoni. Much slower. Very, very slow."

He studied the Jew's face. Unfortunately, the slackness of his skin, the ravages of his well-deserved stroke, killed all expression.

"I will do nothing. Nothing at all. You will be privileged to stay here, exactly as you are, day after day. In prison I learned about the chains of patience. I'm passing you that knowledge as a gift, old man."

Zopilote shrugged and smiled at Mose Goldman.

"Each moment, you will die a little more. Within an hour or two you will piss yourself. A few more hours, you will shit yourself. All tonight and tomorrow the same.

"Then, nothing. No piss, no shit. None left.

"The first day, hungry and thirsty. The second day, the same. The third, only thirsty. The fourth, parched. The fifth, desperate. Who knows how many days you will last? Ten, twenty . . . ?"

Zopilote walked close and turned the wheelchair. "I will leave you faced to the south, straight into the sun. Tied, you can't move. You can't shade your face from the nasty rays. You can only suffer.

"You will want to die. You will ask to die soon. You will beg.

"But there will be no relief, no hope."

He stood tall in front of the old man.

"Hope? Oh, wait. Yes. I have hope. And *only* I have hope."

He waited.

"I hope you live, on this very spot, for twenty-five more years."

He walked away, climbed in the truck, drove across the sandstone to the road, and slept. It was the best sleep he'd had since the night before he discovered his wife's treachery.

And his most delectable pleasure was yet to come. When the old man was dead, and drying in the desert air like a piece of jerked meat, Zopilote would return. He would sit beside the body, imagine the old man's suffering, and relish his handiwork. Then, like a true buzzard, he would imagine eating of the flesh of the dead. It was all part of the drumbeat of Darkness Rolling. It was important to stay right on that beat, his path, Zopilote thought.

Nineteen

Mom actually fell into the backseat of the car, laughed at herself, and laughed up toward the moon, at the joy a party brings. She crawled over to make room for me. Julius drove.

"Three times! One of them a waltz!" cried Mom. "And he dipped me."

"I saw the way he looked at you."

"Oh, silly. Think how many hours he's spent in front of the mirror perfecting that look. And it has so mesmerized the actresses in Hollywood that they don't notice he's slipping their clothes off at the same time." She hooted again. "And I danced with Victor Mature. He's so sexy, the sexiest man I ever saw. He looked at me and I felt . . .

"I never had so much fun!"

Pause.

"You know what I'm thinking?"

She wasn't going to slow down. I said, "I almost hate to ask."

"Right now he's got Linda Darnell's clothes off. And you're a bachelor again, aren't you?"

"Thanks for mentioning it," I said. I pictured Rulon standing guard outside the cabin while— I snipped off my thought. Cut, don't print.

"Really, you don't have to be a bachelor," Mom said. She leaned her head on my shoulder.

I wondered who she'd picked out to end my bachelorhood. At the same time, I didn't want to know.

"Iris's sweet on you," Mom said.

"Actually, she's got a case on Colin," I said.

Mom shrugged. "He won't be around much longer."

"And she's my *aunt!*" I added.

"No, no, you know . . ."

After a long moment's wait, I realized I wasn't going to have to hear the rest. Mom had passed out on my shoulder.

I leaned to make her more comfortable. I ran photo memories of Iris in my head. Then Iris with Colin. I was doing more of that when Julius said, "We're here."

I shook myself to wake up. For some reason I said to him, "Thank you, sir." Julius chuckled, the first time I'd heard that.

I slid my arms around Mom and eased her out and onto her feet. She blinked over and over.

Then I saw something odd. The door to the living room was standing wide open and the light was on.

"Julius, will you hold Mrs. Goldman steady here for a moment? I'd better take a look around."

"You got it."

I pulled out my .45.

Iris was lying on the floor, facing the open doorway

between the living room and the bullpen. She was bound head and foot, and gagged. When she saw me, she started kicking like a madwoman and trying to shout something through the cloth.

I cut her gag with my pen knife.

"A Navajo broke in. He kidnapped Grandpa." Tears gushed. "Kidnapped Grandpa!" Sobs heaved. Then, softer, "And he killed Cockeyed."

I squatted down to hold her, to listen, to hear what horrific events were unfolding in the center of our lives. To understand that our home was no longer a safe haven.

❖❖❖❖

Julius, Mom, and I sat, riveted and made stone-cold by Iris's story. We asked plenty of questions, she told us about the sounds Grandpa made. Something like "odd" and "dick."

Iris was exasperated with us. Distraught, hating to repeat details. But the picture she painted was clear enough. She raged at us to run into the night, not to worry about her, to find Grandpa. Julius told her details were important— there was no time for dead-end leads.

We learned very little, but it was something. A Navajo man, in his fifties, spoke English fairly well. He was vicious— what other kind of person could kill her cat and hang it? Would kidnap an old man?

I could only begin to imagine Iris's heartache. The bastard had said something about taking Grandpa to a "pot of gold," and that went right by me. I was thinking that we were targets. Sitting ducks.

The shot-gunned radio was junk. Julius headed back to Goulding's, his tires spitting gravel.

The other help I thought we could rely on was Jake Charlie. He was out with the sheep, carrying a deer rifle. I tried the pickup, and all I got was a whirring-nothing sound. Opened the hood. No distributor cap. Mom ran into the shed and hurried out with one. Every trader keeps spare parts. Sometimes that felt like a matter of life and death. This time it was.

I hurried the women into the truck. I was not letting them out of my sight, and I would give that beat-up old truck as much juice as she could take.

In half an hour we rumbled back with Jake Charlie in the truck bed, rifle at port arms.

Amazement. Julius, Colin, and Rulon were there with what seemed like a small miracle—a radio. Colin was setting it up in the kitchen. Iris sat down at the table, head in hands, paying no attention to him or anything else.

Julius said, "I got through to the tribal cops, but the only squad car they have on duty is all the way in Red Mesa, and there's no telling when they'll be back."

Mom made strong black coffee and she said, "I have one idea."

I raised an eyebrow at her. We were all sleepless and beyond tired.

"About the pot of gold. I thought of Rainbow Bridge, that's where rich tourists, or serious photographers, or geologists want to be packed in to."

I nodded. I'd gone along on those pack trips myself, helping Grandpa out.

Mom plunged ahead. "Remember, Dad used to say that Rainbow Bridge was going to be our pot of gold. That we can't make money off people who don't have any, meaning Navajos. But white people who wanted to go to Rainbow Bridge? That would be worth something."

I heard Rulon talking to someone on the radio. He roared into the room like a diesel engine. He said, "Mr. Hughes is volunteering to fly his plane and start searching for Mr. Goldman at first light."

"Thank God. What about Miss Darnell?" I said. "Is she protected?"

Julius took over. "Mr. Ford has moved everyone in the cabins into the tent dormitory. He has two guards on duty there, and I'm driving back to stay right beside Miss Darnell."

"And so am I," said Rulon. "Orders from Mr. Hughes."

Nothing made sense. A maniac who had brutalized Linda, who had killed Iris's cat and then kidnapped my grandfather. But that's what a true maniac inspires. Absolute chaos, fear, mania. A moaning world, gone to its side, huddled in a ball, waiting for something to turn it right again.

Julius said, "Hughes doesn't know the country. How's he going to find him?"

I said, "The only clue we have is that the kidnapper may have taken Grandpa to the west on the Rainbow Bridge Trail." *May* have . . . "Grandpa knows that country best, by far. I'm a distant second, but I'm second."

"It's up to you, then," Julius said.

Leaving my mother. Leaving Iris. To hunt for one outlaw and one heroic old man in five hundred square miles of canyons. Leaving Jake Charlie and Colin here with Mom and Iris. It didn't make me feel easy, but it was the best we could do.

"Okay. I'll fly with Hughes and scout the country." So much slickrock, and so much of it looked the same. "If it doesn't work first time around," I said, "we'll start making concentric circles." Over five thousand square miles of red-rock desert—one hell of a lot of circles.

"Straight on," Julius said. "*Make* your luck good." He stuck a pair of high-powered binoculars in my hand.

Julius worked best in a take-charge mode. I liked that.

Twenty

Mose Goldman took his time. When he got the job done—yes, *when*—he would sleep a little. And then he would go. *Go.*

He shoved at the belt buckle. Pushing with his left hand was no problem. Holding the other end with his right hand was driving him crazy. His fingers clasped a little, but they tired quickly, and when he forced the issue, they cramped. Still, he would get it done.

It was a simple mechanism, common in the century he was born in, uncommon now. The buckle, which was on the left side, had been custom-altered by a good leather man. Beneath the buckle, sewn into the heavy leather, was a three-inch blade. When you buckled the belt, you slid the blade into a sheath sewn onto the underside of the other end. If you needed a knife in a hurry, one hard push of the two ends of the belt together, a mechanical release, a fierce jerk of the belt out of its loops, and behold—armed and deadly.

He'd always worn belts of slick leather. Every time he bought a new belt, he took the blade to a Navajo leather-worker—he was now in his third generation of these men—and had the blade and sheath sewn on.

Pop! He felt it release. He let out gallons of breath, shook his right hand, and let it rest.

With his left hand he pulled the belt hard, and with his right he jiggled the leather enough to keep it moving through the loops. Soon he had the belt off. From there, cutting his bonds was easy.

He looked up the hill. He would have to inch the wheelchair up. Somehow. *Maybe I should start now. Maybe.*

No. Too risky, not being able to see. And if I don't sleep, I won't have the strength.

For the moment, everything else could wait.

As he drifted off to sleep, a lopsided smile smeared his face.

◼◼◼◼

He woke at the first glimmer of light, the new sun pinging dull off the iron and wood of the wheelchair.

Adikai? Do I have a surprise for you.

With his strong left arm he pivoted the chair toward the opening in the cleft. Then, slowly, half a foot at a time, he rolled upward.

◼◼◼◼

At first light I was driving the pickup toward Goulding's. Hughes wouldn't be able to land on our section of the road—too many curves.

I was relieved to see him doing something to the plane when I drove up. I parked and ran over.

Without preliminaries, he said, "Preflight check."

We didn't say a word while he did this and that. It took too damn long. And the checks hadn't saved him, according to the newspapers, from a near-fatal crash. Well, maybe that was why he was extra-careful now.

Finally, he said, "All right, let's turn the plane around."

Those frail-looking crafts, made of struts and sheet metal—they're heavy, but we got her turned with sweat and willpower.

We lifted off, made a wide 360, and lined up with the road headed west. I'd never been up in a small plane, but right now I didn't care about how it felt, only about what I could see. Which was a lot.

"This is what you want," he said. He had the air of a man with his mind on his business.

"To start with," I said. "If we're lucky, he didn't take Grandpa more than ten or twelve miles beyond the trading post."

"And if we're not lucky?"

I shrugged but didn't let myself say *needle in a haystack*. I wanted everything I could get out of this man. Finally, I said, "Depends on how much gas we've got."

"We're full," he said. "And Harry Goulding keeps aviation fuel on hand."

Yeah, he would, for film companies. I hadn't thought of that.

When we passed it, I said, "There's our trading post. He could be anywhere west of here."

"What do you say we fly loops?" Hughes said. "The kidnapper wouldn't hide your grandfather right on the road."

"Good idea."

We flew westward in the kind of wide curves that a meandering river makes. Took more time, but it was more thorough. I had a feeling that whatever Hughes did, he did very well.

But well enough? To match this country? That might be another story. And, somewhere in this country was Grandpa. Hope was slim, but my grandfather wouldn't give up hope. I wasn't about to, either.

⧓⧓⧓⧓

The rise slanted a little more upward, and Mose Goldman quickly discovered that his good left arm would not do the job. The top was too far. Such a long way. But he felt confident.

Maybe after a rest, he told himself, knowing better. *Maybe, but maybe not.*

Breaths in and out. Thoughts in and out. Fears in and out. Wondering where, exactly, the monster disguised as a man was now. Mose was not a religious man, but he prayed. He prayed for his daughter first, for Nizhoni, the center of his world. Also the center of that beast's crazed revenge.

Then a good idea. A risky one. He said to himself, *I am the toughest man in this whole damned desert. Anyone to say different?* Quiet from all lizards, potsherds, and buzzards.

He needed that pep talk.

Adikai will rape and kill Nizhoni.

He didn't let the details—exactly what Adikai had sworn to do—nibble at the edges of his mind.

He shoved himself forward to the edge of the seat of his chair. A deep breath. He pushed himself off onto the rock, knees first. Pain.

The chair started rolling backward.

He grabbed for the hand brake, felt his hand glance off it, then watched the chair career back down the slope. Mose shouted all the cuss words his upbringing allowed.

After about thirty feet it hit a low boulder and flipped. It landed on one side, upper wheels spinning against the bottle-blue sky.

Mose rested. Then, inch by painful inch, he crawled downhill to his chair. His left knee supported him, but he had to lie on his side all the way down—weight on his right shoulder and hip, then slide his left knee up, and then do a kind of push-up to get his knee under him and gain another foot of ground.

After at least one thousand years he got back to his chair. Lying on his back, he managed to right it. He set the brake and used the oak frame of the arms to hoist himself onto his left knee. Then, with his left arm alone, he pushed himself high and got his left foot underneath him. He pivoted and plopped back into the chair.

He laughed and hollered and raised his good arm to the sky and garbled, "I am the toughest man in this whole damn desert."

He's going to rape and kill Nizhoni.

Then he thought of Iris. Believing Mose dead, and after killing Nizhoni, Adikai would snuff out the last witness, Iris.

Mose forced himself upward, inch by inch.

Short of where he'd been before, he stopped the chair, set

the brake—*Remember this time, you fool!*—and scooted forward to the edge of the chair. He stood on his left leg.

Awkwardly, he scooted the chair around in front of him. Then, making a quick lurch forward on the right leg and getting the weight back onto the left one, he used the chair as a walker. And crept upward.

On every step forward, he sounded one word in his mind, an echoing, aching cry. *Nizhoni. Nizhoni.*

◈◈◈◈

Driving east to his grand, destined moment, Zopilote was surprised—the sound of an engine. He spotted a small airplane off to the north. Were they searching for the old Jew? A fat lot of good that would do them. When he thought about it, it was more likely that the Gouldings were flying tourists to Rainbow Bridge. Good money for the traders. Pack trips were probably old-fashioned now.

Onward to the inevitable confrontation, what I have dreamed about for years, face-to-face with my betrayer.

He didn't care who else might be there. He still had the shotgun, the derringer, and his knife. No one could stop him.

◈◈◈◈

Mose Goldman crested the rise. He could hardly believe it. It felt like a triumph beyond anything that he dreamed he could do.

Now an easy roll downhill to the road, with some tricky steering around boulders, then lots of ups and downs along the Rainbow Trail toward home. Maybe a truck would come along.

Nizhoni.

Home.

Nizhoni.

Home.

He pushed the chair a foot or two forward, and something . . . *Oh, hell.* He hadn't imagined he would take off so . . .

The speed banged his front left wheel off a knee-high rock and turned him around.

Now he swerved madly backward downhill, blinded. He crashed into something and catapulted head over heels. He crash-landed and skidded to a stop somewhere below, sprawled facedown.

He took inventory. Clothes shredded. Skin torn, lots of it. Some blood. But conscious and—he made the struggle—able to get to one knee.

Mose cut loose with his version of a hee-haw and started crawling back up.

Nizhoni.

Home.

He crawled back to the chair, and finally hefted himself into the seat. Maybe a combination. Braking, rolling slowly, braking . . .

He was happy. And damn glad to be alive. A flat-out miracle, that's what it was. Maybe it had been that prayer. He didn't know or care.

Nizhoni.

Home.

Nizhoni.

◈◈◈

Zopilote saw Jake Charlie at the front door of the trading post, lever-action rifle in one hand, keeping guard. They'd gotten the word out. Who else was here?

Jake Charlie would know this pickup, stolen from the neighbor to the east.

Zopilote let his stolen truck roll to a stop in front of the trading post, got out on the driver's side, away from Jake Charlie's sight, and knelt down beside the left front wheel.

Jake Charlie came around the front bumper, rifle dangling.

Head down, then rising, in one motion Zopilote sat up and rammed his knife deep under Jake Charlie's ribs. The sheepherder died without a sound.

Zopilote bundled the body into the truck, across the seat, and onto the floor on the passenger side. He was about to abandon this hearse.

Time to reconnoiter.

He drove back west a hundred yards, pulled the truck well off the road, got his binoculars, and kept a low profile as he walked up to his hiding place behind the well.

Twenty-one

"Movement," said Hughes. He pointed off to the right. "Look. Over on that slickrock."

He put the small plane into a gentle turn in that direction.

I saw something but couldn't make it out. I trained the binoculars that way and then needed a moment to bring the object into focus.

"My God!" I said. "Holy shit!"

"Tell me, man!"

"A human being tumbling . . ."

I couldn't believe what I saw. A person was rolling down the rock, sometimes spinning like a log in a river, sometimes toppling end over end in cartwheels.

I stammered a few of those words out to Hughes, who began to circle.

The figure slammed into a big rock, knees first, flung the

length of its body onto and over the boulder, and splattered on the slickrock like a paper doll.

I got an idea, raised the binoculars a hundred yards up the slope, and saw the wheelchair upside down, wheels in the air.

"It's my grandfather," I said in a squeezed voice.

"Amazing," said Hughes. We each took a huge breath. "I can't land, though. No straight place."

"Fly over as low as you can," I begged.

He did.

No sign of life.

"Again!"

He did a 360, passed over even lower, and tilted my side of the plane down to give me the best view.

A forearm rose.

"He's alive!" I screamed.

Hughes jerked his headset off. Maybe I'd just deafened the man.

Another circle and another low pass.

Grandpa was up on an elbow now.

I waved madly. Hughes waggled the wings.

Grandpa dropped back and wigwagged his left arm at us.

I was sure he was grinning. A very crooked grin. God, how I loved Mose Goldman.

Hughes lifted my headset off, set it in my lap, and put his own back on.

"Goulding's, come in. Goulding's, come in, please."

"This is Mike Goulding."

"Mose Goldman located alive."

"Roger, located alive."

"Injured, helpless. No place to land. Send a truck to Oljato."

"Vehicle coming ASAP."

Hughes flew directly over Grandpa and read out the numbers of where we were, exactly, in degrees, minutes, and seconds.

"Also call for an ambulance."

"Roger that, ambulance."

I told him, "I'll ride in the Gouldings' truck. First aid."

"Mike," he said, "in a couple of minutes I'll land at your place. "Yazzie Goldman will join your driver there. He's trained in first aid. Then I'll fly west along the Rainbow Bridge Trail and lead your driver straight to the spot."

"Roger that."

"Tell her to call Mom," I said softly.

Hughes said, "Last. Radio Mrs. Goldman and tell her we've found her father alive."

"You betcha," said Mike. Mike was one hell of a woman.

Mr. John had sent Janey, the location's nurse, to drive the pickup to the spot where my grandfather was, and I asked her to press that gas pedal down hard. Why couldn't a damn pickup go a couple of hundred miles an hour, like a plane? It was driving me crazy, and I'd have bet Hughes was getting damn tired of circling around and around to be slow enough for us.

As we drove by our trading post, I didn't see Jake Charlie at the front door, but a figure was standing guard south of the post and above it for a good view, where I'd suggested.

From the short, thick shape, I figured it was Colin. Maybe Jake Charlie was inside taking care of something or on the radio or in the outhouse.

I hoped Janey was up to doctoring whatever injuries Grandpa had. Hell, I would do whatever was needed, period. *Save Grandpa!*

❖❖❖❖

Zopilote took his time studying the situation. It looked like he was luckier than he thought. But to decide that too quickly might be very unlucky.

After about half an hour, he was sure. Only one guard left. *Fools, all of them.*

He circled around, well to the south. Step by soft step, from cedar to cedar and boulder to boulder, he worked his way down the slope toward the red-haired young man. The fellow packed a .38 police special. It would do him no good in its holster.

Every several minutes the guard looked at his watch and slowly, very slowly, turned in a circle with sure, balanced steps. He stopped at the west, south, then east, taking about thirty seconds facing in each direction to end up with a 360-degree survey. He must have been trained to do that. It was dumb.

Zopilote slipped gently downward. When the guard faced the post, the Buzzard moved toward him fast. For the thirty seconds the guard was turned south, where Zopilote was, he laid flat behind a cedar.

He got within about twenty steps. The guard turned to the trading post, away from Buzzard.

Zopilote took his last steps in silence. When he got close, he kicked a stone to make a noise.

The guard whirled, jaw dropping.

Zopilote seized the man's lower jaw and teeth in front and skull in back, and gave a single quick, hard twist.

He heard the satisfying crack. The eyes glazed, and Buzzard smiled.

In prison you learned to survive. He had killed half a dozen enemies the same way.

He took the .38 special. Six more talons to use in his attack.

✂✂✂

When we got within hearing distance, Grandpa yelled something and shook his fist.

The chair was obviously wrecked, useless.

When we got close, I saw that in the middle of the shin his strong leg turned like a hockey stick. I hated to think about the bones sticking out in his pant leg, but Janey checked it. "Not much blood, so no arterial bleeding," she said.

I bent over him, and she helped me lift him into a fireman's carry. Right then, I was glad that he'd lost weight in the last five months. Grandpa kept yelling one word I couldn't make out, sounded like "ah." Or sometimes he'd yell another word, sounded like "dick."

He seemed mad as hell at the two people saving his life, and I had no idea what he was saying.

We got him into the front seat of the truck, in the middle.

"Ah!

"Dick!

"Ah!

"Dick!"

He wouldn't quit.

I clicked the ignition and started home.

Finally Grandpa reached across Janey and tried to open the glove box with his left hand.

She did it for him.

He grabbed a wrinkled, raggedy piece of paper, laid it in his lap, and made a writing motion.

"You want to write something?" she said.

He nodded vigorously.

She rummaged in the glove box and found a two-inch pencil without a point. I gave her my penknife to sharpen it, and she handed the pencil to Grandpa.

Laboriously, he wrote, YR DAD → KILL MOM!!!

Fear squeezed my spine like a constricting snake.

"What? I don't . . . What?"

My mind whirled like a squirrel-cage wheel.

"My father?"

Grandpa thumped my chest with two fingers, hard.

"Mine?"

Grandpa nodded *big.*

A low whisper came out. "You sure!?"

More nodding.

The house of my entire life collapsed on my head.

I tried to stand up in the rubble. Disbelief made me dizzy. This could not be happening. I stupidly forced out the words, "*Whose* mom?"

Grandpa thumped my chest with his fist, his eyes boring into me.

"*My* father is with *my* mom? *Now?*"

Grandpa's head, arm, fist, and every part of his body that could move jumped up and down hollering, *Yes.* Then he scribbled on the paper, ADIKAI.

Then one more scribbled word—BAD!

I ran the truck off the road onto scrub desert.

I had no fucking idea what . . .

I said to myself, loud, "Drive like a madman."

And I did.

Twenty-two

The radio was sounding off, but Zopilote ignored it. He herded them both into Nizhoni's bedroom, the .38 pointed at them, the shotgun still loaded with one shell held loosely in the other hand, the derringer in his pocket.

A gun barrel is very persuasive, and he wanted Iris to see everything. Maybe he could shoot her in a way so that she would live just long enough to tell about what she saw. Or maybe not. He would decide.

The familiar room, the familiar bed. Our room, not hers. *Ours.*

He put a hand on the young woman's back and shoved her toward a corner. With the barrel he motioned Nizhoni to the bed.

She laid down on her back. She knew what was coming.

"Yes, my unfaithful mate. But before it happens, you must picture every detail of your own death. You must feel every touch in your mind, imagine all the fear, all the loathing. You will experience my throbbing orgasm. You will feel the ulti-mate moment of terror rage through your body."

Maybe those were the most words in a row for him in twenty-five years.

He signaled the young woman to sit down. She did, eyes wide open. She didn't mewl, didn't even whimper. He would have to keep an eye on her.

Buzzard drew his hunting knife out of his belt, gripped the hem of Nizhoni's skirt, slit the cloth from bottom to waist, and laid it open. She wore that silly underwear. He cut it off.

He took her blouse in both hands and ripped it wide, pop-ping the buttons. A brassiere. He cut it, deliberately tickling his wife's throat with the tip of his knife, so that a single tear of blood dribbled sideways.

He feasted with his eyes. He hadn't seen her naked in a quarter of a century. He liked it. She was his wife, and she was still beautiful.

He undid his belt, dropped his pants, and stepped up close to her face. *See my full power.*

Nizhoni looked, paralyzed.

Zopilote whirled his head toward Iris. Sure enough, she was pushing herself to her feet.

He fired a pistol shot within an inch of her head. The sound in the room made his blood thump.

Iris sank back to the floor.

Nizhoni began to cry.

He straddled her chest.

"Now, my dear, my betrayer, my whore, give your atten-tion to what I am about to do. My words will be the last you hear in this world. My hands will be the last touch you will feel. Well, not quite the last touch you will feel, Nizhoni."

Still straddling her, holding the gun in one hand and with the other squeezing the cock almost touching her eyes, he told her everything he would do, in detail and as lasciviously as possible.

Then Zopilote said, in a throttled voice, "I love you."

Twenty-three

I surveyed my home, and it didn't take long. Colin was lying dead on the ground behind the post, his neck broken. Jake Charlie was gone, probably dead, too. "Go back to the truck, lie down on the seat, and stay there," I said to Janey. She went.

My skin rolled into spasms. I had to approach carefully, had to see, had to understand. Otherwise I could not save Mom. Or Iris. I would just be another victim. No help in that.

Must be calm. At any moment I might hear a scream or a gunshot that would mean my mother was dead. I would not let that thought come into my mind again.

I chose her bedroom window, looked inside.

Mom lay spread-eagled on the bed, naked, knees up, legs wide. A stranger—my blood father?—knelt between her legs.

Vertigo whirled me around once. I squeezed my mind tight and ordered it to be still.

A pistol was in my father's hand, Grandpa's shotgun propped in a corner. Iris slumped in the opposite corner.

I took four steps back, bulled forward, leapt, and crashed through glass into the bedroom.

Chaos!

I hit the floor and rolled.

My father shot at me and missed.

My mother rolled away.

I grabbed a chair and hurled it at the center of the bed.

The monster dived off the end of the bed and twisted to get another shot.

Iris dived at my father as he aimed at me. His shot numbed my ears.

A spurt of blood from her chest—she'd been hit. The two of them rolled and thumped across the floor.

I used the bed to cannonball myself right onto my goddamned father's chest. My hip knocked Iris aside, and my butt got him hard. He squealed like a stuck pig.

I went for the pistol. He slid it far under the bed.

Iris ran to the shotgun.

My father and I grappled. I grabbed him by his long hair, but he got one hand on my throat. He didn't choke me. On either side of my Adam's apple he dug his fingertips in. Agony.

I jerked his head forward and pounded it hard against the floor.

Iris was aiming, but she could get no clear shot.

"No!" I shouted.

Probably she'd never fired a gun and might hit either or both of us.

We rolled a couple of times, and I splayed my legs to end

up on top. From outside I heard Janey yelling. I couldn't make out the words and didn't give a damn.

He was about to rip my Adam's apple out.

Iris fired.

My father bellowed, lurched, and lost his grip on my throat. I felt buckshot sting my calf, and he must have taken the brunt in his knee.

I gouged my so-called father's eye with my thumb.

He screamed.

I had the bastard. I kept that thumb where it could pop his eyeball out in an instant.

"I want some answers, now, you asshole."

At that moment Grandpa lurched into the room on a two-by-four crutch and fell facedown on the floor, his head whacking my father's elbow.

Grandpa raised—of all the goddamn things—his belt.

"Answers," I bellowed at this fake father.

Then, with his good left hand, Grandpa slammed sharp the tip of the belt into the father-monster's throat.

Twenty-four

The father-man was breathing. I wanted to memorize his face, to hear his voice, to get his words. I sat on the floor next to him. Bright arterial blood spouted from his neck.

"That man is about out of time," Janey said.

So I had only a couple of minutes, out of a lifetime, with the man whose blood ran in mine. I said, "Why?"

His eye, bloody, stared into mine. "It was me raped your fancy woman." His voice was a rasp.

"Why?"

"I hate your mother," he whispered.

"Why?"

"Betrayal," he wheezed.

"I am your offspring," I said. That word seemed better than "son." "Do you have anything to say to me?"

He racked with coughing, and his blood splattered my chest. A gift for his son.

He squeaked out, "I curse you for being born."

His face contorted into something strange and terrible. Maybe elation, maybe horror. Maybe the real face of evil arriving from a place we know nothing of.

He tried to clutch at his throat, twisted, and convulsed. And was still forever.

Twenty-five

Mom was weeping, lying in a ball. A torrent of quiet pain, fear, and humiliation ran from her eyes to her neck.

"Are you hurt?"

The volume of my voice jolted even me.

Mom shook her head no.

Next, Iris.

"Never mind your modesty," I told her. "I'm pulling up your blouse."

She raised her arm on the side of the wound. No sign of penetration into the chest. I felt carefully along—

"Ow, that hurts!"

Janey's hands pulled my arms away. She said, "Let me do that."

She palpated the length of the wound. "Nothing but ribs," she said. "X-rays will show whether any of them is cracked, and that would be the worst case. Very lucky."

It was hard to live inside this scene and think that anything could be called lucky. But I hoped Janey was right.

I bent over Grandpa, who seemed half in another world. His left leg was still bent and crooked. I couldn't imagine how he managed to crutch his way into the house. His will. His amazing will.

I looked at Janey.

"He did it by himself." She shrugged. "I couldn't stop him. I yelled at him, but . . ." Some embarrassment on her part. I guessed she was thinking, *A small woman, but a crippled man—why couldn't I control him?*

I took off my cowboy boot and found two pellets just below my knee. Several more had gouged the top of the boot. I flipped the two out and said to hell with all that.

Another look at Mom. She was murmuring to Janey, voice soft as birds' wings, her breathing rhythm ragged, saying that she was all right. Janey was bending over her, making comforting sounds. "She's okay, physically," Janey told me.

Which meant the damage was emotional. And it was serious.

❧❧❧❧

The ambulance got there in time to confirm what we already knew. My fake father was dead, and Grandpa would have to go to a hospital to get his leg set, but Iris could be patched up right there.

I told her, straight out, no time for delicacies, "Colin's dead. Broken neck."

A flicker of shadow streaked her face at an angle, like a storm-tossed sky's gray sheet through a windowpane.

Then it was gone. She squared her shoulders and became a force.

"Mr. Goldman is not going in any ambulance," she told the driver and Janey, "and he's not going to Flagstaff. I'm taking him to Santa Fe myself."

Grandpa nodded and grumbled his approval.

"But your ribs . . ." I said.

"Yazzie, I'm sure nothing is broken. I am taking Grandpa to Santa Fe, and do not argue with me."

"You," Iris said to Grandpa, "you're going to get physical therapy while you're there, and there's no arguing about it."

Grandpa made a raspy "O" sound, which may have been an attempt at no. But he wasn't going to win this one.

The ambulance guys forced pain meds down his throat. On their way out, I asked them to bring us news of Jake Charlie. Dead or alive, he had to be close by.

Sitting up on the bed, Mom spoke her first words. "While we drive, we'll talk. And eat. And be thankful for our true family. And then I will tell you a story."

Mom and Iris may not have been related by blood, but they sure were by courage and determination.

Mom sat at the table while I threw together a meal for the drive. I suppose it was some kind of therapy for me. I wanted my mother to rest. I wanted to be the person taking care of her. After all, I had left her alone. I wanted her to scream or give voice, in some way, to the horror that took place inside our house. For myself, I could find no words, no cries. I was dry as the desert.

Iris and I shouldered Grandpa to the pickup. Mom carried the basket of fried Spam sandwiches, potato salad, and gherkins.

As we walked out, Officers Cly and Etcitty spun their squad car into the yard. I didn't ask where the hell they'd been. Simply said, "We're leaving, no questions now." I pointed to my grandfather. "Look at that leg."

They saw.

"We'll give our statement to the cops at the hospital." I didn't say which hospital.

"But—"

"I'm not asking you, I'm telling you. At the hospital."

They nodded and left.

With four people in the pickup, the front seat was crowded. I drove, and Grandpa sat with his back against the truck's passenger window and his legs across Mom's and Iris's laps. Somehow it was comfortable, all of us jammed together.

No one knew what to say.

Iris spoke first. "What the hell happened there?"

Between Mom and Grandpa, looks of emotion passed that I couldn't decipher.

Finally, Mom told the story in a bare-bones, dry-fact way. The man who was not my true father, who was a rapist, a killer, a destroyer of lives, who was another reason I would have to do an Enemy Way ceremony—this monster was Adi-kai Begay, which in Navajo means Son of Gambler. The name explained Grandpa's mangled utterances, "odd" and "dick."

My so-called father came from the Chuska Mountains to the east, a handsome fellow when he was young. A man who liked the ladies. Though people in our part of the rez didn't know him, he was a bronc rider, and a hell of a good one. Mom met him one weekend at an Indian rodeo, went to another rodeo the next weekend to be with him, and the next day married him in Flagstaff—a rare non-Navajo wedding that had county paperwork attached to it. Grandpa never met him until she brought him home to share her bedroom.

"My declaration of independence," Mom said, words awash in irony.

I could hardly believe she'd been such a rebel, or that she was able to form the words to tell this story.

Her new husband didn't do a lick of work around the trading post. He disappeared most weekends to go rodeoing, and then he'd be gone for two or three weeks to play poker and get drunk.

Mom added, "And probably to whore around."

Before long he disappeared for six or seven weeks, and finally for three months. After nine months and four days of marriage Mom agreed with Grandpa to put his belongings outside the door. Navajo divorce, and screw the paperwork. Grandpa would play papa to the unborn child.

A curator from the Wheelwright Museum in Santa Fe, a friend of the family, came up that summer to see the post's art, go out and meet artists, and acquire quality items for the museum. Mom fell in love with him. He proposed. They would get married at our family home in Santa Fe.

Except that Adikai Begay killed him.

Both Mom and Grandpa testified at the trial. The sentence was life in prison. They thought they'd never see him again. And they took an oath never to speak his name again.

"Family secrets," Iris said in a voice curdled with anger.

Both Grandpa and Mom nodded and touched each other's hands.

Mom's going to need more than that, I thought.

Twenty-six

Grandma Frieda was waiting for us at the hospital in Santa Fe. She was a complete surprise. I'd have taken her for a Gypsy, not a Jewish lady, and for forty-five years old, not sixty. All her clothes seemed to be scarves. I wondered if she was entirely decent when the wind blew. Plus, she spewed words like a machine gun. Spewed instructions, I should say.

Two of the three women played commanding officer, Grandma Frieda and Iris. Just try to talk back to women like that—even Mom couldn't. Half the Navajo men I knew had more than one wife. I couldn't figure how they survived it.

We all sat in a waiting room while the doctors X-rayed, poked and probed, and then repaired Grandpa's leg. I could hear his protests all the way down the hall.

Finally, a white-coated guy came out and introduced himself as Dr. Such-and-So. After the navy and the FBI, I had to squelch my impatience with uniforms and assertions of rank. His summary was compound fracture of the right leg, which we knew. Now the skin was stitched up and the bone set. Probably two months in a cast. And then?

The doc introduced a physical therapist who asked us questions about how much Grandpa tried to talk, how often we could understand his sounds as words, how active he was in the walker, how much he was using it, and on and on. Endless, all of it.

When we'd told him, he said that the partial progress indicated Grandpa could recover from the stroke a lot more than he had. Then he began a recitation of the treatments Grandpa needed.

Frieda and Mom took turns interrupting the man. The gist of it was that Grandpa would stay in Santa Fe as long as needed and show up for his therapy every day.

"Mr. Goldman doesn't seem to want to do that," the therapist told us.

Mom spoke quickest. "Mr. Goldman isn't running this show. How long?"

"Probably six months."

Frieda said, "A full house." She grinned at us. "Won't that be fun?"

When the PT guy left, I said to Mom, "It's okay with you to close the trading post that long?"

She said, "What trading post?"

They gave Mom an appointment with a psychiatrist in two days. She shrugged. I wondered how many times she'd actually go to see him.

I was charmed by our family home. She was one block off the plaza, a dowager of fading grandeur.

"I could fix her up," said Frieda. "I have the money but not the time."

"The time!" Mom said. "What are you doing?"

"Hey! You don't know . . . Saint Michael's College," Frieda said. Her tone changed. "So exciting. We do music, creative writing, theater, art, graphic design, movies, costumes, sets, and photography. With the talent I have, it's perfect. I love it. And, oh, our string players."

She embraced the whole house with spread arms. "Yes, I know. I'm sorry, you beauty, you old darling." She shrugged. "I've neglected you, and you take care of me still."

Frieda walked Mom through the rooms, one by one, Iris and I trailing behind them. There was a grand living room with a fireplace made of petrified wood from the Painted Desert. Also a genuine crystal chandelier that looked like it hadn't been dusted in centuries, a more private sitting room, a kitchen where you could cook for fifty, a library that would serve a department of professors, a dozen bedrooms, and best of all, a walled garden with a fountain and shaded chairs. Grandpa had always wanted a walled garden at the trading post. He claimed that "walled garden," in the language of Persia, was another expression for paradise. Mom said that a walled garden would do her more good than any psychiatrist.

She spoke of putting one of Grandpa's rugs here and this one there, a certain pot here and a certain one there, a ceremonial basket over every door, with the traditional weaver's path in each basket pointing east, naturally.

She would like it here.

Grandma Frieda showed me to a small bedroom on the third floor that had a panoramic view of the town.

"Beautiful," I said.

While I was reading on the bed in the late afternoon, I heard Iris unpacking in her room, which seemed to be across the hall. I liked that. For a while I would live in a fine house in a real city.

Why make plans in this life? As soon as you do, the currents change, the wind shifts, the waves come up, and off you go where the ocean wills, for better or for much worse. But you ride the waves, you stay afloat, you survive, you thrive.

Twenty-seven

I hurried down the hallway. A rug from Belgium ran its length, and a small carved table sat in the center under a mirror.

"Seaman Goldman, please." It was a female voice of some authority, probably a secretary to a bigwig.

"This is him." A telephone in the downstairs entryway—imagine having a phone in your own house.

She said, "Mr. Leland Chapman, as you may know, is director of security for the Atchison, Topeka, and Santa Fe Railroad."

"Yes." Jack Ford had called an hour ago to tell me about it. He had called the president of the railroad to recommend me as a security officer—a railroad dick! In a tone of amusement, Jack added, "Howard Hughes made the same call for you." Probably after Jack suggested it, I thought.

The secretary continued. "Would you be available at the

depot office in Lamy, New Mexico, on Tuesday next at ten
A.M.? Mr. Chapman would like to speak with you."

'Tuesday next'—that was how ritzy people talked. I said,
"Sure."

Lamy was eighteen miles south of Santa Fe. Crazy but
the main line of the Atchison, Topeka & Santa Fe didn't go
to Santa Fe, the capital of New Mexico. The last eighteen
miles of mountains, they'd decided, were too steep and too
rough. Either that, or the railroad magnates didn't have
what it took to build that track.

◤◢◤◢

Somehow, during the next few days, Iris and I found time
alone together to talk about what we had seen, heard, and
felt. About the horrible deeds that had smashed the peace of
our home, about almost losing Grandpa, Mom, and about
Iris's own near brush with death. It was all just too much to
think about at once. What we both needed was comfort from
another person who'd also gone through it. And that's what
Iris was—comfort, home, and warmth.

And what about her painting dreams? She had left her
painting haven behind, a land that inspired her and ener-
gized her. I had left future dreams and also my past behind.
New dreams were being born, but they still had small voices.
I had gained Mr. John. My feelings for him crept up on me
and were a surprise. Truth is, he felt like an uncle.

At noon, the day before my railroad interview, Grandpa
came home from the hospital. After that, he would go to the
hospital every morning. Otherwise, he was at the house. Unable to use his walker yet, but he was home and he could soak
up the beauty of the walled garden, the paradise.

I had gone to a wonderful shop in Santa Fe and bought a surprise for my grandfather to keep on hand when he came home. Grandma Frieda brought out a bottle of champagne. "Welcome home, Mose!" she declared, and popped the cork.

A couple of lifts of champagne flutes all around, and the bottle was empty.

Now I brought out his real homecoming gift, a gift that was his alone. "My turn to welcome you home, Grandpa."

I walked across the room, and I pulled it out of the closet. It wasn't wrapped, because Grandpa couldn't do much about wrapping paper with only one good working hand. It was a brand-new Underwood typewriter. I set it right where his plate had been.

Grandpa's hand dived straight for his chalkboard. He wrote, CAN'T.

Meaning he couldn't type.

"You'll learn," I said.

Iris pulled a stack of paper from beneath her chair, her collaboration with my surprise. "One-handed peck," she said, and rolled a blank piece of paper into the Underwood.

"And after a while two-handed," I pitched in. "Your therapist says typing will be good exercise for your right hand."

Grandpa studied the keys. I thought the look on his face was more surrender than eagerness. He wrote on his board, WHAT?

Meaning, 'What on earth would I write?'

"Write whatever you want to."

Grandpa pulled out his chalkboard. NO IDEAS.

"Then start here: Tell the adventure of you and The Monster." I had decided to call my nonfather by that name, having promised Mom never to say his actual name, although I said it in my head a few times and then pushed it away. "Adikai Begay" sounded too human, too real. The man was a monster. Let him be called that.

I went on, "Tell how Monster kidnapped you, took you out to that place on the slickrock, tied you up, and abandoned you to die, slowly, of starvation and thirst.

"Then how you freed yourself, struggled one-handed and one-legged up that hill, then cut loose on a crazy ride downhill, crashing and breaking your leg. *After* you'd gotten near the road, where we couldn't help but find you.

"It's a heroic story, Grandpa. One that everyone in the family should know about and remember."

He tried to say something. "Kah" came out. He tried again and managed, "eroh."

I couldn't guess it.

On his blackboard he wrote, QXTE.

"Right. Exactly so. Don Quixote, sometimes comic, sometimes heroic."

Always heroic, that seemed more like the truth to me. He gave his nutty grin.

I spread my hands. "You are the Don. Overcoming all odds, you kicked the windmill down."

He pointed a finger at me. "Pan."

I bowed to him. "And I, at your service, am Sancho Panza."

With his good hand he clapped the lame one.

❖❖❖❖

That afternoon Grandpa and I played chess. We talked. Or I talked. So many feelings to get out, dreams, stories.

I would have loved to hear his voice. But some part of me liked talking and getting nothing but nods and wise looks in return. Left me free to do my own thinking, and get his nods, growls, or cheers.

"They all want to know what I'm going to decide." He knew I meant our three women. "Go to work on the railroad or stay here and do . . . whatever. Sleep in Pullman cars all the time or be with my family. Stay in Santa Fe and find work or go home and reopen the trading post."

Every day the post was closed was another day local people took their trade to Goulding's, we all knew that. In a couple of months we'd lose most of our business. But we thought we could get it back. Goulding's looked to sell to white people. We aimed at red people. Mom was right—there was enough family to work it out one way or the other.

Besides, I couldn't imagine selling Grandpa's life's work to Harry and Mike, as much as I loved them. Or worse, selling the trading post to a stranger.

The way things were going right in front of me, I wouldn't have to imagine getting beat at chess again—it was about to happen.

"I definitely need something to do. A real, paying job," I said. "But working for the railroad? Do I want to leave my family again? Still, shoving furniture around the house, hanging curtains, patching stucco, painting walls—that's no way to live."

Silence. "Eating on white tablecloths is," I said. Then I took thought. "Of course, we do that here."

Santa Fe, the house, my family—yes, I loved it.

"What should I do, Grandpa?"

He gave me his big grin, and while I made what I hoped

was a surprise move with my knight, he wrote on his chalk-board, LISTEN SONG HEART.

I said, "But which song?"

He shrugged and took my queen. His grin was starting to look less weird.

I picked the Underwood up from a side table and set it in front of him. Now it was my turn to grin. "Get to it. No excuses."

At dinner that evening Iris volunteered to drive me to Lamy the next morning.

I said, "Sure."

That night I went to bed early. I didn't sleep. I tried to think, but nothing added up. I did a lot of fretting.

The next morning I put on dress whites. It struck me that I should wear a suit and tie—the railroad would surely require that—but I didn't own such clothes.

As soon as she started the truck, Iris said, "What are you going to decide?"

"I don't know."

Pause. "Do you have to be so chintzy with your words?"

"Grandpa said to listen to the song in my heart. But what I'm hearing is more like the banging of pots and pans."

We drove in silence. She parked at the depot and looked at me with an expression I couldn't read. Iris said, "I'll be right here." She gave me a little wave, got out, opened a big pad, and starting sketching.

Mr. Leland Chapman wore not only a suit and tie but a vest. His tailored English clothes made him look entirely too elegant for the station master's office.

He introduced himself. "Cigar?" he said, extending one.

I had no doubt it was Cuba's finest, but I said no.

From there he was direct. He spoke like the job was a done deal.

"You are well recommended. Also, you speak three languages common in the Southwest. We have no one else who can do that." He ahemmed. "So I am able to offer three kinds of positions. Two are riding trains."

"I've always wanted to ride the Super Chief."

"That is protecting the well-to-do passengers against those who would prey on them. It's a good job.

"The other riding job is on our regular trains. There you protect the passengers, protect the freight, and keep hoboes off. A lot of work, and sometimes rough. Good for a man who likes to be active."

Since it sounded to me like Jack and Hughes had nailed the top railroad deal down, I went for it. "Tell me more about the Super Chief."

"It's specialized. We need men to ride all the way from Chicago to Los Angeles and back. That's forty-one hours straight on duty, a night at a hotel in L.A., one we have an arrangement with. Then, another day and a half back to Chicago. Two weeks of work in three and a half days."

Wow. "A guy does this every week?"

"No. Since the round-trip is two weeks of work, we give eight days off."

That sounded good.

"What's the pay?"

"Three hundred a week, and all Santa Fe employees get passes, and their immediate family also gets passes, to ride the railroad at any time and wherever it goes."

Twelve hundred a month. Eight days off at a time. Free trips when I wanted. Unbelievable.

Now I was going to use that silly word. "What if the dick lives in Santa Fe?" I'd worked it out that, starting from Chicago, Santa Fe was about 60 percent of the distance to LA.

"Easier if he lives in Chicago, but one guy does it from Amarillo, which is right at halfway. He just starts by riding overnight, in a berth we provide, to Chicago. Then he works the eighty-hour shift and sleeps his way back home. Same number of hours working, plus sixteen on the train unpaid, off duty, and sleeping. Then the days off and start the routine over."

"Pretty good money."

"Seaman Goldman, we only hire la crème de la crème."

Flattery or intimidation in that?

I thought for maybe too long. Finally I said, "Tell me about the other job, not riding the trains."

Chapman grimaced. "It's straight PI work, whenever we need it. We have, say, a robbery—God forbid, an assault or a killing. We fly you by private plane to the scene, you go wherever the investigation leads, find the perpetrators, recover the property, and turn the criminals over to the police. We fly you home. You must be available whenever we need you. We pay a retainer of three hundred dollars per month. When you're working, we pay a hundred a day plus expenses. Guarantee of a minimum of five days of work a month."

So eight hundred a month, at least, unpredictable hours,

but probably more time off. "With a pass to ride the railroad?"

"Yes. I must say, this is a job for a man with a taste for adventure. Imagine every crime in the Four Corners that can touch on the railroad."

Long breath in, long breath out. "It's a lot to think about. I'll call you."

He blinked at me, maybe surprised. Then he stood and offered his hand. I shook it firmly, white-man style. Do as the Romans do.

"Let me know by the end of business on Friday."

Twenty-eight

"So what did he say?"

Iris put it in gear and hit the gas pedal hard.

I told her, in detail, every nook and cranny. The further I went, the more interested, and interesting, her questions became. We were coming into Santa Fe when she got to the big question.

"What in the world are you going to decide?"

I hesitated, made one sound, and hesitated again. "I've always wanted to ride the Super Chief. I guess that settles it." Funny, but I didn't sound sure, even to myself.

"About fifteen days at home a month?"

"And twelve hundred bucks."

"Pretty terrific," she said, "and what would you do with that time off? Would you spend it in Santa Fe or Oljato or . . . ?"

She pulled into a parking spot on the plaza. My head

turned toward the facade of La Fonda, said to be the finest hotel in New Mexico.

She looked at me oddly. "Yazzie, I want to take you to La Fonda for lunch. My congratulations on the new job."

I looked at her. Simply looked. *You know what your heart's song is, dummy.*

I reached out and put my hand on hers. "What will I do . . . ?" I said. "I think I'll read, spruce up the family house, and spend lots of time getting to know you better."

What on earth had I just said?

I felt her hand jump a little.

I squeezed it to show that I'd meant every word.

She studied my face.

"Are you kidding? You're talking crazy."

"Iris, what can I say? It kind of snuck up on me. Now's the time, and it just came out. I don't know if I should apologize."

"Jeez, you are so romantic. I can hardly contain myself."

She looked out the window, back at me, back to the people on the street. Probably thinking up another wise-ass remark. I hoped so.

Out with it, open my heart. "Iris Goldman," I said, "will you let me court you?"

Time to listen and watch, not just to hear her words, but to watch her body speak.

Finally, she said, "We could start over lunch."

I nodded yes and we walked inside, surrounded by swirling, dancing murals.

A white-coated waiter seated us and brought us menus.

"How would we work this? Wait," she said, "courting means finding out whether we want to get married, right?"

The word stuck in my throat like a hot hard-boiled egg in its shell.

"Yes."

"I'm glad to date you and have a good time," Iris said, "but where would we live that would be close enough to see each other?"

"After Grandpa's done with rehab, we can live here in the family house, go to Monument Valley, or go back and forth. Whatever you want."

Iris looked at me for a long time. "There is an awful lot of the 'we' word in this conversation." She smiled. "Don't take 'we' for granted, Yazzie Goldman." And then she played footsie with me. She gave me coy glances. She downed a margarita. She glowed.

Finally, she leaned over and kissed me lightly, but with a lover's touch.

"You'd be gone a lot."

She looked at me under shelved eyebrows like there was a challenge coming.

"I guess."

"So, are you willing to hear a better idea? Or note one?"

A beat passed. "Yes."

"Yazzie, you're being silly. You're passing up the best job. What if you took the off-and-on PI work? Some months you might be gone ten days, some none. And guess what? Any time, *any* time in between, we could ride the Super Chief all we wanted. We could go everywhere and see everything. And while we were living the high life, you wouldn't be working."

She grinned at me, showing the impish front tooth. "How about this for a first date? We ride the Chief to

Chicago and spend a few days there. I've always wanted to see the Art Institute. They have a fabulous collection of impressionist paintings. I'm dying to see them, sketch them, understand."

After there had been about a hundred years of silence between us, I said, "A first date in a single sleeping compartment?"

"Oh, I think there's enough space, don't you?" She wiggled her whole body.

She was proposing a pretty big form of courting. I had no idea why, Iris being Iris, that surprised me.

"Let's face it," she said, "we do have a certain charge between us, and we can have everything we want, the whole shebang. Why not jump?"

I wanted right then to say, "Iris, will you marry me?" I choked back the words.

"Are you saying yes?"

I managed to stammer, "Yes."

"Yes to me, or yes to the other job?"

"Yes to both. Let's jump, and let's do it in a big way."

She nodded her head, slim smile. I thought she figured this was exactly the way it would turn out, and I sure wasn't about to argue.

"Okay," Iris said, "I have two conditions. That you start work as soon as possible so we can see if we like the arrangement. And that you take me upstairs right now."

I looked around at the white tablecloths and uniformed waiters. "You wanted lunch."

"Did you ever hear of room service?" she said, nodding toward the elegant, curving staircase that led upstairs.

I took her hand. She let me have a little kiss and pushed me back gently.

She said, "And we can stay for breakfast if you want."

❖❖❖❖

On the day of the summer solstice, a time of coming to maturity, I sat in a forked-stick hogan with Grandpa, Mom, and Frieda. Slowly, ceremonially, Bitsui and his family joined us. He was the staff bearer, the chief singer of the Enemy Way ceremony I needed and needed and needed. Outside the hogan sat Iris, dressed in shawls, robes, fabrics, and buckskin, my unofficial mate playing her role. We began singing the words of the ancient song:

"Sa'ah naagh'éi, Bik'eh hózhó . . ."

When we finished the songs and prayers, I stepped out of the hogan so that the round dancing could begin and the ceremony would come to its climax. I walked in the steps of *hózhó*. Many gifts would be given, and we would offer a lavish feast.

After a month and a half of trying the arrangement out, as Iris put it, a clerk of Santa Fe County gave state sanction to the union of Yazzie and Iris Goldman. This mattered much less to us than the afternoon several days later when another medicine singer came to our family house in Santa Fe and united us in a house-blessing ceremony, followed by another feast.

Iris and I had reserved a berth to ride the Super Chief to Chicago for our honeymoon. I was fine with watching her go crazy over the Impressionists. I loved the times when we looked at each other, and held each other. No details here, except one—it was the true high life, and it was a damn sight more fun than anything that had ever happened on a movie set.